Diane Gaston

The VANISHING VISCOUNTESS

D1363798

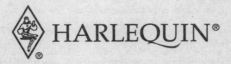

HARLEQUIN®

TORONTO • NEW YORK • LONDON
AMSTERDAM • PARIS • SYDNEY • HAMBURG
STOCKHOLM • ATHENS • TOKYO • MILAN • MADRID
PRAGUE • WARSAW • BUDAPEST • AUCKLAND

ISBN-13: 978-0-373-29479-4
ISBN-10:   0-373-29479-4

THE VANISHING VISCOUNTESS

First North American Publication 2008

To Mallory Pickerloy,
a lovely reader whose name is worthy of a heroine

Chapter One

October, 1818

The gale roared like a wild beast. Under its savage attack, the ship creaked and moaned and begged for mercy. Shouts of the crew echoed the ship's distress as men struggled to work the pumps and save the rigging.

Adam Vickery, the Marquess of Tannerton, or Tanner, as he was known to his friends, sat with the other passengers in the packet ship's cuddy, awaiting his demise. He remained still, arms crossed over his chest, eyes closed, reviewing his life.

He found it wanting. He'd left no mark on the world, no son to inherit his title and lands, no child to carry on his bloodline. All he had done was maintain what his father, grandfather, great-grandfather, and all the Marquesses of Tannerton had built. If he were truly honest with himself, he would say he'd not even done the maintaining. Other men did that work for him: his estate managers, men of business and secretaries. They toiled while Tanner enjoyed his gaming, his sport, his women.

A loud crack sounded and a thud on the deck shook the whole ship. A woman wailed. Tanner opened his eyes to see the woman clutching an infant and a small boy to her breast. The cabin was filled with many women like her, shaking in fear, and men, like Tanner himself, cursing their helplessness. There was no way to stop the storm, no way to calm the sea, no way to hold the timbers of the ship together.

His gaze fell on one woman who neither wailed nor cowered from the storm. With an expression of defiance rather than fear, she stood next to a Bow Street Runner, leather shackles on her wrists, obviously his prisoner. Only a few hours ago, at the beginning of this voyage from Dublin to Holyhead, Tanner's gaze had been drawn to her, so dignified in her plight. What crime had she committed to warrant her escort from Ireland? He'd been too blue-devilled to bother inquiring about her, however. Now he wished he'd spoken to her, or at least smiled at her. She seemed every bit as alone as he.

When the winds began their fierce assault, the first mate had gathered all the passengers into this cabin. He'd told them they were close to the Anglesey coast. Of course, the Anglesey coast could be rocky and treacherous, although the man neglected to mention that part.

What could be worse? Tanner wondered. Plunging into the cold depths of the Irish Sea? Or being dashed upon some craggy rocks?

Either would mean death.

The first mate popped in a second time when the storm intensified. "All will be well," he reassured them. None of the passengers believed him. Tanner could see it in their eyes. He felt it in his own soul. Tanner watched a man remove a miniature from his pocket and stare at it, a portrait of a loved one he would never see again, of someone who would soon be grieving.

Who would grieve for the Marquess of Tannerton? His friend Pomroy would likely drink a toast to his memory now and then. A mistress or two might consider him a fond memory. Perhaps the Duke of Clarence or even the Regent himself might recall him after the space of a year or two, but more likely not. Algernon, his fribble of a cousin, would be terrified at the prospect of inheriting the lofty title and its responsibilities. Tanner rubbed his face, regretting he'd never taken Algernon in tow and taught him how easy it all was. Algernon could busy himself with purchasing new coats or the latest fashion in boots or all the watch fobs and stick pins he fancied.

The Bow Street Runner began pacing, Tanner noticed, and the prisoner flashed the man an undisguised look of contempt.

Would she have anyone to mourn her?

She stood with her chin high and her startling blue eyes vigilant. He disliked thinking of what the sea would do to her, turning her body all bloated and white.

He glanced away, shaking that horrible image from his mind, but no matter where he looked, his eyes were drawn back to her.

She was tall and slender, with the same dark hair and piercing blue eyes of the woman who'd briefly captivated him a year ago. That was where the resemblance ended, however. Rose O'Keefe had made the right choice when she'd chosen Tanner's former secretary, Jameson Flynn, over Tanner himself. Flynn had offered the Vauxhall singer marriage, something Tanner would never have done. Flynn had also loved her.

Tanner laughed inwardly at the irony of it all. The secretary preferred over the marquess. He could not muster any resentment, however. Rose had picked the better man.

He frowned and bowed his head. Tanner's zeal had not been to love Rose, but to outwit another rival for her favours. Three people had died as a result. Three lives on his conscience because of his heedless selfishness.

Purchasing the Dublin theatre for Flynn and Rose did not make amends for the destruction Tanner had set in motion, but it did give the married couple the means to a new life. That was the very least Tanner could do. He'd travelled to Dublin for their opening performance, and now he was crossing the Irish Sea again, heading back to England on this Holyhead packet.

The ship had been scheduled to land hours ago, but the storm stalled them and now the day was late. He pulled his timepiece from his pocket. It was near nine p.m.

Another shuddering crash came from above. Tanner stuffed his watch back into his pocket and glanced at the prisoner. Her eyes flashed with alarm. Tanner could not blame her. Her life—and his own empty one—appeared to be edging towards the end.

The cabin door sprang open and the first mate, drenched and dripping on to the wooden floor, yelled, "Everyone on deck! To the boats. Women and children first."

The death knell. The captain no longer expected the ship to remain intact. It was time to risk the lives of the women and children in the small boats.

There were quick anguished embraces as goodbyes were tearfully said. Panicked men tried to push in front of mothers clasping the hands of terrified children. Tanner rushed forward and pulled the men back. He used his stature and strength to keep the way clear. The prisoner was the last woman out of the door, her Bow Street Runner pushing her on, his hand firmly clamped around her arm. The man could have at least untied her shackles. What could it matter now? At least allow her to die free.

Tanner was the last person to come up on deck. As he stepped out into the air, the rain sliced him like knife blades, the wind whipping in all directions. The ship's masts no longer stood tall and proud, but lay like snapped twigs on the deck.

The sails, now in tatters, resembled nothing more than rags flapping haphazardly in the tempest. Tanner stepped over pieces of wood, remnants of sails and other debris. A loose barrel rolled towards him. He jumped aside, nearly losing his footing on the slick surface of the deck. More than once he had to grab hold of whatever was near to keep from falling.

Tanner pushed his way through to where the women and children were being loaded into boats. Although he feared the effort futile, Tanner pitched in, helping lift women and children over the side of the ship to crewmen waiting in the boats. Lightning flashed, illuminating the shadow of the shore, so distant when the sea churned like a cauldron, violently pitching the ship. The boat's fragile passengers would have a treacherous ride.

Let these people survive, he prayed.

He lifted a child into waiting arms and her mother after her. This was the last boat, and the crewmen manning it were already starting to lower it to the sea. Tanner reached for the woman prisoner, who, outwardly calm and patient, had held back so the others could go before her. Tanner scooped her into his arms to lift her over the side, but, at that same moment, the Bow Street Runner shoved them both, knocking them to the deck, jumping into the boat in her place. Tanner scrambled to his feet, but it was too late. The boat had hit the water, the crewmen rowing fast to get it away.

"Bastard!" Tanner cried. In the howling wind, he could barely hear his own words.

The prisoner's eyes blazed with fury and fear. She struggled to stand. Tanner grabbed her arm and pulled her to her feet.

"The ship's going to break apart!" the first mate cried, running by them.

Tanner glanced wildly around. Some of the crew were lashing themselves to pieces of mast.

"Come on," he shouted to the woman, pulling her along with him.

Tanner grabbed rope from the rigging and tied her to a piece of broken mast. He would be damned if that scoundrel Bow Street Runner survived and she did not. He lashed himself next to her, wrapping one arm around her and the other around the mast. The ship slammed into rocks, sending them, mast and all, skittering across the deck.

The vessel groaned, then broke apart in a cacophony of cracks and crashes and splintering wood. Their piece of mast flew into the air like a shuttlecock, the wind suspending them for several moments before plunging them into the churning water.

The impact stunned Tanner, but the shock of the needle-sharp cold roused him again. The howling of the wind, the hissing of the rain, the screams of their shipmates suddenly dulled to a muffled growl. The water was inky black and Tanner had no idea which way was up, but his arm was still around the woman. He had not lost her.

Their wooden mast began rising as if it, too, fought to reach the surface. Tanner kicked with all his strength, his lungs burning with the urge to take a breath.

When they broke the surface of the water, it was almost as great a shock as plunging into its depths. Tanner gulped for air. To his relief, he heard the woman do the same. She had survived.

Then a wave crashed over them and drove them forward.

Tanner sucked in a quick gulp of air before they went under. Again they resurfaced and were pushed forward and under once more.

When they popped to the surface, Tanner had time to yell, "Are you hurt?"

"No," she cried.

He tightened his grip on her as another wave hit. If the sea did not swallow them, the cold would surely kill them.

Or the rocks.

This wave thrust them further. Through the sheen of rain and sea, Tanner glimpsed the coast, but jagged rocks lay between, jutting up from the water like pointed teeth. Another wave pelted them, then another. The ropes loosened and were washed away. The woman's grip slipped from the mast. Tanner could hold on to the mast or the woman. He held on to the woman.

Her skirts were dragging them down and her bound wrists made it hard for her to swim. Tanner kicked hard to keep them above the water, only to see the rocks coming closer. He swivelled around to see if other survivors were near them, but not a soul was visible. No one to help them. No one to see. Perhaps no one to survive.

The next wave drove them into one of the rocks. She cried out as they hit. Another wave dashed them into another rock. Tanner tried to take the blows instead of her, but the water stirred them too fast. He lost feeling in his arms and legs and he feared he would lose his grip on her.

Not another death on his conscience. Tanner could not bear it. *God, help me save her,* he prayed. *Help me do something worthwhile. One last bloody something worthwhile.*

He slammed into a jagged rock and everything went black.

When Tanner opened his eyes, he felt cold wet sand against his cheek. He could see the water lapping the shoreline inches from his face. Its waves sounded in his ears, and whitecaps seemed to wink at him. There was hard ground beneath him, however. Hard solid ground.

The woman! He'd lost her. Let go of her, damn him. Despair engulfed him as surely as had the Irish Sea. His limbs felt heavy as iron and his soul ached with guilt. He'd let go of her.

A light glowed around him, bobbing, then coming to a stop. Suddenly someone's hands were upon him, rough hands digging into his clothes, searching his pockets.

He seized one of the groping hands, and his attacker pulled him upright, trying to break free. Tanner's grip slipped and he fell back onto the sand. The man advanced on him, kicking him in the ribs. Tanner rolled away, trying to escape the blows, but the man kicked him again.

"Your money," the man snarled as he kicked him once more. "I want your money."

Every English coast abounded with wreckers, people who flocked to the shore eager to see a ship founder, so they could seize whatever bounty that washed ashore. Tanner had never thought to meet one.

He curled himself against the onslaught of the man's boot, as he struck again and again. A loud thwack sounded and the man collapsed on top of him. Tanner shoved him off and sat up.

The woman stood above them, a long piece of wood, part of the ship, no doubt, in her trembling, still-shackled hands.

Marlena Parronley stared at the prone figure, the brute who had so violently attacked her rescuer, the Marquess of Tannerton. She'd hit the villain with all her remaining strength.

Perhaps this time she really *had* killed a man.

Tannerton struggled painfully to his knees, staring at her, holding his sides, breathing hard.

Marlena had recognised Tannerton immediately when she'd first seen him on board ship, but he'd shown no signs of remembering her.

Thank goodness.

That first Season in London—her only Season—he'd attended many of the entertainments, but he was already a marquess and she was a mere baron's daughter, a Scottish baron at that. He'd provided her and Eliza with some excitement in those heady days, however. They'd called him Tanner, as if they had been admitted to that close circle of friends he always had around him. They'd peeked at the handsome marquess from behind their fans, he so tall, his brown hair always tousled. And his eyes! They'd been in raptures about his mossy green eyes. She and Eliza had devised all manner of ways they might meet him, none of which they'd dared to carry out.

Too bad they had not thought of being caught in a gale on a ship that broke apart and tossed them in the sea.

We forgot that one, Eliza, Marlena silently said.

"Have I killed him, do you think?" she asked the marquess.

Tanner reached down to place his fingers on the man's neck. "He's alive."

Marlena released a breath she'd not realised she'd been holding.

Tanner rose to his feet.

"Are you injured?" he asked, his breathing ragged.

She shook her head, sending a shiver down her body. He still showed no signs of recognising her. He pulled off his wet gloves and reached for her hands to work on the leather bindings. When she'd been on the ship they had chafed her wrists, but she was too numb to feel them now. Her teeth chattered and she started trembling all over, making his task even more difficult. He leaned down to loosen them with his teeth.

Finally the bindings fell to the sand and she was free. Marlena rubbed her wrists, but she could not feel her hands.

"We need to find shelter. Dry clothing." He glanced around.

They were in a small cove, dotted with jutting rocks and a small patch of sand. Steep black cliffs imprisoned them as certainly as the walls of Newgate Prison.

Tanner touched her arm. "If that fellow managed to get in here, we can get out."

She nodded, but suddenly any strength she'd possessed seemed to ebb. It was difficult to think. The cold had seeped into her very bones.

He rubbed her arms, then pressed a hand on his ribs and winced. "Come now. We'll be warm and dry very soon."

He picked up the man's lantern and circled their prison walls. She could do nothing but watch. A huge wave tumbled ashore, soaking her feet again, but she could only stare at it swirling around her ankles. He crossed over and took her arm, pulling her away from the water.

He'd once danced with her, she remembered, although he never knew it. Lady Erstine had held a masquerade ball, a respectable one, and she and Eliza attended, having spent many agonising hours deciding what costume to wear. Tanner had danced one dance with Marlena without knowing who she was. Eliza had been green with envy.

"Stay with me," he said, holding her firmly.

What looked like one massive black rock was really two, with a narrow corridor between them. He held her hand and pulled her through. They climbed up smaller rocks that formed a natural stone staircase. When they finally reached the top, they found flat and grassy farmland. The storm had passed at last, but in its wake blew a cool wind that made Marlena's clothes feel like ice.

In the distance they spied one light. "A farmhouse," he said. "Make haste."

Marlena had difficulty making sense of his words. She liked his arm wrapped around her, but disliked him making her walk, especially so briskly. He made sounds with each breath, as if every step brought pain. Pain would be preferable to feeling nothing, Marlena thought. She was no longer aware of her arms or her legs.

The light grew nearer, but Marlena forgot what it signified. Her mind felt full of wool and all she wanted was to sleep.

She tried to pull away from him. "Rest," she managed to say. "Sleep."

"No." He lifted her over his shoulder and carried her.

They came to a cottage with a lone candle burning in the window. Tanner pounded on the door. "Help us! Open the door."

Soon a grizzled man in a white nightcap and gown opened the door a crack.

"Quick. I must get her warm," Tanner told him.

"Dod i mewn," the man said. "Come in, come in."

Tanner carried her inside and made her stand in front of a fireplace. The dying embers on the hearth gave heat, but the heat felt painful after the numbing cold.

"Bring some blankets," Tanner ordered. "I must warm her."

The man tottered into another room, and Tanner began stripping her of her clothing, which seemed a very odd thing for him to do, but nice, because her wet clothes were so very heavy, and she wanted to feel light again.

Suddenly dry cloth covered her shoulders and Tanner made her sit in a chair close to the fire.

The old man threw more lumps of coal into the fireplace,

and poked at it with the poker, which only made it hotter and more painful.

"M'wife and son are at the wreck," the man explained.

Oh, yes, Marlena dimly remembered, as shivers seized her. She had been on a ship that had broken apart. She remembered the shock of the cold water.

A cat ambled by, rubbing its fur against her legs. "Cat," she said to no one in particular, as her eyelids grew very heavy.

Marlena woke to find herself nestled in a nice warm bed with heavy bedcovers over her. She did not seem to have on any clothing at all, not even a shift. Next to her, also naked and holding her close, lay the Marquess of Tannerton.

Chapter Two

The woman felt warm against him, warm at last, when Tanner had thought never to be warm again. He slipped his hand down her smooth back, savouring the feel of her silky skin under his fingertips. He could still smell the sea on her, but they were both blessedly dry. And warm. He had saved her from the sea, thank God.

Thank God.

A shuffle sounded in the room and a murmur, and the woman pushed away from him with a cry.

He sat up like a shot.

The woman slid away to a corner of the bed, clutching the blanket up to her chin. Morning light shone through the small window and three pairs of eyes stared at them both, the wrinkled old man who had opened the door to them the night before, a wrinkled old woman and a younger, thick-chested man.

"What the devil?" Tanner growled.

The spectators jumped back. The old man gave a servile smile. "M'wife and son are back."

Tanner glared at them. "You disturb our privacy."

In actuality, he and the woman were the intruders. Tanner had given the old man little choice but to relinquish what was surely the bed he shared with the old woman. The night before all Tanner could think of was to cover the woman in blankets and warm her with his own body—and be warmed by hers. He'd left their clothing in a pile in the front room and carried her to the little bedchamber behind the fireplace, ordering the poor man to bring as many blankets as he owned.

The younger man—the farmer's son, obviously—rubbed his head and winced, and the hairs on the back of Tanner's neck stood on end. The son, he would swear, had been his seaside attacker. Tanner frowned. Their place of refuge suddenly seemed more like a lion's den.

He quickly regained his composure. "What are you doing in this room?" he demanded again, checking his finger for his gold signet ring and feeling under the bedcovers for the purse he'd had sense enough to remove from his coat. He held it up. "Were you looking for the purse?"

The younger man backed away to where clothing hung by pegs on the plastered walls above two wooden chests.

"We merely came to see if you required anything, that is all." The old woman simpered.

Tanner scoffed. "All three of you at once?"

The young man gave a chagrined expression and inclined his head.

Tanner glanced at his companion, still huddled under the blanket. He turned to the others. "Leave us," he commanded.

The old man and woman scurried towards the door. Their son moved more slowly, his hand returning to his head.

"We require our clothing." Tanner added.

The woman paused in the doorway. "Your things are still damp, m'lord." She tipped her head in a servile pose. "I've hung them out in the sun and the wind. 'Twill take no time at all to dry."

"Good." Tanner's tone turned a shade more conciliatory. "Treat us well and you will be rewarded." He lifted the purse.

The son smiled. "What else do you require, m'lord?"

"Some nourishment, if you please."

The man bowed and closed the door behind him.

"They thought they could nick my purse," Tanner muttered, rubbing the stubble on his chin. He did not have the heart to worry her with his suspicions about the farmer's son. "How do you fare, miss? Are you all right?"

She moved beneath the blanket as if testing to see if all parts of her still worked. "A little bruised, but unharmed, I think."

Her eyes flicked over him and quickly glanced away. Tanner realised he was quite bare from the waist up. From the waist down, as well, but the covers concealed that part of him. He reached for a blanket and winced, pressing a hand to his ribs.

"You are bruised," she cried, reaching towards him, but immediately withdrawing her hand.

He looked down at himself, purple bruises staining his torso like spilled ink. "Nothing to signify," he said, although his breath caught on another pang of pain.

He glanced at her again and the humour of the situation struck him. It was not every day he woke up in a naked embrace with a woman whose name he did not know.

He gave her a wry smile. "I do not believe we have been introduced."

Her eyelids fluttered, reminding him of shy misses one encountered at Almack's. "No, we have not."

He made a formal bow, or a semblance of one there in the bed only half-covered by a blanket. "I am Tannerton. The

Marquess of Tannerton. Tanner to my friends, which, I dare say—" he grinned "—I had best include you among."

The blue of her eyes sparkled in the morning light. "Marquess—" She quickly cast her eyes downward. "My lord."

"Tanner," he corrected in a friendly voice. "And you are…?"

He had the feeling her mind was crafting an answer.

"I am Miss Brown, sir."

It was a common name, and not her real one, he'd wager.

"Miss Brown," he repeated.

She fussed with the blanket, as if making sure it still covered her. "Do you know of the others from the ship? Did anyone else survive?"

He gave her a steady look. "The Bow Street Runner, do you mean?"

She glanced away and nodded.

He made a derisive sound. "I hope he went to the devil."

She glanced back at him. "Did any survive?"

"I know nothing of any of them," he went on, trying not to think of those poor women, those helpless little children, the raging sea. "We were alone on the beach, except for the man who tried to rob me." The man who had just left this room, he suspected. "We made it to this cottage, and all I could think was to get you warm. I took over the farmer's bed and must have fallen asleep."

She was silent for a moment, but Tanner could see her breath quicken. He suspected she remembered the terror of it all.

"I believe I owe you my life, sir," she whispered.

Her blue eyes met his and seemed to pierce into him, touching off something tender and vulnerable. He glanced away and tugged on the covers, pulling off a faded brown blanket. He wrapped it around his waist and rose from the bed. "Let me see about getting you some clothes. And food." He turned towards the door.

"A moment, sir," she said, her voice breathless. "Do—do you know where we are? Who these people are?"

"Only that we are in a farmer's cottage," he replied, not entirely truthfully. "There was a lamp in the window. I walked towards its light."

She nodded, considering this. "What do they know of us?"

His gaze was steady. "I did not tell them you were a prisoner, if that is your concern."

She released a relieved breath. "Did you tell them who you are?"

He tried to make light of it all. "Last night I only saw the old man. I fear I failed to introduce myself. My manners have gone begging."

"Good," she said.

"Good?" His brows rose.

"Do not tell them who you are."

He cocked his head.

"A marquess is a valuable commodity. They might wish to ransom you."

She was sharp, he must admit. Her mistrust gave even more credence to his suspicions. He had thought to bully these people with his title, but he now saw the wisdom of withholding who he was—as well as who she might be.

He twisted his signet ring to the inside of his palm and put his hand on the door latch. "I will not say a word." Her lovely face relaxed. "Let me see about our clothing and some food and a way out of here."

She smiled and he walked out of the room, still holding the blanket around his waist.

* * *

It took Marlena a moment to adjust when he left the room. The marquess's essence seemed to linger, as well as the image of him naked. She and Eliza had been too naïve to speculate on how the Marquess of Tannerton would look without clothing, but she could now attest that he looked spectacular. Wide shoulders, sculpted chest peppered with dark hair that formed a line directing the eye to his manly parts. She'd only glimpsed them upon first awakening, but now she could not forget the sight. He was like a Greek statue come to life, but warm, friendly and flirtatious.

He might not recognise her as the notorious Vanishing Viscountess, subject of countless Rowlandson prints and sensational newspaper stories, but he did know she'd been a prisoner. He would, of course, have no memory of the very naïve and forgettable Miss Parronley from Almack's.

She hugged her knees. As long as he did not recognise her, she was free. And she intended to keep it that way.

She had no idea what piece of shore they'd washed up on, but it must be closer to Scotland than she'd ever dared hope to be again. She longed to be in Scotland, to lose herself there and never be discovered. A city, perhaps, with so many people, no one would take note of a newcomer. She would go to Edinburgh, a place of poetry and learning. Who would look for the Vanishing Viscountess in Edinburgh? They would think her dead at the bottom of the sea.

She'd once believed she'd be safe in Ireland, in the ruse she and Eliza devised, governess to Eliza's children. Not even Eliza's husband had suspected. Marlena had been safe for three years, until Eliza's brother came to visit. Debtors nipping at his heels, Geoffrey had come to beg his sister for money.

Marlena would have hidden from him, or fled entirely, but

Eliza and the children had been gravely ill from the fever and she could not bear to leave. Geoffrey discovered her tending to them. He'd recognised her instantly and suddenly realised he could raise his needed funds by selling the whereabouts of the Vanishing Viscountess.

Geoffrey had long returned to London the day Marlena stood over Eliza's newly dug grave in the parish churchyard, the day the magistrate's men and the Bow Street Runner came to arrest her.

She swiped at her eyes. *At least we nursed the children back to health, Eliza.*

She rose from the bed and wrapped the blanket around her like a toga. The room was tiny and sparse, but clean. There was no mirror, so she tried to look at herself in the window glass, but the sun was too bright. She felt her hair, all tangles and smelling of sea water. It was still damp underneath. She sat back on the bed.

She must look a fright, she thought, working at her tangled locks with her fingers, still vain enough to wish she appeared pretty for the handsome Marquess of Tannerton.

Except for the bruises on his chest, he had looked wonderful after their ordeal—his unshaven face only enhancing his appearance, making him look rakish. She inhaled, her fingers stilling for a moment with the memory of how his naked skin had felt, warm and hard with muscle.

Her whole body filled with heat. It had been a long time since she'd seen a naked man and a long time since a man had held her. She tried to remember if she had ever woken naked in her husband's arms. Perhaps she never had. He usually had fled her bed when he finished with her.

So long ago.

The door opened and the old woman entered, the scent of boiling oats wafting in behind her.

"Your gentleman says to find you some clothes, ma'am. Yours are ripped and would take too long to mend." She handed Marlena her stockings, which had somehow remained intact. "I told your gentleman I've just the thing for you in here." The woman rummaged through one of the wooden chests. "I've put the kettle on as well, and there is some nice porridge boiling."

Marlena slipped on her stockings. Porridge sounded as heavenly as ambrosia at the moment. Until she'd smelled it, she'd not known she was ravenous.

"That is very kind," she said to the woman. "What is your name?"

"I'm Mrs Davies, ma'am." The woman leaned over the chest, still looking through it.

Marlena made her voice sound friendly. "Thank you, Mrs Davies. Where are we, might I ask?"

"At our farm, ma'am." The woman looked at her as if she were daft. Her mouth opened, then, and she finally understood the question. "About a mile or so from Llanfairynghornwy."

Marlena blinked. She had no idea where that was, nor did she think she could repeat its name. "Is there a coaching inn there?"

"There is a coaching inn at Cemaes."

"How far is that?" Marlena asked.

"About five miles, ma'am."

Marlena could walk five miles.

The old woman twisted around, leaning on the edge of the chest. "But if I think of it, you'll want to reach Holyhead, not Cemaes."

Holyhead was the port where the ship had been bound. "How far is Holyhead?"

"Ten miles or so the opposite way, to reach the ferry, that is. You'll need a ferry to take you to Holyhead, ma'am."

Marlena nodded. Holyhead would likely be where other survivors would be bound, making it the last place she'd wish to be.

The woman turned back to her rummaging, finally pulling out a shift and tossing it to Marlena, who quickly slipped it on. Next the woman pulled out a faded blue dress.

"Perhaps this will do." She handed it to Marlena.

The dress was made of wool in a fine, soft weave that seemed nothing like a farm wife's dress. Marlena stood up and held it against herself. The dress was long enough for her, although she was taller than most women and certainly a good foot taller than Mrs Davies. The dress would totally engulf the farm woman and would be big on Marlena as well.

Some other woman from some other shipwreck had once worn this dress. Marlena whispered a prayer for that woman's poor soul.

"It will do very nicely," she said.

The woman straightened and thrust something else at Marlena. "Here's a corset for you."

"Thank you." Marlena smiled. "I am so very grateful to you."

The woman started towards the door.

Marlena stopped her with another request. "I would like very much to wash. Would it be too much trouble to bring me some water?"

The woman looked heavenwards, as if she'd been asked for the moon, but she nodded and hurried out of the door.

Marlena inspected the corset. Its laces looked as if they could be tightened to fit her. She lifted the dress to her nose and was grateful that it smelled clean. She was eager to be clean herself, eager to wash the salt from her skin. What she would not give for a nice long soak in warm bathwater, but she would content herself with a quick wash from a basin. She paced the room, thinking, planning. She could easily walk to Cemaes this very day, but what would she do then? She had no money.

She must beg money from Tanner, she decided. It was her only choice. She was uncertain of him, although it was a good sign he'd not betrayed her to this farm family. If he discovered she was the Vanishing Viscountess, however, he would certainly want to turn her over to the local magistrate. It was best to slip away as soon as she could do so.

A knock sounded, and Tanner walked in with her basin of water, a towel over his arm like a valet. She grabbed the blanket and wrapped it around the shift. He was dressed in what looked like his own shirt and trousers. His hair was damp. Marlena touched her still-tangled hair, envious that he had been able to wash out the salt and the memory of the sea.

"Your clothes are dry?" she asked.

"Dry enough." He placed the basin on a small table in the corner of the room. "I thought you might like this." He pulled a comb from the band of his trousers. "I've washed it, although these people seem clean enough."

She took it from him. "Oh, thank you!" She immediately sat back on the bed and attacked her locks. "Have they told you anything of the shipwreck?"

He shook his head. "These people are a close-mouthed lot. The son left, but I hope it was merely to return to the beach. I gather these people are wreckers."

Like the man who attacked Tanner. The man she hit on the head. She remembered that suddenly, but it was like a murky dream.

"The mother and son were out there during the storm last night." He walked towards the door. "Is there anything else you need?"

"My shoes," she replied. "But do not leave yet."

He waited.

She took a breath. "I need to ask you—to beg you—to let me go."

His brows rose.

She went on quickly, "Mrs Davies—the wife—says there is a town five miles from here with a coaching inn. You may go on to Holyhead, but let them all think me dead. Please. I want only to go home. That is all I desire." Not all she desired. She needed money, but she'd make that request only if he gave his permission to flee.

He leaned against the door. "Where is home?"

"Scotland," she said truthfully and an image of her Scottish home jumped into her mind. *Parronley,* home of her ancestors and her carefree childhood.

He peered at her. "You do not sound Scottish."

"I was sent to school in England." This was true, as well. At lovely Belvedere House in Bath, where she'd met Eliza. She'd been very keen to rid herself of any traces of a Scottish burr in those days, so eager for the other girls to like her.

He pressed a hand against his ribs. "Tell me why the Bow Street Runner was bringing you back to England."

Marlena flinched, feeling his pain. Her mind raced to think of a story he would believe. She borrowed one from a Minerva Press novel she and Eliza once read. "I was a lady's companion to a very nice elderly lady. I was accused of stealing her jewellery."

His mouth twitched. "And you did not do it."

"I did not!" She was not guilty of stealing jewellery or any other crime. "I was wrongly accused, but there was no way to prove it. Her son placed the jewels in my room."

How she wished she had been accused of the theft of jewels. Far better that than standing over the bloody body of her husband and being accused of his murder.

She made herself face him with a steady gaze. "I ran away to Ireland, but they sent the Bow Street Runner after me."

His eyes probed her. They were still that lovely shade of mossy green she remembered from those giddy assemblies at Almack's. "They went to a great deal of trouble to capture you."

She gave a wan smile, but her mind was racing to recall the details of the novel. "Not all the jewellery was recovered. My lady's son sold the rest. He made it look as if he was trying to recover it all, going so far as having me tracked down in Ireland for it." She glanced away from Tanner, and her voice came from deep in her throat. "He placed the blame on me."

In truth, it had been her own cousin who contrived to have her blamed for Corland's murder, and her cousin Wexin had once been a member of the Marquess of Tannerton's set. That had been seven years ago, when Marlena and Eliza had had their first Season, but for all Marlena knew Tanner could still count Wexin among his friends.

In that lovely Season, when she and Eliza had been so full of hope, she'd begged Wexin to present them to the handsome marquess. Wexin refused, although she and Eliza had been undaunted.

"Who were these people who employed you?" he asked.

"I cannot tell you," she replied truthfully again. "For all I know, the son may be one of your close companions." Like Wexin had been. "You would believe them and not me." She fixed her gaze on him again. "Let me go, I implore you. Let me disappear. Let them think I am dead."

He stared back at her, not speaking, not moving. Panic spread inside her like a wild weed.

"You have no money. How will you get on?" he asked.

She took a breath. "I would beg a little money from you."

He gave her a long look before speaking. "First wash and dress and eat. We shall both leave this place, then we will decide what to do next." He opened the door and walked out.

Her nerves still jangled. He had not precisely agreed to help her, but he had not sounded as if he would turn her in, either. She had no choice but to wait to see what he would do.

Marlena washed and dressed and managed to get her hair into a plait down her back. When she walked out of the bedchamber in her stockinged feet, the smell of the porridge drove all other thought and emotion away. She sat in a plain wooden chair across from Tanner at a small table. The old woman set a bowl of porridge in front of her. Marlena's hand shook when she dipped her spoon into the steaming bowl. The first mouthful was too hot. She blew on the next spoonful and the next and ate as quickly as she could. Tanner ate as hungrily as she.

The old farmer and his wife watched their every move.

When they finished, Tanner turned to them. "Bring the rest of my clothing, my boots and the lady's shoes. The lady also needs a cloak. You will undoubtedly have a cart. I should like you to take us to the nearest town."

"Holyhead?" the farmer asked. "You'll need a ferry to reach it."

Tanner reached into the sleeve of his shirt where he had tucked his purse. He opened it and took out a sovereign. "Very well."

The farmer's eyes grew wide at the sight of the coin. Both he and his wife sprang into action, leaving Tanner and Marlena alone.

Marlena gave him an anxious look. "I will not go to Holyhead. Just leave me, I beg you. I will not even ask you for money."

He shook his head. "I'll not leave you." He leaned closer

to her. "But I have no intention of going to Holyhead either. Let them think that is where we are bound."

Warmth spread through her, and she did not think it was from the porridge. She wanted to throw her arms around him in gratitude. Instead she composed her emotions. "Mrs Davies told me Cemaes is five miles from here in the opposite direction from Holyhead."

"Then we shall go to Cemaes." He smiled.

Mrs Davies brought Tanner's coat, waistcoat, boots and Marlena's half-boots. She rose and took her shoes from the woman's hands. They were still damp and the leather tight, but she did not care. Tanner was going to help her to get to Cemaes.

Arlan Rapp sat in front of the fire in the inn at Llanfwrog, sipping hot cider, waiting for his clothes to dry through and through. He puzzled what he should do next.

All he really wanted was to return to London and get paid for his work, but he'd better not do that until he discovered if the Viscountess Corland had been lost with most of the other passengers and crew, or if she had by some miracle survived.

The Vanishing Viscountess had vanished again. That would make a good story for the newspapers, he'd wager, but he'd rather it not be widely known he'd been the one to lose her.

He stared into the fire and pondered the choices he'd made. He refused to feel guilty about taking her place in the last boat. She'd been as good as dead from the moment he first put her in shackles. He would have taken her back to a hangman's noose, nothing less. The Vanishing Viscountess had killed her husband in a jealous rage. Everybody knew her husband rutted with any female he could find. The Viscountess had been caught red-handed. Her cousin had discovered her standing over Viscount Corland's dead body, bloody scissors in hand. There was no doubt that she'd committed the murder.

She had escaped, however. The guilty always ran away if you gave them half a chance.

She'd escaped again, Rapp thought, rubbing his face. He hoped drowning was an easier death than hanging by the neck.

He took another gulp of cider. A log sizzled in the fireplace. He glanced around for the serving girl, who seemed to have disappeared. Rapp's stomach growled, ravenous for breakfast. He was also bone weary from being up all night, pulled out of the sea by local folk and sent to this inn in a wagon with the handful of other survivors.

Rapp bowed his head, thinking of the women and children in his boat. They had not been strong enough to hang on when the wave washed over them.

Rapp suddenly wanted to hurry home to his wife and children. He wanted to kiss his wife, hug his two sons, hold his baby girl. It was only right that he'd seized the chance to survive. His wife and children needed him.

Only eight passengers survived, as far as he knew, and a few more crewmen. The Vanishing Viscountess was not among them. If her body lay at the bottom of the sea, it might never wash up on shore. Rapp cursed the storm. Wexin would not pay him without proof that the Viscountess had perished.

He'd have to investigate, make absolutely certain she was among the dead. He was a Bow Street Runner. It should be a simple matter for him to discover who survived the shipwreck.

The serving girl finally set down a plate with bread and butter and thick pieces of ham.

He nodded his thanks. "Bring me paper, pen and ink," he asked her.

He'd pen a letter to Wexin, reporting the shipwreck, and one to his wife, as well, telling her he loved her, but that he must delay his return to London until he had searched up and down the Anglesey coast.

Chapter Three

By the time Mr Davies's old horse pulled the cart to the front of the cottage, Tanner was more than ready to leave this place. He had no wish to tarry until the son returned.

Tanner pressed a hand to his still-aching ribs, remembering the strength of the man's boot. He had no wish to meet young Davies again.

He stepped aside for Miss Brown to walk out ahead of him. The red cloak the old lady had found for her was threadbare, but Tanner supposed it would keep her warm enough. His lack of a top coat did not worry him overmuch. The temperature was not that harsh and would keep him alert.

Mrs Davies trailed behind him. "You promised us payment, sir."

He turned to her. "I will pay when your husband delivers us where we wish to go." He strode on.

She skipped after him. "How do we know you will pay? Your lady is walking away wearing my clothes. We can't afford to give our possessions away. Times are hard."

He stopped again and the old woman nearly ran into him. "You will have to trust my word as a gentleman, will you not?" He walked over to where Miss Brown waited next to the cart.

He did not know how much of her story to believe, but he'd be damned if he'd turn her over to a magistrate. No matter what she had done, she'd paid for it by what that deuced Bow Street Runner made her endure, leaving her to die while he saved himself. As far as Tanner was concerned, that alone should give her freedom.

Saving her life absolved him, in part, for the other deaths that weighed on his conscience. He would see her safe to help repay that debt.

He touched her arm. "I will climb up first, then assist you."

His ribs only hurt mildly as he got up next to the old man. He reached for Miss Brown's hand and pulled her up. As she settled next to him, he wanted to put his arm around her. He wanted to touch her, to keep fresh the memory of their naked embrace. He remembered the feel of her in his arms as he lay between sleep and waking. Her skin, soft and smooth and warm. Her curves, fitting against him as if tailored to him.

"Let us go," he told the farmer.

Mr Davies snapped the ribbons and the old horse started moving.

"You make him pay, husband!" Mrs Davies shouted after them.

The old horse pulled the cart past the vegetable garden, colourful with cabbages and kale. Wheat was already planted for the winter crop and a rook swept down and disappeared into the field of swaying stalks. The cart rolled at a slow speed finally reaching a road, leaving the cottage some distance behind.

At the road, Tanner turned to Mr Davies. "Take us to Cemaes."

The old man's head jerked in surprise. "Cemaes is north. You'll be wanting to go south to the ferry to Holyhead."

"We wish to go north. To Cemaes," Tanner said.

Mr Davies shook his head. "You want to go to Holyhead, I tell you."

Tanner felt a shiver crawl up his back. He'd wager the old man had some mishap planned on the road to the ferry. He held up the sovereign, which glittered in the sunlight. "If you wish to earn this coin, you will take us to Cemaes." He returned the coin to his pocket. "If not, we will walk from here." Tanner began to stand.

The farmer gestured for him to sit. "I'll take you to Cemaes," he grumbled and turned the horse and cart north.

The road, still muddy from the rains, wound past more farmland and other small cottages like the Davies's. Sometimes Tanner could glimpse the sea, looking calm this day, like a slumbering monster that had devoured its fill. The old man kept the frown on his face and did not speak. Miss Brown gripped the seat to steady herself as the cart rumbled along, but she, too, was silent. The cart jostled her against him, from time to time, keeping Tanner physically aware of her.

Her face was obscured by the hood of the cloak, and Tanner missed watching the play of emotions on her face. He'd seen her angry, earnest, frightened and relieved. He would enjoy hearing her laugh, or seeing passion light her face.

He also wished to discover her real name and the names of the people from whom she had supposedly stolen jewels. If she confided in him, he could help her. Even if she was guilty of the theft, he could make her troubles disappear. Money, power and influence overcame justice most of the time. If he repaid the son for the jewels, he'd wager the theft would be totally forgiven.

Tanner could not gaze at her without being obvious, so he settled for the warmth of the sun on his face, the scent of the fresh sea air and fragrant fields, and the sight of the peaceful countryside. It was not precisely an Arcadian paradise, not with men toiling in the fields and cottages too small for comfort, but it was solid and timeless and vastly preferable to the cold, fickle sea.

As the sun grew higher in the sky, they passed a windmill spinning in the breeze, and a standing stone placed there by Celtic people long erased from history. Tanner guessed the time to be about noon. He dug his fingers into his pocket for his timepiece. It was no longer there.

His head whipped around to the old farmer driving the cart. The old man had gone through his pockets, he'd wager. "I wonder what time it is," he said.

The old man's jaw flexed.

Tanner coughed and winced as the pain in his ribs kicked at him again. Miss Brown looked over at him with concern in her eyes. He returned a reassuring smile, before glancing back to the old farmer.

He ought to deprive the man of the sovereign he'd promised, glad he'd had the presence of mind to hang on to his purse after he'd peeled every piece of wet clothing off his body, making a sopping pile on the cottage floor. Miss Brown had been shivering so violently, Tanner had been desperate to make her warm.

Mr Davies flicked the ribbons and glanced at Tanner nervously, fearful, no doubt, that Tanner would challenge him on the theft of his timepiece.

Tanner glanced back to the road. Let the man keep the watch, he said to himself. As payment for his bed. Tanner would have given the man anything for that warm bed. For *her*. To save her from the killing cold as he had saved her from the killing sea.

* * *

Two slow hours passed and Tanner suspected they could have walked faster than the old horse moved on the muddy road. Finally rooftops and a church bell tower came into view.

"Cemaes," said the old man, lifting his chin towards the town.

Miss Brown leaned forward. What was she thinking? Tanner wondered. What plan was she making for herself?

They came to the first houses, gleaming white, edged with chrysanthemums and marigolds. Up ahead the buildings became thicker and Tanner could see people walking about.

Miss Brown put her hand on Tanner's arm. "May we stop here?" She gave him that earnest look again.

He drank it in for a moment, then turned to the old man. "Mr Davies, you may leave us off here."

The old man's bushy brows shot up. "It is no distance to the inn."

"Good!" Tanner responded in a jovial voice. "Then it shall be only a short walk for us. Stop, if you please."

The farmer shrugged and pulled on the ribbons, halting his horse. Tanner climbed down and reached up for Miss Brown. Putting his hands on her waist, he lifted her down to the road and was reluctant to let go of her. He fished in his pocket for the sovereign and handed it up to Mr Davies, who grabbed it quickly, as if fearing Tanner would change his mind. Without a word of farewell, the man flicked the ribbons again, and the old horse clopped its way into town, to the inn and some refreshment for them both, Tanner suspected.

"You gave him a sovereign." Miss Brown said in a disapproving tone.

Tanner kicked a pebble into the street. "Yes."

She rolled her eyes.

"Too much?"

"I dare say," she responded. "Half that amount would have been generous."

He tilted his head, somewhat chagrined. "Especially since the man also stole my watch and I highly suspect his son was the man you hit over the head."

Her jaw dropped. "Tell me it is not so." Outrage filled her face. "How shabby of them to take such advantage."

This was an odd reaction for a supposed thief, Tanner thought. "Well, it is done…" He glanced around him, at the cobblestones in the street, at the tidy houses. "Why did you wish to be let off here?"

The sun illuminated her features and made her eyes sparkle like sapphires. He felt momentarily deprived of breath.

"I wanted a chance to talk with you." She gazed at him intently. "To prepare."

It took a moment for him to respond. "Prepare for what?"

She frowned in concentration. "I cannot enter that inn saying I am Miss Brown off the shipwrecked packet from Dublin, the prisoner escorted by a Bow Street Runner. I must think of some fiction to tell them."

Tanner nodded. He'd not thought much beyond being rid of Mr Davies and finding an inn with good food and a comfortable bed, but, then, he was not much accustomed to thinking ahead while travelling. The next meal, the next bed and the final destination were all he considered, and half the time they were arranged by his valet or his secretary.

She went on. "And I cannot walk in as the companion of the Marquess of Tannerton."

He felt a bit like a rejected suitor. "Would that be too scandalous?"

"It would be too foolish." Her expression turned patient,

as if speaking to a dull child. "The Marquess of Tannerton is sure to create a great deal of interest, especially if the marquess almost drowned. If I am seen with you, I will become an object of curiosity as well, and that I cannot have. I must slip away without anyone noticing me."

This woman must never look at herself in a mirror, Tanner thought. Surely she could not go anywhere and not be noticed.

"I see." He nodded, trying not to be distracted by his vision of her. "What do you propose?"

Her expression gave the impression of a mind turning like the intricate gears of his stolen watch. The road forked a few paces away and led to a stone bridge over a stream. She gestured for him to walk with her. They strolled to the bridge, where they stood side by side, leaning on the wall, gazing into the stream, swollen and brown from the previous day's storm.

She turned to him. "I—I must be on my way. The sooner I leave Anglesey, the sooner I will be forgotten. I want it thought that I drowned in the shipwreck. If they think me dead, no one will search for me."

Tanner disliked hearing her speak of being "on her way."

"Where will you go?" he asked. "Scotland is a big place."

She searched his face for a moment before turning her gaze away. "It is best for me not to say."

He frowned, unused to anyone refusing an answer to his question. Her mistrust wounded him when she so clearly needed a friend.

She turned back to him, her voice low and desperate. "I need some of your money."

He stared at her.

Nothing would be easier for him than to hand over the entire contents of his purse. He could get more money for himself later, on the mere strength of his name. Even in this remote place someone would extend the Marquess of Tannerton credit, enough to arrange for a post-chaise to carry him back to London. He could return to his townhouse in a matter of days.

He usually solved his difficulties by handing over money and letting someone else take care of it. Ironically, one of the rare times he'd taken it upon himself to solve a problem, three people died.

Perhaps he ought to leave her here in Cemaes.

Suddenly some of the colour drained from her face and her breathing accelerated. "Forgive my foolish request," she whispered. "You have done more than enough for me. I do not need your money."

She spun away from him and started to walk away.

He seized her arm. "Wait."

His conscience could not let her go, even with his purse in her hand. He knew he could help her. His name and influence—and his money as well—could save her from the hangman's noose or transportation or whatever fate might befall her if she was caught again.

"I have another proposal." He spoke in a low voice. "Come to London with me. Let me use my influence to help you. Whoever has caused you this trouble is not likely to have friends as highly connected as my friends, nor as much money as I possess. I am certain I can settle this matter for you. My power and influence are considerable."

She stepped away from him. "No!" She took a deep breath. "No," she said more quietly. "I thank you, but—but—you are mistaken. My trouble is—" She clamped her mouth shut on whatever it was she had been about to say.

He kept his gaze steady. "No matter what your trouble is, I assure you, I can help."

She shook her head. "You cannot know—" Again she stopped herself from speaking. "It is safer for me to run. No one will look for me, because they will think me dead. They will forget me, and I may start my life anew."

She gazed at him with such intensity Tanner felt the impact resonate deep inside him. He moved towards her. What made her think *he* could forget her? What made her think he could let her be dead to him now when he'd refused to let her die in the sea?

"Surely you cannot travel alone," he tried.

"Of course I can." She glanced away, and he could sense her mind at work again. "I might be a governess travelling to a new place of employment. Who would question that?"

He did not like this idea. Some men would consider an unescorted governess fair game. "Someone would ask who employed you, for one thing. They would ask where you were bound."

"Then I would fashion answers."

She was slipping away. He remembered that horrible moment when he'd woken up on shore and thought she had slipped from his grasp. He did not want to let go of her now any more than he had wanted to then. True, he might easily return to his comforts, the diversions of London, the hunting parties he and Pomroy planned to attend, but how could he be content now if he thought her adrift, alone?

He glanced away, his mind whirling, as he'd fancied hers had done. All he could think to do was delay.

He gripped her arm, holding on to her like he had done in the sea. "I'll give you the money." He made her look into his face. "There is no obligation to pay it back. It is a trifling amount to me, I assure you, but listen to me. I am afraid our taciturn Mr Davies is at the inn this very moment loosening his tongue with a large tankard of ale." He glanced in the direction of the inn. "He will tell everyone we are husband and wife—that is what he and his wife concluded about us and I did not correct their impression. Did you?"

She shook her head. "I did not."

He went on, "Davies will tell them we are from the shipwreck, a husband and wife from the shipwreck. If we act as strangers now, we will increase suspicion about you, not reduce it."

She considered this. "Yes, that would be true."

His spirits rose. He held on to her still. He took a breath. "In this town we must also be husband and wife."

"Husband and wife?" She stared at him, a worry line forming between her brows.

Acting as husband and wife meant sharing a room. Tanner longed to hold her again, longed to again wake with her in his arms, to know he had kept her safe.

He looked into her face, suffused with reluctance, and realised she might not be as thrilled at the prospect of sharing a bed with him as he was with her.

"I will not take advantage of you," he said in as earnest a tone as he could muster, although his body pulsed with desire for her.

She glanced away, and again turned her eyes back to him, eyes as blue as the sky behind her. "Very well. Tonight we are husband and wife."

He heard the unspoken end to her sentence. Tomorrow they would part. Still, his spirits soared. He would have this brief time with her and maybe wherever they were bound on the morrow would reassure him she'd be safe.

He offered her his arm. "Shall we prepare? We must concoct a story for ourselves, must we not? Names. We need to have names, and, to own the truth, I do not think Brown is a good choice."

"Why?" she asked.

"It is the sort of name a gentleman gives to an innkeeper when he does not wish his identity known." He winked.

She gave a light laugh. "Is that so?

"It is." He smiled. "Select another name."

"Smith?" A corner of her mouth lifted.

He rolled his eyes, playing along with her jest. "You are not good at this, are you?" He put his mind to the task, but the only names he could think of were ones too connected to him. Adam. Vick. Tanner. "I am hopeless as well."

"I have an idea," she said. "How about the name *Lir? Lir* is the god of the sea in Irish mythology."

He peered at her. "You know Irish mythology?"

"I lived in Ireland." She cast her eyes down. "I read about it in a book there."

"How do you spell it? Like Shakespeare's King Lear?" he asked. "Because I know how to spell that Lear. The Irish always use—well—Irish spellings."

She gave him a look that mocked the one he'd given her. "You know Shakespeare?"

He laughed.

Her eyes twinkled. "We can spell it like King Lear."

He smiled back at her, his heart gladdened at her mirth. Their first night together had been full of terror. This one ought to be peaceful and happy. He vowed he would make it so.

"I shall be Adam Lear, then. Adam is my given name." He waited for her to tell him her given name—hoped she would say it, so he might have that small piece of her to keep for himself.

She said nothing.

He took a deep, disappointed breath. "I believe I need an occupation as well."

* * *

Marlena enjoyed their short walk to the inn, and their creation of a story to tell about themselves. The Marquess of Tannerton became Mr Adam Lear, stable manager for Viscount Cavanley, Adrian Pomroy's father, although they agreed it would be best to avoid mentioning Pomroy if at all possible.

Pomroy was another name from Marlena's past, from that one London Season. She had not thought of Pomroy in her four years of exile in Ireland or really even three years before that, not since her Season. She remembered him as a most ramshackle young man. She and Eliza thought Pomroy was a relentless flirt, devoid of even one serious bone in his body. They'd laughed at his antics behind their fans, but neither she nor Eliza mooned over him the way they mooned over his good friend, Tanner. Even though they had been very green girls then, they knew an attachment to Pomroy would be a foolish one.

It was unfortunate that Marlena's judgement of character had not been that astute when it came to Corland, but then, her husband had disguised his true nature. Pomroy had been as clear as glass.

As Marlena walked at Tanner's side, she almost again felt like that carefree girl who'd enjoyed every moment of her Season. Tanner made her laugh again, something she'd not done since Eliza took ill. Marlena feared she was much too glad she would be spending another night with Tanner.

Imagine it, Eliza! she said silently. *I will be married to the Marquess of Tannerton. Very briefly, however. In name only, and a false name at that.*

She remembered then how warm his skin had felt, how firm his hand on her body. Her skin flushed with the memory.

She spied Mr Davies's horse drinking water from a trough at the inn, and the truth of her situation hit her once more.

She was the Vanishing Viscountess, trying desperately to vanish once more. She was not the wife of the Marquess of Tannerton nor plain Mrs Lear. She was not even Miss Brown. She was a fugitive, and if Tanner was caught aiding her, he would face the same punishment as she faced, the hangman's noose.

She and Eliza had not known that fact when Marlena had fled to Ireland with her friend and became her children's governess. Once in Ireland, they had read a newspaper that described the penalty for aiding the Vanishing Viscountess, but Eliza had refused to allow Marlena to leave.

Tanner squeezed her hand as they walked in the door of the inn. "How are you faring, Mrs Lear?"

"A bit nervous, Mr Lear," she replied. At the moment, more nervous for him than for her. She stood to earn life from this masquerade. He risked death.

"We shall do very nicely," he said.

She pulled him back, "Tanner," she whispered.

He gave her a warning look. "It is Adam."

She bit her lip. She must not make such a mistake again. "Do not act like the marquess."

He gave her a puzzled look.

"Do not order people about," she explained.

He tilted his head, appearing very boyish. "Do I order people about?"

She nodded.

The innkeeper approached them. "Good day to you! Are you the lady and gentleman from the shipwreck?"

Mr Davies had indeed been talking of them.

"We are," said Tanner, his affability a bit strained. "And we are in need of a room for the night."

"If we may," added Marlena.

"If we may," repeated Tanner.

The innkeeper smiled. "We will make you comfortable, never fear. If you are hungry, we are serving dinner in the taproom. We have some nice pollack frying. You must let it be our gift to you for your ordeal."

Marlena was touched by this kindness.

"We thank you," said Tanner. He laughed. "I confess, a tall tankard of ale would be very welcome."

The innkeeper walked over and clapped him on the shoulder. "Ale it is. For you, m'lady—?"

"Lear." She cleared her throat. "Mrs Lear. I should like a glass of cider, if you have it."

"We do indeed," said the innkeeper.

Soon they were seated, drinks set in front of them. Marlena glimpsed Mr Davies, who gave them a sidelong look before slipping off his chair and walking to the door.

A woman wearing a bright white apron and cap walked over. "I am Mrs Gwynne. Welcome to our inn. My husband said you had arrived. From the shipwreck, are you?"

"We are." Tanner extended his hand. "It is a pleasure to meet you, Mrs. Gwynne."

"You poor lambs." She clasped his hand.

"Have you heard of any other survivors?" Marlena asked.

The woman clasped Marlena's hand next. "Not a one, but if you made it, others may have as well, God willing. Now, what can we do for you? Besides giving you a nice room and some food, that is. What do you need?"

Tanner rubbed his chin, even darker with beard than it had been that morning. Marlena suppressed a sudden urge to touch it.

"All we have is what you see," he told Mrs Gwynne. "Is there a shop where we might purchase necessities?"

She patted his arm. "There certainly is a shop; if you tell me what you want, I will purchase it for you."

"That will not be necessary. I will visit the shop." Tanner glanced at Marlena and back to Mrs Gwynne. "I have thought of something else you might do, however."

"Say what it is, Mr Lear. I'll see it done."

His gaze rested softly on Marlena. "A bath for my wife."

Marlena's mouth parted. There was nothing she could more desire.

Mrs Gwynne smiled again. "I will tell the maids to start heating the water."

She bustled away and soon they were brought a generous and tasty dinner of fish, potatoes and peas. After they ate, Mrs Gwynne showed them to their room, a chamber dominated by a large, comfortable-looking bed. There was also a fire in the fireplace and a nice window looking out at the back of the inn. The best part, however, was the large copper tub half-filled with water.

"There are towels next to the tub, and a cake of soap. The maids are still bringing the water, and one will assist you if you like." Mrs Gwynne folded her arms over her considerable chest.

"Thank you," Marlena rasped, her gaze slipping to Tanner.

"I'll leave you now," the older woman said. "Mr Lear, when you wish to go to the shop, either my husband or I can direct you."

"I will be down very soon," he said.

After the innkeeper's wife left, Marlena walked over to the tub and dipped her fingers into the warm water.

"Am I sounding like a marquess?" Tanner asked.

She smiled at him. "You are doing very well."

He blew out a breath and walked towards her. "That is good. I confess, I am uncertain how not to sound like a marquess, but if I am accomplishing it, I am content." His eyes rested on her. "I should leave, so you can have your bath."

She lifted her hand and touched him lightly on the arm. "Thank you for this, Lord Tannerton."

"Adam," he reminded her, his name sounding like a caress.

"Adam," she whispered.

His eyes darkened and he seemed to breathe more deeply. He glanced away from her. "What ought I to purchase for you?"

She thought the bath more than enough. "A comb, perhaps? A brush? Hairpins?"

He smiled. "I shall pretend I am an old married man who often is sent to the shop for hairpins. Anything else?"

She ought not to ask him for another thing. "Gloves?"

"Gloves." He nodded.

There was a knock on the door and he crossed the room to open it. It was the maid bringing more water.

She poured it into the tub. "I'll bring more." She curtsied and left.

"I will leave now, as well." Tanner opened the door and turned back to her. "Save me the water."

Marlena crossed the room to him. "Forgive me. I did not think. You must have the water first. I will wait."

He reached up and touched her cheek. "You first, Mrs Lear."

By the time she could breathe again, he was gone.

Arlan Rapp trudged down the Llanfwrog road to the blacksmith shop. A huge barrel-chested man, twice the Bow Street Runner's size and weight, hammered an ingot against his anvil. The clang of the hammer only added to the pain throbbing in Rapp's ears. He'd walked from one side of Llanfwrog to the other, but few villagers were even willing to admit to knowing of the shipwreck. He'd recognised plenty of them from when what was left of his boat washed up to shore. The villagers had grabbed crates and barrels. A few had been good enough to aid the survivors. He'd been whisked off to the inn, he and the others who had washed up with him.

He waited to speak until the smithy plunged the piece of metal into water. "Good day to you, smithy," Rapp said.

The man looked up. "Do you require something?"

Rapp smiled, although his fatigue made him feel anything but cordial. "Only a bit of information."

The blacksmith just stared at him.

Rapp cleared his throat. "I am from the packet ship that was wrecked last night."

No understanding showed on the smithy's face, but Rapp doubted anyone in Llanfwrog was ignorant of the previous night's bounty.

He went on. "I am searching for survivors, specifically a woman who had been my companion."

"I know nothing of it," the man said.

"Perhaps you have heard talk," he persisted. "Perhaps someone told you of survivors. I am most eager to learn her fate."

The blacksmith shook his head. He took another piece of glowing metal from the fire.

"I would pay for information," Rapp added, although he much preferred not to part with his still-damp money.

The smith placed the hot metal on the anvil and picked up his hammer. "Bodies wash ashore sometimes."

That was a grisly thought, but if the Viscountess's body washed up on shore, he could cease his search and go home to his wife.

"Where would bodies be taken?" Rapp asked, but the smithy's hammer started again and its din drowned out his words. He gave up.

No sooner had he walked out of the blacksmith shop than a smudged-face boy tugged on his coat. "I can show you bodies, if you want to see 'em."

Rapp squatted down to eye level with the little eavesdropper. "Can you now?"

The boy nodded energetically. "About ten or so."

Rapp took a breath and stood, squaring his shoulders. "Excellent, my good fellow. Take me there now." A few minutes of unpleasantness might mean he could be in London within a few days and still receive his reward.

"It'll cost you tuppence," the boy said.

Smart little cur, Rapp thought sourly. He fished the coin from his pocket and showed it to the boy. "Take me to the bodies and a tuppence you shall have."

Chapter Four

~~~~~~

Tanner's shopping expedition proved to be a novel experience. He'd never shopped for ladies' hairpins before, nor any of his own necessities, for that matter. He typically sent his valet to procure things like razors and shaving brushes and polish for shoes and combs and toothbrushes. He dawdled in the shop for as long as he could to give Miss Brown time for her bath. The shopkeepers and two other customers were full of questions about the shipwreck, unknown to this village before Davies brought news of it. He practised being Mr Lear, although he could answer few questions about how much salvage had washed ashore.

When he left the shop and stopped for another tankard of ale in the taproom, the patrons there had more questions. The extra alcohol made him mellow and, while he talked, a part of his mind wandered to how Miss Brown might appear in the bath, how slick her skin would be, how scented with soap.

Because he had little information about the shipwreck, interest in him waned quickly. He drank more ale in solitude, if not peace. There was nothing peaceful about imagining Miss Brown in the bath. When he eventually carried the packages up the flight of stairs to the room he would share with her, his eagerness to see her made it difficult for him to keep from taking the steps two at a time. He walked down the hall to the door and, balancing the packages in one arm, knocked.

"Come in," she said.

He paused, took a breath, and opened the door.

She was dressed and seated in a chair by the fireplace, pressing a white towel to her long mahogany brown hair. He inhaled the scent of soap and wanted nothing more than to embrace her, soft and warm and clean.

"You are back," she said in a breathless voice.

He felt equally as robbed of air. "I tried to give you ample time."

She twisted the towel around her hair. "I fear you have waited too long. The water has gone quite cold."

He smiled at her. "It cannot be as cold as what we've already experienced."

She shuddered. "No, it cannot." Her eyes lifted to his and held him there.

He mentally shook himself loose from her. It was either do that or do something foolish. "The packages," he said, carrying them over to the table in the corner. He unwrapped one and brought it to her. "I suspect you would like these now." He handed her the brush and comb he had purchased.

They were crafted from simple tortoiseshell. Tanner thought of how many sets of silver brushes and combs he'd had his former secretary, Flynn, purchase for his mistresses. There was nothing so fine in the Cemaes shop, but Miss Brown's eyes glowed with excitement when she took the items from his hands.

"Oh, how wonderful," she cried. "I can comb out the tangles and brush my hair dry."

No gift he ever gave a mistress had been so gratefully received. He grinned, pleased he had pleased her. She was too busy working the comb through her hair to see.

Tanner strolled over to the tub and felt the water, now on the very cold side of tepid. At home, his valet would be hovering with pots of hot water to add, making certain his bath remained warm from start to finish.

She rose from her chair, still holding the comb. "I could ask Mrs Gwynne for more hot water."

They faced each other over the tub and it took Tanner a moment to remember to speak. "You cannot go out with your hair wet."

"I shall put it in a quick plait," she assured him. "I will need to go out anyway so that you can bathe."

He could not help gazing at her. It took time for him to compose another thought, that thought being he did not wish her to leave. "Will not the Gwynnes think it odd that Mrs Lear walks to the public rooms with wet hair?" He reached over and fingered a lock, marvelling at how it already shaped itself in a curl. "They would not expect you to leave your husband merely because he bathes."

She held his gaze, and he fancied her mind working again, mulling over this latest puzzle.

"I believe you are correct." Her eyes were large and round. "I shall position my chair so that my back is to you, and I will comb my hair with the lovely comb you have purchased for me."

With resolution, she marched back to her chair and set it to face the fireplace. Tanner watched her pull the comb through her hair, wishing it was his fingers doing the task.

He shrugged out of his coat and waistcoat and laid them on the bed. Sitting next to them, he removed his boots and stockings. As he pulled his shirt from his trousers, he watched Miss Brown totally absorbed in combing her hair.

He laughed.

Her comb stilled. "What amuses you?"

He had not realised he'd laughed aloud. "Oh, I was merely thinking that when I'm in the company of a woman, undressing is usually a quite different prospect."

She paused for a moment and then began combing again. "Have you been in the company of so many women, Tanner?"

He faced her, naked and aroused and wishing she would turn and see the evidence of his desire for her. He wished she would come to him and let him make love to her right at this moment, to the devil with bathing.

Such thoughts were dangerous. He'd promised her he would not touch her. "I have known enough women, I suppose," he mumbled instead, padding over to the tub, cringing as he tested the water again.

Again she hesitated before speaking. "I suppose you have lots of mistresses."

He frowned at her assumption of him. "I assure you I am quite a success." His attempt at a joke fell flat to his ears. Truth was, he tended to be involved with only one woman at a time, and none but the briefest of encounters in this last year. At the moment he was wondering what the appeal had been in any of them.

She cleared her throat. "Are there towels folded nearby? And the soap?"

He walked around the tub to see them. "I've found them."

Bracing himself, he put one leg in the water, which was as cold as he expected. He forced himself to put the other leg in and began lowering the rest of him, making the water splash loudly in the room.

"Ye gods!" He shot up again when the water hit the part of him most sensitive to temperature. "Ah!" he cried again as he lowered himself a second time, but now it was because his ribs hurt from jumping up so fast.

"It is too cold," Miss Brown said. "I knew I ought to have sought hot water."

"It is tolerable," he managed through the pain and the chill.

He picked up the soap and lathered himself as quickly as he could, grateful for having had the foresight to do a fairly decent job of washing his hair that morning. In his rush, the soap slipped out of his hand and fell into the water. He fished around for it, making a lot of noise doing so. When he finally caught it and lifted it out of the water, it slipped from his hand again, this time clattering to the floor and sliding too far away to reach.

"Deuce," he muttered.

"You've dropped the soap?" she asked from her seat facing the fireplace.

"Yes." This was a damned odd conversation to have when naked with a woman. "It is of no consequence. I believe I am clean enough."

She stood. "I will fetch it for you."

"It is not necessary, I assure you." he told her.

"I do not mind."

Before he could stop her, she turned to face him. Their gazes caught, but she lowered her lashes and searched for the soap, picking it up and bringing it to him. He quickly glanced down to see how much of himself he was revealing at this moment. The water was too cloudy to see anything.

"There you are." She placed the bar of soap in his hand as calmly as if she'd been handing him his hat and gloves. After wiping her hand on a nearby towel, she returned to her chair and resumed combing her hair.

Tanner guessed he was as claret-faced as she'd been un-flappable. "You are not missish, are you, Miss Brown?"

"Mrs Lear," she corrected. "And you are correct. I am too old to be missish."

"Old," he repeated. "How old are you exactly?"

She chose another lock of hair to work the comb through. "Now that is a question no woman wishes to answer."

He shot back. "As old as all that, then?"

She turned her head to him and smiled. "I am twenty-five."

"Good God," he cried in an exaggerated voice. "You are in your dotage!"

She laughed. "And you, sir, are teasing."

He liked the sound of her laughter. He also liked that she was not prone to blushes and foolishness like that. He never could abide the young misses who flocked to London during the Season, looking for husbands when they'd barely been let off leading strings. Miss Brown was ever so much more interesting.

He turned back to his bathing, frowning at what it might mean that she was not missish. What was her experience of men, then?

He realised he was merely sitting in the water, which was turning him into gooseflesh.

"I warn you, I am about to rise from this bath and stand up in all my glory." He started to rise, but stopped. "You may wish to look, seeing as you are not missish."

He tried to make it sound like a jest, although he wanted her to look at him with a desire matching his own of her.

Because of the cold water, however, a part of him was not showing to its greatest advantage. In fact, it had no glory at all.

"I'll look away," She kept her back to him while he dried himself and donned his shirt and trousers.

"It feels glorious to be clean, does it not?" she said.

"Indeed," he agreed, pressing his hand to his ribs. "But I

would be happier if I had a clean shirt." He picked up one of the packages and walked over to the bureau upon which sat a mirror, a pitcher and a bowl.

She switched to the hairbrush and turned around again. "It must be wretched wearing the same shirt."

He smiled at her. "It is not that bad. It merely smells like the devil." He rubbed his chin. "I suppose I shall have to shave myself. Now that is a wretched prospect."

He unwrapped the package and took out a shaving cup, brush and razor. She picked up the soap and brought it to him, her long dark hair falling about her shoulders in soft waves. He wanted to touch it again. In fact, he wanted to grab a fistful of it.

Their gazes caught for a second when she handed him the soap. She lowered her eyes and walked back to her chair.

He took a deep breath and started to lather his face. "It is a fortunate thing my valet developed a toothache on the day we were to leave for Dublin."

"I meant to ask you if anyone accompanied you," she said in a sober voice.

"No one." Thank God, because he did not wish to have more lives on his conscience. Chin and cheeks lathered, he turned away from the mirror to look at her.

"I am glad of it," she murmured.

"I am as well," he responded.

He turned back to the mirror and scraped at his beard. "Pomroy and I once went two weeks without shaving." He made another stroke with the razor. "We went to one of my hunting lodges, but it rained like the devil. There was nothing to do so we drank great quantities of brandy and grew beards."

She giggled. "I wonder you had the energy for it."

"We wagered to see who could grow the longest beard in two weeks." He smiled. "I won it."

"Who was charged with measuring?"

"Our poor valets." He laughed. "We made them switch." He twirled his finger for emphasis. "Pomroy's valet measured my beard and my valet measured Pomroy's. It made the two men very nervous."

He scraped at his cheek some more until his face was nearly clean of soap, except for tiny lines here and there. He rinsed off with the clean water and dried his face.

He presented himself to her. "How did I do?"

To his surprise, she reached up to stroke his face. "You did well," she murmured.

The part of him that had retreated during his bath retreated no more. He leaned closer to her, so close he saw the lines of light and dark blue in her eyes. Her hand stilled, but her fingers still touched his cheek.

He wanted to breathe her name into the decreasing space between them, if only he knew it.

There was a loud knock on the door.

"Deuce," he murmured instead.

He walked to the door. "Who is it?"

"It is Mrs Gwynne, lamb. If you are finished with your bathing, we've come to fetch the tub."

He glanced over to Miss Brown. She nodded.

"You may fetch the tub." He opened the door.

Removing the bath was almost as laborious as filling it had been. The maids had to make several trips. The towels were gathered up for laundering and, when all this was accomplished, Mr Gwynne appeared to carry the copper tub out of the room. Mrs Gwynne remained the whole time, chatting in her friendly way, pleased, Tanner suspected, that she had made her guests so happy.

"Now," the innkeeper's wife went on. "If you would care to come to the taproom, we have a nice supper. We also could give you a private parlour for dining. Or, if you prefer, we'll bring the food to you here."

"It shall be as my wife desires." He turned to Miss Brown.

As his wife desires, Marlena repeated to herself, her heart pounding at the way his voice dipped low when he spoke the word *wife.* He spoke the word softly, intimately, as if he had indeed kissed her as he had been about to do. Her whole body tingled with excitement.

"I should like to stay here," Marlena responded.

She did not want to break this spell, this camaraderie between them, this atmosphere that had almost led to a kiss.

"We are commanded, Mrs Gwynne." Tanner smiled at the woman.

Marlena enjoyed Tanner's teasing manner. She and Eliza had not known of his good humour all those years ago, something that would undoubtedly have given them more to sigh over. Now his light-heartedness made her forget she was running for her life.

Mrs Gwynne said, "We shall be back directly."

After she left, Marlena asked, "Did you truly agree, Tanner? With having supper here in the room?"

He walked back to her, and lowered himself in the chair adjacent to the one she had been sitting in. He winced as he stretched out his long legs. "I wanted to do what you wanted."

She did not miss that his sides still pained him.

"It is just that my hair is not yet dry," she rattled on. "And I do not wish to put it up yet." And also that she liked being alone with him in this temporary haven.

"You do not have to convince me. Your desire of it is sufficient." His eyes rested softly upon her.

Her desires had never been sufficient for her husband to do what she asked. Early in her marriage she'd learned that Corland's desires took precedence and that she must do what he wanted or he would be in a foul mood. Later in their three-year marriage, she had not cared enough to attempt to please him.

It occurred to her that she had been on the run for as long as she had been married. In a way, Corland still directed her life. It was a mystery to her why Wexin had killed Corland, but because of it, she was on the run.

Marlena fiddled with the brush in her hands, disliking the intrusion of Corland and Wexin in her time with Tanner.

How would it have felt if Tanner had, indeed, kissed her?

It had been so long since a man had kissed her. Corland's ardour for her, mild at best, had cooled after the first year of their marriage, after her money had dwindled and his debts increased. After she discovered his many peccadilloes. Actresses, ballet dancers, their housemaid.

Her last sight of her husband flashed into her mind, lying face up on the bed, eyes gaping sightlessly, naked body covered in blood.

She shuddered and glanced at Tanner, so gloriously alive, so masculine even as he slouched in his chair.

His expression had sobered. "What is it?"

She blinked. "I do not understand what you mean."

He gestured towards her. "You were thinking of something. Something disturbing, I'd wager."

She averted her gaze. "Nothing, I assure you."

When she glanced back at him, he frowned, and the peaceful, intimate feelings she'd had a moment before fled.

All she need do was think of Corland and clouds thickened.

There had been a time when she blamed all her woes on her husband. He was to blame for many things—his gambling, his debts, his affairs—but he would never have done to her what her own cousin had done. Who could have guessed Wexin was capable of such treachery?

Was Wexin still among Tanner's friends? she wondered. If she had so difficult a time believing what her cousin had done, surely Tanner would not believe it.

"Do not be angry with me, Tanner," she murmured.

His brows rose in surprise. "I am not angry." He gave her a very intent look. "I merely wish you would tell me what cloud came over you. Tell me your secrets. Trust me. I know I will be able to fix whatever is wrong."

She shook her head.

"Then at least tell me your name," he persisted, putting that teasing tone back into his voice, but still looking at her with serious eyes. "Tell me your given name. I gave you mine. Adam. When we are private together, let me address you with one name that belongs to you."

She stared back at him.

Would he know the Vanishing Viscountess by her given name? Would her name be enough to identify her as Wexin's cousin, Corland's widow, the young girl who'd had such a *tendre* for him at age eighteen that she blushed whenever he walked past her?

Marlena had been named for a distant French relative who'd died on the guillotine in the year of her birth. She had been Miss Parronley to everyone, save childhood friends and family and Eliza. And Wexin, of course. Even the newspapers after Corland's death and her flight had never printed her given name. She could not think of a single instance when Tanner would have heard of the name Marlena and, if he had, would never associate it with the Vanishing Viscountess. She opened her mouth to speak.

Tanner stood, blowing out a frustrated breath. "Never mind." He ambled over to the window. "Forgive me for pressing you."

The moment to tell him had passed. Her body relaxed, but she grieved the loss of the easy banter between them.

"I asked Mr Gwynne about coaches," he said, still looking out of the window. "I told him we were travelling north." He turned to her.

"Yes, I wish to travel north," she said.

"To Scotland, correct?"

She nodded.

"Well, Mr Gwynne's recommendation was to take a packet to Liverpool." He looked at her intently. "Where in Scotland?"

She bit her lip.

He made a frustrated sound and turned away.

"Edinburgh," she said quickly. "I wish to go to Edinburgh."

He turned back, lifting a brow. "Is Edinburgh your home?"

She hesitated again.

He waved a dismissive hand. "I ought to have known not to ask."

She turned away, her muscles tensing. "A ship."

"Could you bear it?" His voice turned soft.

She faced him again and saw sympathy in his eyes. "If I must."

"It sails in the morning."

"I will be ready." She would get on the packet, in any event, no matter if her courage accompanied her or not. She stood, but was hesitant to approach him. "What will you do?"

His brows rose. "Why, accompany you, of course. It would look odd otherwise."

She released her breath. The ship would be a little less terrifying with Tanner at her side.

Liverpool would certainly be big enough a town for her to pass through unnoticed. From there she could catch a coach, perhaps to Glasgow first, then on to Edinburgh.

So close to Parronley. Her estate. Her people. One place for which she yearned, but dared not go.

She was Baroness Parronley, a baroness in her own right.

The Parronley barony was one of the few that included daughters in the line of succession, but Marlena would have preferred not to inherit. It meant losing her dear brother Niall and his two little sons. Her brother and nephews perished of typhoid fever. So unexpected. So tragic.

Marlena had been with Eliza in Ireland when they read the account in a London newspaper that Eliza's husband had had sent to him. Marlena could not even mourn them, her closest family. She could not wear black for them, could not lay flowers on their graves.

With the shipwreck she would eventually be pronounced dead, the end of a baroness who had never had the chance to claim her title, the end of the Parronleys. Wexin would inherit. Her people, the people of Parronley, would be in the hands of a murderer.

Another knock on the door sounded, and Mrs Gwynne herself brought in their supper on a big tray. Two steaming meat pies, a pot of tea, and a tall tankard of ale.

Tanner took the tray from the woman's hands and set it on the table. "Ah, thank you, Mrs Gwynne. You even remembered ale."

She beamed and rubbed her hands on her apron. "After all these years, I ought to know what a man wants."

He smiled at her. "You knew what this man wants." He lifted the tankard to his lips and took a long swallow.

After the woman left, Marlena picked at her food. The camaraderie she'd shared with Tanner had disappeared. They ate in silence.

As she watched him finish the last of the crumbs of the meat pie's crust, she blurted out, "You do not have to travel to Liverpool with me, if you do not wish it."

He looked up at her with a mild expression. "I do not mind the trip."

She sipped her cup of tea. "If it were not for me, you would probably be headed for London tomorrow."

"Probably," he responded.

She regarded him. "I do not even know if there is someone in London awaiting your return."

His eyes clouded. "The usual people, I suppose."

She flushed, embarrassed that she had not considered what his life might be like now. He had been the marquess of her memory, dashing and carefree and unmarried. "Forgive me, but I do not know if you are married. If you are—"

"I am not married," he replied, his voice catching as he pressed his hand to his side. "A delay in my return should not inconvenience anyone overmuch. My affairs are well managed and rarely require my attention."

She felt a disquieting sense of sadness from him. Still, that once innocent, hopeful débutante brightened.

He was not married.

Their meal struggled on with even fewer words spoken until Mrs Gwynne again knocked. Tanner rose stiffly.

"I've come for your dishes, lamb," she said as he opened the door. "But first I have something for you." She placed folded white garments into his hands. "Nightclothes for you."

"Thank you," Marlena exclaimed, surprised again at the woman's kindness. She placed their dishes on the tray.

"That is good of you, Mrs Gwynne." Tanner took the garments and placed them on the bed. "Might we purchase them from you?"

The woman waved a hand at him. "Oh, I hate to ask you for money after all you have been through."

"I insist," he said.

Mrs Gwynne gave him a motherly pat on the cheek. "Then we will settle up tomorrow, Mr Lear. Is there anything else you might require?"

"I can think of nothing." He turned to Marlena.

She shook her head and handed Mrs Gwynne the tray full of dishes. She walked over to open the door for the woman.

Marlena stopped her before she crossed the threshold. "Wait." She glanced over to Tanner. "Would it be possible for someone to launder my—my husband's shirt? He would so like it to be clean."

Mrs. Gwynne brightened. "It would indeed be possible. I'll see to it myself and dry it in front of the fire." She stepped over to Tanner again. "Give it over, lamb."

Tanner glanced at Marlena before pulling the shirt over his head and draping it over Mrs Gwynne's arm. "Thank you again."

The innkeeper's wife smiled and bustled out of the room.

Tanner turned to Marlena. "That was thoughtful of you."

His skin glowed gold in the light from the oil lamp and the fireplace, but he was no less magnificent than he'd appeared that morning or as he bathed. Just as one is tempted to touch a statue, Marlena was tempted to run her fingers down his chest, to feel his sculpted muscles for herself.

She resisted. "No more thoughtful than you asking for my bath. I would say we are even now, except for the matter of you saving my life."

His mouth curved into a half-smile. "We are even on that score, as well. Do you not recall hitting Mr Davies-the-Younger over the head?"

"I am appalled at that family, the lot of them." She shook her head.

He smiled. "You'll get no argument from me on that score."

He picked up one of the garments Mrs Gwynne had brought them and put it on, covering his spectacular chest. "I'll walk down with you to the necessary, before we go to bed."

Go to bed repeated itself in her mind.

The sky was dark when they stepped outside to the area behind the inn where the necessary was located. Marlena was glad Tanner was with her. The darkness disquieted her, as if it harboured danger in its shadows.

When they returned to the room, he said, "Spare me a blanket and pillow and I will sleep on the floor."

"No, you will not," she retorted, her voice firm. There was no way she would allow the man who had rescued her to suffer through such discomfort. "Not with those sore ribs of yours. You must sleep in the bed."

He seized her arm and made her look at him. "I'll not allow you to sleep on the floor."

Her heart pounded as she looked directly into his eyes. "Then we must share the bed."

Chapter Five

Marlena's heart pounded as Tanner stared at her. He said nothing.

She must have made a terrible mistake, must have mistaken the meaning of his almost-kiss. Surely he would give her some sign of wanting to make love to her after her brazen invitation. Not this silence.

She felt the rebuff as keenly as she'd once felt those of her husband. Corland, however, had voiced his disgust at her wantonness. She'd believed him, too, thinking herself some unnatural sort of wife to desire the lovemaking, until she discovered that Corland had no such disgust of other women bedding him.

Tanner's reaction confused her all the more.

Perhaps she was not a temptation to any man. She'd not really had the opportunity to find out while playing governess to Eliza's children.

"I—I ought to speak more plainly," she prevaricated. "I meant we ought to share the bed, which is big enough. I was not suggesting more."

He swung away from her, so she could not tell how this idea—outrageous all on its own—had struck him.

He finally turned back to her. "You wish only to share the bed."

She nodded, wishing she had merely insisted upon sleeping on the floor and been done with it.

"I will turn my back while you undress, then." He faced the chest where the water and bowl were.

Marlena undressed as quickly as she could, although her fingers fumbled with the laces of her corset. She slipped the nightdress over her head and noticed the comforting smell of lavender lingering in the fabric. She laid her clothing over one of the chairs so that it would not wrinkle.

She crawled beneath the covers. "I am done."

He'd been so still as she undressed, adding to her discomfort, but he moved now, removing his boots and the coat he'd donned over his nightshirt when they'd gone below stairs. She peeked through her lashes at him, watching him unfasten the fall of his trousers and step out of them, the nightshirt preserving his modesty.

He walked towards the bed and climbed in beside her. The bed shifted with his weight. When he faced away from her, she wished it could have been as it had been that morning, his arms around her, bare skin touching bare skin. She was certain she would never sleep a wink the whole night, but soon after his breathing became even and rhythmic, she drifted off.

The dream came. She'd not had the dream in ever so long, but now, with all the fear and danger, she dreamt it like it was happening all over again.

She'd been restless, unable to sleep that terrible night. Corland and Wexin made plenty of noise when they returned from their night of debauchery. Wexin often slept off the effects of their entertainment in one of the bedchambers, so it did not surprise her that he stayed the night.

When she finally dozed, a woman's cry woke her. Earlier in the day the housekeeper had warned her that her husband had his eye on Fia Small, the new maid, a girl Marlena had hired mostly because she came from near Parronley and was so very young and desperate for employment. A light shone from beneath the door connecting her husband's bedchamber to hers.

Again in her dream, Marlena rose from her bed and walked to the door. She turned the key and opened it.

A man who looked as if he were dressed in women's clothes grappled with someone, something in his hand, trying to strike with it. Marlena ran and grabbed his arm. The weapon was a large pair of scissors and the person with whom he struggled was the new maid. He swung around to Marlena, slashing the weapon towards her.

"No!" the girl cried, trying to pull him off Marlena.

He flung the girl away.

Marlena fought him, both her hands grasping his arm, holding off the lethal scissors. She finally saw the man's face.

In her dream the face loomed very large and menacing.

It was Wexin. *Her cousin.*

"Wexin, my God," she cried. The dream turned him into the image of a demon. He drove her towards the bed and she fell against it, losing her grip on his arm. He brought the scissors down, but Marlena twisted away.

She collided with her husband, her face almost ramming into his. Corland's eyes were open and lifeless, blood spattered his face, pooling at the wound in his neck.

Before she could scream, Wexin called out, "Help! Someone, help!" He tore off the woman's robe and threw it at Marlena. He thrust the scissors into her hand.

Footsteps sounded in the hallway.

Wexin swung around to the maid. "I'll see you dead, girl, if you speak a word of this. There will be nowhere you can hide. Your lady here has killed her husband. Do you understand?"

Marlena threw aside the robe—her robe, she realised. The scissors in her hand was sticky with blood. Her nightdress was stained with it. Wexin pulled off his gloves and stuffed them in a pocket. He was clean while she was bloody.

The maid glanced from Marlena to Wexin and back again. With a cry, she ran, scampering through the hidden door that led from Corland's room to the servants' staircase.

Wexin laughed at the girl's escape. "There goes your witness, cousin," he sneered. "You have killed Corland and there is no one to say you have not."

Marlena jolted awake, her heart pounding.

The nightmare had not ended, however. A man leaned over the bed and slammed his hand over her mouth.

Tanner woke with a start.

A man, no more than a black figure, had his hands on Miss Brown. Tanner grabbed for the man's coat, knocking him off balance.

The man released Miss Brown and pulled out of Tanner's grip. Tanner sprang from the bed and lunged at him before he could reach her again. They both fell to the floor, rolling and grappling, until slamming against the mantel, the coals on the hearth hot on Tanner's back. They illuminated the man's face.

Davies, the son come back to finish what he'd started on the beach.

"No!" Miss Brown ran towards them, pulling the back of Davies's collar.

"Stay back!" Tanner yelled, although he was perilously close to having his nightshirt catch fire.

Davies released him and scrambled to his feet. Miss Brown backed away from him, but he came at her, clamping one big beefy hand around her neck. Tanner stood and advanced on him.

"Keep away or I'll kill her," Davies warned, squeezing her throat for emphasis, and dragging her towards the door.

"Leave her," Tanner commanded. "The purse you want is in the bed."

The man glanced to the bed, but shook his head, squeezing Miss Brown's neck tighter. "She'll be worth more, I'll wager." The man swallowed. "I saw your ring. Only a rich man wears a ring with pictures on it. You'll pay me more than what's in that purse for her."

Tanner suddenly felt the weight of the signet ring on his finger, the ring that was so much a part of him. He'd tried to disguise it, but Davis had obviously seen it for what it was.

"I'll have you arrested and hanged," Tanner growled.

"I'll kill her first," the man replied.

A choking sound came from Miss Brown's lips. Tanner had no doubt Davies would make good his threat.

"I'll not pay for her if she is dead," Tanner said, playing for time.

Tanner kept his distance as Davies neared the door. He could barely see in the darkness, but he knew one thing. He would never let that man take her out of the inn.

The intruder reached the door, and Tanner could hear him fumbling with the key to unlock it. "Do not raise a din," Davies warned, "or I'll snap her neck and run for it."

He lifted the latch and swung the door open. At that same moment, Miss Brown brought her heel down hard on his foot. *Smart girl!*

Davies cried out in pain and she twisted away from him. Tanner came at him, landing his fist square on Davies's jaw and spinning him around into the hall towards the stairway. The man's hand groped for the banister, but slipped, and he tumbled down the stairs.

Tanner rushed after him. By the time he reached the stairs, Davies was back on his feet and out of the building. Heedless of his bare feet, Tanner ran down the stairway and into the inn's yard, the nightshirt tangling between his legs and hampering his progress. Davies disappeared into the darkness.

"Hell," he yelled, stamping his foot and lodging a stone painfully between his toes.

Breathing hard, Tanner limped back to the inn where Miss Brown stood framed in the doorway.

He hurried to her, touching his hand to her neck. "Did he hurt you?"

She placed her palms on his ribs. "No, but what of you? Has he injured you more?"

He had forgotten that his ribs still pained him. He put his hand over hers and pressed his side. "Nothing of consequence."

He wrapped his arms around her, holding her close with only the thin fabric of their nightclothes between them.

A commotion sounded behind them. The innkeeper and his wife appeared, along with several curious lodgers.

"What is this?" asked Mr Gwynne, in his nightshirt, robe, and cap.

Tanner reluctantly released Miss Brown. "A man broke into our room and tried to rob us."

"Oh, dear!" Mrs Gwynne's hand went to her mouth. "Who would do such a thing? And you with so little. Did he take anything of value?"

Tanner put his arm around his pretend wife. "My purse almost, but we stopped him." He glanced towards the yard. "He ran off."

"Shall I alert the magistrate?" the innkeeper asked.

"No!" cried Miss Brown.

Tanner tightened his arm around her to let her know he understood she would not wish to speak to a magistrate. "It is no use. The man is gone, and it was dark. I'd not know him in the light."

"You poor lambs!" Mrs Gwynne ushered them inside and closed the door. "What can we do for you?"

"We need only to return to sleep. I am certain he will not come back." Tanner blew out a breath and reconsidered her offer. "I might appreciate a glass of port, come to think of it."

"I'll fetch you a whole bottle," said Mr Gwynne.

The other lodgers crowded around them with questions, sympathy and speculation. Tanner suppressed his natural inclination to merely order them away. He was not precisely sure how Mr Lear the stable manager might act in such a situation, so he merely answered what he could and thanked them for their concern.

Acting as a husband came easier. Tanner kept a protective arm around Miss Brown and walked her through the entrance hall to the staircase. He only released her when Mr Gwynne handed him a bottle of port and two glasses. She hurried up the stairs and Tanner followed.

When they reached their room, the door was ajar and a breeze blew through from the open window, undoubtedly how Davies had gained entry.

As soon as Tanner closed the door behind them, he faced her. "Are you certain he did not hurt you?"

She gazed up at him. "Very certain."

He wanted to touch her, to examine her all over, to reassure himself she was unharmed, but his hands were full and he was fairly certain his touch would not be welcome.

For a fleeting moment earlier that night he'd believed she'd invited him to do more than share the bed. Thank God he had not acted on that belief. A second later he realised he'd presumed too much.

"Would you like some port?" He placed the glasses on the table and pulled out the bottle's cork. "I am in great need of it."

"Yes." She put her hand over his, and his desire for her flared anew. "But I will pour for you."

She took the bottle, and Tanner paced. The encounter with Davies had set his blood to boiling and he had not yet calmed down. He still burned to pummel his fists into the bastard's fleshy face and beat it to a pulp.

All that unspent energy was in grave danger of being misdirected. Not in violence, but in passion. He surged with desire for this woman who again had been in danger. Tanner felt the need to have her. Now.

He shuddered. He must force himself to remain civilised.

He walked over to the window, closing it and taking a taper from the fireplace to light the lamp on the table. Anything to keep his hands off her.

"The money!" he cried, nearly dropping the taper.

She looked up, holding a glass in midair.

Tanner rushed over to the bed and groped under the pillow. The door of the room had been open for several minutes. Anyone might have walked in. He exhaled in relief as he pulled out the purse.

Her arm relaxed. "Thank goodness." She held out the glass to him. "Was it the money he was after—or—or me?"

He returned the purse to its place under the pillow and took the drink from her. "I would not have let him take you," he murmured, brushing a lock of hair off her forehead.

She looked up into his eyes, and he felt the surge of passion return.

She poured port into the other glass. "Do you think Davies knows who I am?"

Tanner took a sip, the sweet, woody wine warming his throat, but not cooling his ardour. "*I* do not know who you are."

She averted her face. "I mean, he still seemed to think me your wife, did he not?"

"My wife," he murmured.

He took a gulp of the port. The light of the fireplace behind her revealed the outline of her body beneath the thin white fabric of her nightdress. A vision of her naked filled his mind, full high breasts, narrow waist, flat stomach, long silken legs.

Lust surged through him. Curse him, she'd already made it clear that sharing a bed meant only sharing a bed.

He glanced away from her, but looked back again to see her lips touching the glass, her pink tongue darting out to lick off a stray droplet of port. He downed the contents of his own glass and walked over to the table to pour another one.

With his back to her, it was easier to speak. "Davies saw my ring when we were at the farmhouse, evidently. I doubt he could identify the crest, although someone more knowledgeable might do so. I've since turned it around on my finger."

"So he thought me your wife?" she asked again.

"I believe he did." It fitted with what Davies had said about wanting Tanner to pay for her.

She finished her port. "What time does the packet ship sail?"

He turned around to answer her, but a sharp pain pierced his ribs. He leaned on the table until the worst of it had passed. "Mid-morning," he answered in a tight voice. "And another one later in the day. Mr Gwynne said we should be at the docks by ten o'clock for the morning departure."

She put down her glass, and crossed over to him. "You are hurt." She gently touched his ribs. "Is it where he kicked you? You must go back to bed."

She put his arm over her shoulder to help him over to the bed. Instead, he turned and wrapped his arms around her, taking pleasure in merely holding her.

"Let us both go back to bed."

She looked up at him, a question in her eyes.

He garnered more strength than he'd used to battle Davies. "To sleep?"

She stared at him. "To sleep."

She doused the lamp, and helped him to the bed, sweeping the covers back and waiting for him to climb in. She moved to the other side and climbed in next to him, covering them both with the blankets.

This time, rather than turn away, Tanner faced her. He put his arm around her and drew her close. The pain protected him from doing more and finally exhaustion brought him sleep.

Lew Davies stumbled into the cottage as dawn peeked over the horizon. He did not trouble himself to be quiet, still too angry at this latest failure. The other wreckers had found all sorts of treasure. Crates of cargo and bits of jewellery, coin, clothing from the dead. Why did he have to find a fellow who was alive? The only thing his family had to show for the best shipwreck in years was a bloody timepiece with that same picture on it that had been on the man's ring. Davies did not even know where they might sell such a thing.

He shrugged out of his coat and let it fall to the floor. His foot pained him like the very dickens from where the woman had stomped on it, his jaw ached from the man's fist, and his muscles were sore from the tumble down the stairs. He'd been lucky to escape.

He was sick of being foiled by these two fancy people. First on the shore, then on the road to the ferry when his father's cart never showed up for him to ambush, and finally in Cemaes. He flopped down into a chair and pulled off his boots, tossing them into a corner.

He'd been stupid to decide to take the woman instead of the purse. The idea just came to him suddenly when he'd grabbed her. He should have left as soon as the man saw his face. If he was lucky the gentleman wouldn't go to the magistrate about him.

From now on, he'd stick to wrecking and hope for another storm off shore very soon.

The bedchamber door opened and his mother tottered out. "Well, did you nab the purse?"

He rubbed his jaw. "No, they woke up. I was lucky to get away in one piece."

She clucked her tongue. "We need that money."

"I know, Mam." He dragged a hand though his hair.

She crossed the room and picked up his coat, hanging it on the peg on the wall. "Well, I want you to try again, but this time take the woman."

He gaped at her. "Take the woman?"

"You heard me." She stood with her fists on her hips. "A man came asking questions after you'd gone. Looking for the woman, he was." She pumped some water into the kettle and placed it on the fire. "He bought her clothes from me, if you can imagine it. More like rags they were, but I'd not have got a half-crown for 'em elsewhere."

He sat up. "He gave you half a crown for them?"

"Well, yes, he did." She opened the tin box where she kept the chicory and took out a piece of the root.

"Half a crown." Davies still could not believe it.

"That fellow told me she was running from the law and

that he is supposed to bring her to London. I'll wager there is a big reward or else this fellow would not pay half a crown for her rags."

"A reward?" Davies's foot started paining him and he lifted it on to his knee to rub it. "What about the gentleman she was with?"

"I told the fellow about the gentleman, but he didn't have anything to say about him." His mother shrugged as she plopped the chicory into a tea pot. "I did not tell we had the man's timepiece."

Davies put his foot back down and sank his head into his hands. He could have earned a big reward if only he had not let go of her.

"So this is what you have to do," his mother went on. "You go back to Cemaes and get the woman. If she's gone, follow her until you find her and bring her back. We will take her to London for the reward."

He looked up at her. "You'll have to give me money."

She checked the kettle, which was starting to hiss. "I'll give you the sovereign the gentleman gave us, but you must find her before that man does."

"Did you tell him they went to Cemaes?"

She glared at him. "I'd not do anything so daft, but I reckon he'll find out before the day is through."

Young Davies reached for his boots. "I'll do it, Mam. I'm going back to Cemaes right now."

His mother waved a dampening hand at him. "First you have some chicory tea and some bread and cheese. I'll not send you out again without something in your stomach."

He leaned back in the chair. "Yes, Mam."

He'd obey his mother, but as soon as he'd eaten, he'd walk back to Cemaes and wait for the perfect time to nab the woman. He did not think he could get in her room again, but he could follow her and the gentleman wherever they went. He didn't care how long or how far it might be.

With a big reward at stake, he'd nab her, all right.

Chapter Six

Marlena gripped the ship's railing as land came into view, a welcome sight indeed. She'd felt the whole trip as if she had been running, rather than merely scanning the sky for storm clouds and the sea for surging waves. Tanner remained next to her the entire time, unwavering and as solid as land beneath her feet.

She supposed it was good to board a ship so soon after another one broke to pieces around them, like remounting a horse after being thrown off its back. When she'd first seen the ship, her fear had tasted like bitter metal in her mouth, but she'd forced one foot in front of the other, gripping Tanner's arm all the way, and she'd made it onboard.

"We should be close to landing," he said, gazing out at the land, still just a line of green and grey on the horizon. For the last hour they had seen more and more sails in the distance, other ships traversing to and from the busy port of Liverpool.

"Yes," she responded. Words had not come easily to her during the voyage, but he did not seem to mind, making comments here and there that demanded no more of her than monosyllables in return.

She felt him flinch and knew another pain had seized him. It was no use for her to beg him to go below and sit; he would not leave her side, and she could not leave the deck where she would at least not be surprised if danger descended upon them again.

He remained beside her while the day waned and the land came closer and closer. The nearer they came to the port, the easier it became to breathe, but, at the same time, Marlena felt like weeping. Setting foot on the solid ground that was Liverpool also meant parting from Tanner and continuing her journey alone.

She glanced at him. The plain felt hat Mr Gwynne had given him looked incongruous with his expertly tailored coat and trousers.

He must be cold, she thought. Why did he not leave her and go below?

He turned his head and caught her watching him. He smiled. "What is it? Do I have a smudge on my nose?"

She looked away. "No." She decided against asking him one more time to leave her and seek somewhere warm. "I was merely thinking that the hats you have in London must be so much finer than this one."

He cocked his head. "Perhaps, but, I tell you, this hat is quite comfortable. I may not give it up."

"The Gwynnes were dear people," she said.

Both Mr and Mrs Gwynne insisted they keep their money and send payment for the room when they reached their destination. "You'll have many expenses," the innkeeper had said. "We can wait for payment." The Gwynnes had also insisted they take the nightclothes with them and a small satchel in which to carry their meagre belongings. And the hat.

Tannerton's eyes, now the colour of the sea, turned soft.

"Never fear. I shall see the Gwynnes are well rewarded for their kindness."

If things had happened differently, she could have done the same. Baroness Parronley ought to have been a wealthy woman. The last she knew, her brother had well managed the family's estate and fortune.

There was no use repining what could never be.

"I wish I could repay them," she murmured.

How would Parronley fare under Wexin? Would he gamble its fortune away as he seemed bent to do when he and Corland went out together night after night? Wexin had never liked Parronley. He used to tease Marlena and her brother Niall that they lived in a savage land.

Who was the savage in the end? Wexin's face flashed before her once more, and Corland's bloody body.

"You've gone off once more."

Tanner's voice startled her. She glanced back at him, feeling as if she'd just awoken from the dream.

One corner of his mouth lifted. "I surmise you will not tell me what you were thinking."

She turned back to stare out at the land, very close now, the mouth of the Mersey River in plain view. "I was thinking of nothing at all."

She felt his position shift and his arm brushed against hers. "I dare say it was not nothing." He paused. "Do not fear. I will not press you." He tilted his head, looking boyish in the floppy hat. "I do wish you would tell me your name. I dislike calling you Miss Brown."

She made herself smile and tried to make the topic into a joke. "You ought to be calling me Mrs Lear, at least for a little while longer."

The expression he gave her was impossible to decipher, something resembling disappointment or, perhaps, wounding.

She turned away from him again. Soon she would part from him and she would not see his face again. She blinked away tears. It was for the best. Perhaps he would never discover he had aided and abetted the Vanishing Viscountess.

A shout went up from the first mate and soon the deck was teeming with crewmen, all busy at their stations as the ship sailed into the mouth of the Mersey River towards the docks. It suddenly seemed as if a multitude of ships dotted the water, like a swarm of insects all flying towards a lamp.

The activity freed her from having to talk with him further as they sailed up the river. Liverpool's buildings came into sight, a town swollen with brick warehouses and a sprawl of lodgings for the people whose lives depended on this busy port.

"Oh, my!" She swivelled around in alarm as a large ship loomed up on the opposite side of the packet, dwarfing their vessel and looking as if it would collide with them.

"Do not fear." Tanner touched her arm. "I am certain these captains have navigated this port many times without mishap."

She found it hard to breathe again, nonetheless. Even so, there was so much to see, so much going on, that time passed more swiftly than it had on the open sea. Soon the packet ship reached its dock and soon after that, they were among the first of the passengers to disembark.

The docks were bustling with activity, even as the daylight waned. Cargo was unloaded and carried into the warehouses. Raucous shouts came from nearby taverns, where seamen tottered from the doorways, swaying on their feet. Marlena was one of but a handful of women on the dock, and it seemed to her that all the men stared at her. Some of them looked like the pirates of storybooks, dark and dangerous and, above all, dirty.

She felt a *frisson* of fear travel up her back at the prospect of facing men such as these without Tanner at her side, but soon they must come to more civilised streets. At least she felt quite anonymous in this motley crowd. If Tanner left her at this moment, no one would notice.

Tanner stopped and looked around. "We need to discover where to go."

Marlena tried to breathe, but not enough air reached her lungs. "Perhaps we should part here. Say goodbye."

He scowled at her. "The devil we should. I should feel as if I am leaving a lamb to be slaughtered."

As if to prove his point, a huge sailor stumbled towards them, but Tanner was quick enough to step out of the man's way.

"See?" He pulled her to safety. "I'm not abandoning you to the mercy of such miscreants."

The man paused a moment, glancing back at them before weaving his way in the direction of another one of the passengers on the packet.

A pickpocket, she realised. "Take care for your purse," she warned Tanner.

"I have it well concealed," he reassured her. 'Come." He increased their pace.

Leaving the warehouses behind, they found the road where a line of hackney coaches waited.

Tanner approached one of the jarveys, who was leaning against his vehicle. "Take us to an inn, man. A respectable one for the lady."

The jarvey gave Marlena an assessing look. "A respectable inn, eh?" he said lazily.

Marlena knew she must present an odd picture in her ill-fitting dress and shabby cloak. Tanner was not much better for all his once-elegant coat and trousers had endured.

"Looks more like Paradise Street, if you ask me." The man chuckled.

Marlena guessed this Paradise Street housed less-than-respectable ladies. She pulled at the hood of her cloak to disguise her face.

"A respectable inn, sir," Tanner repeated in a firm voice.

"Aye." The man roused himself to open the door of the coach.

Tanner helped Marlena inside and climbed in beside her. She straightened her skirts and glanced out of the window of the coach as it started to move. "When we arrive at the inn, perhaps you can wait a bit and we will walk inside at different times."

"I think not," Tanner said.

Marlena's head jerked back to look at him. "Very well. We can say we merely shared the coach."

He gave her a level stare. "We will remain together."

Her heart beat faster, although she did not know if his words were the cause or the intensity of his eyes. "I do not understand."

He shifted his gaze to look around him. "After last night, do you think that I would allow you to make your journey alone?"

"But that was merely the Davies's son. I daresay such a thing could not happen again." She tried to make her voice sound nonchalant.

"The Davies's son is not the only man who might endanger you." He caught her in his gaze again. "Did you not see how the sailors looked at you on the docks?"

She blinked. "But we are not at the docks."

He gestured to the front of the coach. "Neither is the jarvey who is driving us. You recall his impertinence, do you not?"

She indeed recalled it. Her fingers fiddled with her skirt. "I shall be all right. I can look after myself. I did so with Davies, did I not?"

He shook his head. "I'll brook no argument. I am staying with you until you reach a place where I might safely let you go. I could not look myself in the mirror if I did not."

She clutched his sleeve and pleaded with her eyes. "You do not understand. If I am caught again and you have been found to have assisted me, you could suffer the same punishment." She shook his arm. "Think of it. What would be my punishment for stealing a wealth of jewellery? Never mind that I really did not do it."

He turned to her, placing his hands on her shoulders. "I have no fear of that. My position and my money will be enough protection. Let me take you back to London. I have told you, I can make the whole matter disappear."

She turned away. Perhaps a marquess could make a theft disappear by paying back the amount lost, but there was no way to pay back the murder of a peer.

Three years before, the newspapers that reached her and Eliza in Ireland had for weeks detailed everything about the murder. The bloody robe, the scissors from her sewing basket, her bloody hands. Wexin's eyewitness account. No one would believe anything except that she was the murderer.

Even if she could find Fia Small, the maid who'd shared her husband's bed that night, who would believe a maid over an earl?

Fia had run that night, the same as Marlena, and Marlena could not blame her. She hoped the girl had escaped, because, if not, Wexin had probably killed her, too.

She turned back to Tanner. "Do not risk yourself for me, Tanner, I beg you."

He reached up to caress her cheek. "I will finish what

began on the ship from Dublin, Mrs Lear," he murmured. "How could I do any less?"

Fia Small hoisted four tankards of ale at once in her two hands and carried them to the table where men she'd known her whole life sat for a bit of rest after a hard day's work.

"We thank you, Fia," said Lyall, giving her a long and significant look.

"Ay, we thank you," echoed his twin, Erroll.

She knew who was who only because Erroll had a scar across his forehead, but as a child it had taken her years to remember which name went with which boy.

"Well, aren't you two talking like honey's pouring from your lips?" Mr Wood, one of the nearby crofters, shoved Lyall and laughed.

The Reverend Bell grinned from his seat on the other side of the table.

"You know they are merely being polite," Fia retorted. "You might take a lesson or two from them, Mr Wood."

Errol and Lyall laughed, and Lyall shoved Mr Wood in return.

It was plain as a pikestaff that both Lyall and Erroll were sweet on her. Fia did not take their interest seriously. They were merely at an age when they wanted to be married. Almost any passably handsome and biddable girl would do. She'd turned down proposals of marriage from other men in the village these past three years and those men always found another girl to marry. True love did not last a long time.

At least that was what the songs said, old Scottish songs of love sung sometimes in the taproom, unhappy love that usually ended with somebody dying. Sometimes when Mr. McKenzie, a tutor to some of the local boys, had too much whiskey in him he recited the poems of Robert Burns:

O my Luve's like a red, red rose,
That's newly sprung in June.

Ha! She much preferred it when he recited "To A Louse On Seeing One On A Lady's Bonnet at Church." That poem made her laugh and had more truth in it.

There was no such thing as love, Fia knew. Men mistook lust for love, but it really was merely lust.

"Fia!" one of the men on the other side of the room called to her. "We're thirsty over here."

"I'm coming over." She walked towards the man, knowing Lyall and Erroll's eyes were on her back.

Once Fia had pined for the excitement of the city, travelling all the way to London and begging for work from Miss Parronley—Lady Corland—the Baroness, she meant. If only Fia had been content with her little part of Scotland.

She liked working in her uncle's tavern. It was hard work, and it kept her very busy most of the time. No time left over to think.

She trusted the twins would soon tire of making moon eyes at her and they'd turn their two heads towards some girls who might believe in true love. Or in the need to have a husband.

Fia next served some strangers staying at the inn. There were never many travellers passing through Kilrosa, but sometimes the laird had people come to see him. Most people travelling in this area stopped at Peebles where the coaches came through. Even Parronley, five miles down the road, received more visitors than Kilrosa. She eyed the strangers carefully, but they did not seem to take any special notice of her.

A part of her would always fear that *he* would find her and silence her for good. Lord Wexin, an equal to the devil in her mind.

She scooped up empty tankards and walked into the kitchen, greeting her aunt, who was busy stirring the stew that would feed anyone asking for a meal.

She carried the tankards into the scullery, pausing when she saw the huge man standing there with his arms elbow-deep in water, his shirtsleeves rolled up so that she could see his muscles bunch as he scrubbed a pot.

She gritted her teeth and entered the room. "More for you."

Bram Gunn swung around and wiped his arms on his apron. He smiled at her. "I'd say thank you, but I would not mean it."

He took the tankards from her, and she gave an awkward nod of her head as she turned to leave.

"How is it out there this evening?" he asked her. "From the dishes that have come back to me, it is a busy one."

He always tried to engage her in talk, ever since he had come back from the Army. He'd come home from France only a week ago, leaving the 17th Regiment behind him, so he said. He planned to stay in Kilrosa and help with the inn now that her cousin Torrie was in Edinburgh becoming educated.

It shouldn't be so hard to talk to him. She'd grown up with Bram, after all, like he was her own kin. He was her uncle's son, born to her uncle's first wife who died birthing him. Fia's aunt, her mother's sister, raised him. It seemed to Fia that Bram had always been around when she was a wee one, until he left to be a soldier.

"'Tis busy enough," she said.

He grabbed a large tray. "Shall I clear tables for you?"

Bram was always trying to do nice things like that. Fia told herself he was being a good worker for his father, not being nice to her.

"If y'like," she said.

She started to leave again, but this time he stopped her with his huge hand upon her arm. "Wait, Fia. Have I done something to anger you?"

She stepped back. "Nay."

He shook his head. "Then did I do something to frighten you, because you always seem in a hurry to be away when I'm near?"

"Don't be foolish," she retorted.

But there was too much truth in what he'd noticed. She felt both afraid of him and angry, though she could not explain it, not even to herself. He did not look on her with that same sort of wanting that Lyall and Erroll had on their faces, but those lads did not make her think about being a woman like Bram did. She could feel her breasts when Bram was near. She felt her hips sway when she walked. And she ached sometimes, down *there,* and the remembering would come. Lord Corland. And Lord Wexin.

Bram walked close behind her through the kitchen. Even with the scent of the stew cooking, she fancied she could smell him, the fine scent of a man.

"If something troubles you about me—or anything else— you can tell me, y'know." His voice was low pitched, rumbling so deep Fia felt it as well as heard it.

"Nothin' troubles me but getting the work done," she told him, entering the taproom and walking to the bar. "Nothin' troubles me at all."

The hackney coach pulled into a coaching inn whose sign depicted a black man in exotic garb.

"It is not too late for us to enter separately," Miss Brown said.

"Say it no more." Tanner placed the strap of the satchel

over his shoulder. "I will stay with you until you have reached safety in Scotland, if that is the only help you will allow me to give you. We can hide behind being Mr and Mrs Lear or any fiction you wish to create. It matters not to me, but I'm not leaving your side."

The intensity of her frown dismayed him, but he was determined. If he parted from her, he would always fear harm had come to her. He refused to have her life on his conscience adding to the tally.

He climbed out of the coach first and turned to assist her. The coach driver called down from the box, "This is the Moor's Head, a place respectable enough, with all the coaches coming and going."

Tanner handed the man some coins. The inn looked adequate. He took Miss Brown by the elbow and escorted her inside.

They registered as Mr and Mrs Lear again, but this time the innkeeper had little interest in them, except to ask for payment in advance. He called a maid to show them to the room.

When the maid left and shut the door behind her, Tanner put their satchel down on a chair. Miss Brown, a frown still on her face, removed her cloak and hung it on a peg.

He'd hoped for gratitude from her, at least.

A lie. He hoped for more than gratitude.

He wanted her. She fired his blood in a way totally new to him.

His interest in women typically burned very hot upon the first encounter, at which time he would do anything to make the conquest. Flynn had been excellent at assisting him at this stage, purchasing the correct gift, finding the correct housing if matters went that far, arranging perfect liaisons. Tanner's love life had not been quite the same since Flynn left, but, then, Tanner had not found a woman to interest him until now.

Tanner could not deny he burned hot for Miss Brown, whoever she really was, but the difference was, he cared more for saving her than winning her.

Typically, hesitancy on the woman's part served to increase his resolve to win her. Miss Brown's hesitancy merely brought back the loneliness he'd been wallowing in shortly before the shipwreck.

Tanner gave himself a mental shake. No matter that she affected him differently, the important thing was to preserve her life, the life he'd saved in the storm.

He glanced at her. "Are you not hungry? I'm famished. Shall I have the innkeeper secure us a dining parlour and some food?"

She swivelled to face him, elbows akimbo, looking the tiniest bit resigned, but not liking it at all. "If you insist on making this journey with me, no matter how unnecessary—no, *foolish*—it is, then we ought to consider how much money you possess before eating in dining parlours."

Tanner almost smiled. That tirade seemed better than an I-wish-never-to-see-your-face-again one. In fact, it seemed quite sensible.

He fished out his purse and dumped the coins on the bed. She walked over to stand next to him to count the money.

"Thirty-one pounds!" she cried.

He frowned. "It is not much, is it?"

"It is a great deal to some people." She recounted it. "But we'd best save where we can."

That would be a novel experience. Tanner was unused to saving. In any event, he was made quite happy by her use of the word *we*. "What do you suggest?"

"For one thing, no private dining room. We should eat in the taproom."

"Very well." He scooped up the coins and returned them to his purse.

The taproom was crowded and noisy, which did not bother Tanner overmuch, except for it being unpleasant for her. It was not much different from White's on a crowded night, except the smells were different. Neither better nor worse, necessarily, merely different.

They could talk little during their meal, at least about how they were to go on, because they risked being overheard—if, that is, they could even hear each other above the din. Tanner bought a bottle of port to take with them above stairs. When they returned to their room, he lit the lamp, removed his boots and settled in a chair by the fire with the port. Miss Brown sat in a chair next to him.

He poured her a glass. "We should create a plan."

She took the glass. "If you insist on coming with me, perhaps you have considered how it may be done."

He had not, really, but he could be roused to do so. He took a sip of his port. "I believe I can discover a way to travel to Edinburgh."

Chapter Seven

It should be astonishingly simple to reach Edinburgh, Tanner thought. The only limitation would be the amount of money remaining in his purse, but he had no doubt he had enough to get her safely to Edinburgh.

He wished Miss Brown would be as pleased to extend their acquaintance as he was. The look she gave him before crawling between the covers made it clear she was still peeved with him for not leaving her.

He ought to be amused by the irony. Women usually had their hysterics because he *did* leave them. Those women were easily consoled when money was offered to them. This woman refused the help his wealth could offer.

It made for a fitful night's sleep. During the hours that he lay awake, acutely aware of her warm body so close to his, he puzzled over the best way to get her to Edinburgh, to a place where she could be forever buried in the identity of someone she wasn't. Forever Miss Brown, perhaps.

He could not even toss and turn for fear of waking her, so he slipped out of bed and walked to the window, which faced the street, quiet now in the dead of night.

They ought to sail to Glasgow, that was what they ought to do. It would be fast. They'd be in Edinburgh in under a week if travelling first by ship to Glasgow, then by coach.

He had not yet suggested sailing to Glasgow, however. She'd been terrified enough on the ship to Liverpool. He'd been afraid as well, if truth be told. If he never sailed again, it would not trouble him in the least.

He took a deep breath and set off a spasm of pain that encircled his chest. He stood still, waiting for the spasm to pass. Davies's boot had done proper damage to his ribs. Tanner did not know what disgusted him more, Davies kicking a man who'd barely survived a shipwreck or Davies putting his hand around Miss Brown's throat.

Yes, he did know. His blood still boiled whenever he thought about Davies touching her, hurting her. Tanner's own hand curled into a fist with the memory.

The tensing of his muscles set off another spasm. He groaned and pressed both hands to his ribs and held them there until it subsided.

She stirred in the bed and he feared he'd wakened her. She murmured something and rolled on to her back. Dreaming, he realised.

"No," she cried suddenly. "No. Do not do it. Do not." She thrashed her head to and fro. "No!" she cried louder, her hands grasping at the air.

He rushed to her side and clasped her hands in his own, folding them against her chest. "Wake up, now," he said, trying to sound calm. "Wake up, now. It is a dream."

Her eyes flew open and she gasped, staring at him for a moment, still in the dream. Then she sat up and threw her arms around his neck. "This time he was going to kill you," she cried, burying her face into his neck.

He let his arms encircle her and he held her close, holding

her as if she were a small child. "See, I'm all in one piece. It was only a dream."

Curse Davies, he thought. Frightening her into nightmares like that.

"It always seems so real," she said, clinging to him.

The notion she was like a small child vanished like smoke through an open flue. She felt all woman to him, all soft, warm woman. How the devil was he to control his response to her trusting embrace?

"Just a dream." He carefully pulled away from her. "Lie down now and try to go back to sleep."

She grabbed his hand. "You will not leave me?"

He smiled at the irony of her speaking the same words they'd argued over half the evening. "I'll not leave you."

Thinking it would be wiser to go in search of some frigid bath water, he nonetheless crawled into bed beside her.

She moved over to him, lying like a nesting spoon against him. "Hold me, Tanner. Do not leave."

He took a bracing breath at the exquisite pleasure of it and made his ribs hurt all the more. It was not only his ribs that tortured him, however, but another much sweeter torture.

Her body trembled in his arms, and, among other needs, the need to protect her surged through him. He waited to hear her fall asleep before he placed his lips on her smooth, soft cheek.

"Mmm," she said, snuggling closer.

His last waking thought was a renewal of his vow to get her safe to her destination, to make certain the life he'd saved remained saved.

Marlena had a vague memory of waking during the night and asking Tanner to hold her, but she was not certain of it and dared not ask him if she'd done so. Instead she slipped from the bed and dressed and was pinning up her hair when he woke, stretching and giving her that lazy smile of his.

"Good morning." His voice was rough with sleep.

He rubbed his face, shaded again with his dark beard, and she wished she could rub it, too, to feel it scratch her fingertips.

He sat up and winced.

She frowned. "You are still in pain."

The corner of his mouth turned up again. "Only when it hurts." His eyes glittered with amusement at his joke. He stood. "I merely have to start moving again."

He walked over to the satchel and removed his shaving things, carrying them to the bureau upon which sat the water pitcher and bowl. She could not help but watch him. He glanced in the mirror after soaping his face, catching her at it.

She quickly turned away and busied herself with straightening the bed covers.

After he was dressed they went below stairs for breakfast. Tanner told the serving girl their belongings had been stolen rather than lost in a shipwreck. He asked where they might purchase clothing.

"You are fortunate," the girl responded. "It is not far." She gave them the direction.

The taproom was nearly empty at this hour, so after the serving girl walked off to fetch their food they were free to talk as they wished.

"I have been thinking about the trip to Edinburgh," Tanner said. "I dare say the fastest way would be by ship to Glasgow."

Marlena's heart seemed to rise into her throat. "Indeed." She swallowed. "How long on board?"

He tilted his head. "More than one day, for certain."

"Oh, my," she whispered. She picked up her teacup, but held it in two hands because she was shaking. She mentally scolded herself for her cowardice.

Setting her chin, she gave him a direct look. "If we must go by ship, we must."

His eyes seemed to shine in the low light of the taproom. "We do not have to travel by ship. Perhaps public coaches would not be more than a day or two longer."

She glanced away. "It must be your pleasure, since you insist upon being my escort." And, of course, his money would pay for the trip.

He took another sip of tea. "If you are not in too great a hurry, public coaches will do."

Two more days with him would be heavenly.

She glanced around, but no one seemed within earshot. "You must need to return to London as soon as possible. They will think you dead."

His brows knitted. "I have thought on this. Flynn, the man I visited in Dublin, was the only one to know I was on that ship. I dare say he won't learn of the wreck for two days or more, and then it will take a few days for a letter from him to reach London. I suspect no one will worry overmuch even then. I should have more than a week before I need to send word of my survival. My presence is not required. I may stay away as long as I wish." A bleakness flashed through his eyes, but so fleetingly she thought she must have imagined it. "We may travel by coach."

Marlena's muscles relaxed. No sea journey and two extra days with him. She ought to chastise herself for being selfish.

She met his gaze again. "Thank you, Tanner," she whispered.

His expression softened. "We are decided, then."

They finished their meal and left the inn in search of the clothes market where the serving girl had directed them.

"I need only a shirt or two and other underclothes," Tanner said. "And a top coat."

She glanced over at him. "You need a coat and trousers as well, if you wish to look the part of a stable manager."

He paused on the pavement to look down at himself. "Is my coat too shabby now?"

She examined him as well. "On the contrary, your clothes are too fine. Your coat fits you as perfectly as if it was made by Weston, and your trousers by Meyer."

He grinned. "They were."

After walking several minutes they found the street with its clothing traders, one stall after another, all calling to passers-by to come to examine their wares. Marlena found two dresses almost right away, and she picked through a box until she found two shifts that would fit her that looked tolerably clean. At another stall, she discovered corsets of all shapes and sizes and selected one that she could put on without assistance.

He walked away briefly, but soon returned to her side carrying a portmanteau. "I purchased this. We can pack as we go along."

She placed her purchases inside.

At other stalls Marlena picked up small items: a proper hat to shield her face from the sun, a sturdier pair of gloves, a spencer so she would not always have to wear the cloak. When they turned their attention to men's clothing, Tanner took the task in his stride, though he must never in his life have worn clothing that had once belonged to another. They found him a good brown coat and a pair of wool trousers, as well as a caped top coat, all that had seen better days. When he slipped on the coat to check its fit, she realised that it was the man who made the clothes, in his case, not the reverse. He looked every bit as handsome in a plain brown wool coat as he did in the one that came from Bond Street.

It was afternoon by the time their battered portmanteau was filled with clothes. Marlena could not remember when she had so enjoyed a shopping expedition, even though neither of them could have ever imagined making such purchases a short time ago. They dropped the portmanteau off at their room in the Moor's Head and ate dinner in the taproom before venturing out again to discover the schedule of public coaches.

Lew Davies left his dark corner of the taproom and hurried through to the outside door. He'd not yet found the right opportunity to snatch the woman. This time he'd be smarter and catch her alone and unawares, rather than break into their room at night.

In Cemaes, he'd followed them to the docks and boarded the same ship to Liverpool as they'd boarded. On the ship he'd watched them as best he could without them seeing him. He'd followed them off the ship in Liverpool and caught a hackney coach to follow behind the one they had got in. He even took a room at this same inn and had been following them all day, but everywhere they went, too many people were around, especially at that clothing market.

Davies watched the man drop some coins on the table as he and the woman rose to leave the taproom. Davies waited a moment before following them into the street, but he'd waited too long. They were no longer in sight. Not to worry. They would return to the inn eventually, and he'd already scouted out a good place to catch her unawares.

He returned to the taproom to have one more tankard of ale.

By the time he and Miss Brown had returned to their room in the inn, Tanner felt a pleasant sort of weariness. He lounged in a chair, the pain in his ribs settling into a tolerable ache.

He'd enjoyed this afternoon's adventure. Haggling with vendors had been much more enjoyable than he could have imagined, and he did not know when he had been required to figure out the best coaching route to anywhere.

Tanner watched her unfold their nightclothes and other thoughts filled his mind, infinitely more carnal. He'd have a few more days with her, a few more days to burn with wanting her. It occurred to him to merely ask her for what he craved from her with his body and his soul, but how was she, so indebted to him, to refuse him?

She stood in front of the mirror and removed the pins from her hair. Tanner watched her dark, touchable curls tumble down to her shoulders. If that were not enough, she drew her fingers through her locks and shook her head so that her curls bobbed a quick dance before settling again.

Dear God.

He blew out a breath. "Let me know when you wish to walk down to the necessary."

She turned around, now brushing her hair.

He shifted in the chair.

"In a little while." Her voice was soft. Caressing. "Unless you wish to go now."

At least the topic of the conversation was sufficiently dampening. He did note, however, that she gave the decision back to him. Even in this matter she would acquiesce to his wishes. It would be no different if he asked for a kiss. Or more.

"No need for haste on my part," he said.

A few minutes later he followed her down the stairs, through the corridor to the back of the inn and through the door to the yard where the necessary was located. Adjacent to the stables, it was convenient for those whose carriages and coaches merely stopped for a quick change of horses, as well as those staying at the inn. She'd donned her newly purchased spencer against the crisp chill of the night. The horses in the stables nickered as a door slammed in the distance.

She entered first and, as he waited for her, he kicked at pebbles in the cobbled yard and listened to the muffled voices coming from the taproom. He laughed to himself that this was yet another example of the intimacy he shared with the secretive Miss Brown. Except for the obvious ultimate intimacy about which he could not stop thinking, he'd never been closer to a woman. And he did not even know her blasted name.

She came out and he smiled at her. "I'll be only a minute."

When he finished, he heard muffled sounds from outside and rushed out.

She was gone.

Another sound came from a dark, narrow passageway next to the building. He hurried in that direction and, in the darkness, could barely make out a man walking at a fast clip, carrying a bundle over his shoulder.

Tanner charged after the man, who broke into a run, reaching the alley behind the buildings. Tanner caught up with him and seized him from behind. The bundle slipped from the man's shoulder, a blanket wrapped haphazardly with rope. The bundle's contents were struggling to get free.

Tanner swung the man around. There was just enough light to see it was Davies.

"You!" Tanner growled, pushing him back against a wall. "If you have hurt her—"

Davies seized a wooden box stacked up next to him and slammed it into Tanner's already injured ribs. The jolt of pain loosened Tanner's grip, and Davies squirmed out of his grasp and ran down the alley.

Tanner turned to the bundle. "It is me," he reassured her, pulling at the ropes.

They loosened easily and she threw off the blanket and pulled out the cloth Davies had jammed in her mouth.

"Ah," she cried, taking deep breaths. "Who was it? Who was it?"

He pulled her to her feet. "Davies." He felt her neck, her arms. "Are you hurt?"

She shook her head, still breathing hard, eyes flashing in alarm.

He clutched her to him. "I thought I'd lost you." But this was not the time to panic. "Come. We must leave here."

He retraced his steps back to the inn and they hurried inside and up the stairs to the room.

"Pack up everything. We are leaving now," he said.

"Now?" she cried.

He scooped up his razor, soap and shaving cup and shoved them into the portmanteau. "Now."

She picked up her hairpins while he rolled up their nightclothes. They stuffed everything into the portmanteau and hurried down the stairs. They crossed the empty entrance and went out into the street.

"We'll go to another inn. I noticed one on the way to the clothes market." He held her arm, and they walked along at a brisk pace, trying at the same time not to call attention to themselves.

Tanner watched for Davies, but it was impossible to tell if he was following them or not. There were too many dark places for a man to hide.

They finally reached the inn and entered the taproom to ask for the innkeeper. His brows rose in surprise at the request for a room at such a late hour, but he took their money and showed them a room two flights up.

It had little more than a bed and a table and two wooden chairs, but Tanner did not care as long as it kept her safe. He dropped the portmanteau on the floor and waited while the innkeeper laboured at lighting a fire. When the innkeeper left and closed the door, Tanner brought one of the chairs to it and wedged the back of the chair under the door latch. Then he crossed over to the window and looked out. A man would need a ladder to climb up to it.

Tanner turned back to her. "I think this is safe."

"Tanner…" Her voice cracked and she stared at him with pleading eyes.

He stepped towards her and took her in his arms. "You are safe now, I promise you. I promise you." He held her as close as he could and she moulded herself to him, clinging as if they were one person.

God forgive him, he'd lose his battle with his carnal desires if she did not break away from him.

When she did pull away, he threw his head back in frustration and relief, his breath ragged. He closed his eyes, trying to compose himself.

Her hands, fingertips soft and warm, closed on the back of his neck and pulled him down to her, down to her waiting lips.

The floodgates of his desire were nearly unleashed with the touch of her mouth against his. He forced himself to kiss lightly, trying with all his strength not to take more than she offered. Perhaps all she wanted to give was a mere kiss of thanks for thwarting Davies again.

They separated, and into the breach she breathed his name again. "Tanner." She closed the distance between them and this time pressed her mouth against his, opening her lips, taking his breath inside her.

He groaned and spread his legs, his hands reaching around her to press her against him. Her tongue touched his teeth, like a tapping on a door. He flung the door wide and invited her inside, letting her tongue dance with his. Her fingers dug into his hair, massaging his scalp, sending shafts of need to his loins already so on fire he might torch them both.

She made small noises as she kissed him, the sound rousing him even more.

"Make love to me," she murmured against his lips.

He broke away to stare at her, uncertain if he had heard her correctly or if his own desire merely rang in his ears.

She grabbed fistfuls of his hair and found his lips again. "Make love to me," she repeated.

He tilted his head, trying to see into her eyes. "Do you mean this?"

"Yes. Yes," she said, pulling him by his hands to the bed. "Now, Tanner. I want you to."

"You are certain?" he asked again.

She laughed. "Yes."

Now that the invitation was clear, he could barely move. Irony, again. "Have—have you done this before, Miss Brown?"

She backed into the bed and still pulled him towards her. "Yes, I have done it before."

His mind started whirling. She'd said she was a lady's companion. Since when was a lady's companion experienced in lovemaking?

"Oh, very well," she cried, suddenly pushing him away. "I did not mean to offend you."

"Offend me?" He was totally confused now.

"By throwing myself at you." She looked as if she would cry. "Forgive me."

"Forgive you?"

"Stop repeating what I say!" She whirled around and pressed her forehead against the window frame.

"Repeating—" he started, but caught himself.

He had mucked up something, but he was uncertain what. All he knew was, he'd been on fire for her—was still on fire for her—and he had somehow sent her skittering across the room.

"What the devil is going on?" His voice came out harsher than he intended.

Her fingers fiddled with the curtain. "I forgot myself." She took a shuddering breath and turned, hiding half her face with the curtain. "It has been a long time."

"A long ti—" He shook his head. "Talk plain, Miss Brown, or I may be echoing you into the next decade."

A small giggle escaped her lips.

Now he was really confused.

"I am sorry, Tanner." She gave him a wan smile. "I—I was so upset about Davies and having to run here. I did not mean to be so forward. I know you do not…think of me in that carnal way. I think I must have just needed—"

"Not think of you in that carnal way?" he repeated, then shook his head again. "What makes you think I do not think of you in a—carnal way?" Good Lord, he could hardly think any other way when he was with her.

"You looked at me so."

"Looked at you so?" He lifted his hand when he realised he'd repeated again.

She laughed.

He smiled. "I seem to have some affliction."

She waved a dismissive hand and walked back to the bed. "Perhaps we ought to go to sleep. It has been a long day."

When she passed close to him, he grasped her arm. "Let me clarify one thing," he murmured. "I think of you in a carnal way, Miss Brown." He made her face him and he rubbed his hands down her arms. "And I would very much like to know you in a carnal way, if you would wish it."

"If I would wish it," she repeated. She smiled. "I would wish it very much."

Chapter Eight

Marlena waited, her heart pounding, hoping. She longed to let her fingers explore where her eyes once wandered, to feel the muscles of his chest, the ripples of his abdomen, the roughness of his cheek, shadowed now with beard. She dared not act the hoyden again. He might change his mind; if he did, she might shatter like glass.

His eyes looked dark and soft in the dim light of the room. He gently lifted her chin with his fingertips and lowered his face to hers. With soft, gentle lips, he brushed her mouth, and, though her heart pounded, she remained still while he sampled, wishing he would instead take more of what she yearned to give.

The emotions of the night still stormed inside her: Terror at being captured, rage at being bound, frenzy at their impulsive flight. Marlena burned with the need to release all the passion her emotions ignited. If she stayed quiet and still much longer, she would surely combust.

Tanner broke off the kiss. She drew in a breath and held it. If she pulled him back to her, she feared he would withdraw altogether. To her great delight and relief, he, instead, slid his hands to her shoulders and gently turned her around. He untied the laces of her ill-fitting dress and pulled it over her head, tossing it aside. Next his fingers lightly brushed her as he loosened the laces of her corset. When freed, she grasped his hands and held them against her ribs, relishing the warmth of them, the strength of his fingers. She longed to move his hands to her breasts, but she feared showing so much wantonness.

She turned back to face him. "Shall I help you now?" she asked. She could not resist placing her hands upon his broad shoulders, sliding them down to his chest and underneath his coat.

One corner of his mouth lifted in a half-smile, but his words were breathless. "Recall, my coat fits well. You must peel it off."

She looked into his eyes. "I shall be delighted to do so."

She slid the coat off his shoulders and then pulled on first one sleeve, then the other. Reluctant to stop touching him for even an instant, she flung the coat over a chair. Tanner's half-smile was replaced by eyes that seared her with smouldering fire. She could not look away as she unbuttoned his waistcoat.

He stood very still while she removed it, and again she feared appearing too eager for him, wanting just to rip it off.

"Do you make your valet do all this work?" she asked, trying to slow herself.

He looked down at her with his half-smile. "My man would be shocked if I did not. A marquess must not undress himself, after all."

She undid the Dorset buttons at his neck and pulled his shirt from the waistband of his trousers. As she lifted it, the white cloth of the shirt billowed out to form a canopy that enclosed them both.

From inside the canopy, while the blood was racing through her veins, she laughed softly. "You are Mr Adam Lear now, are you not?"

His half-smile fled. "But who are you?"

It seemed as if the blood in her veins turned to ice. She continued to pull his shirt over his head, but she turned away to place it on the chair with his coat, and to retrieve his waistcoat from the floor.

She heard him move away, the ropes of the bed creaking as he sat upon it.

She turned back towards him and saw him pulling off his boot.

"I will do it." She crossed over to him and tugged at the heel of his right boot. It reluctantly parted from his foot. The left boot did the same.

"They are in sad need of polish, are they not?" he remarked, but the warmth had gone out of his voice.

Marlena suddenly felt as if thousands of tiny doors had quietly closed on all the impassioned emotions of a few moments before. She'd heard the doors latch the second he asked, *But who are you?*

With her head bowed, she turned and set the boots next to the chair. She dearly wished she could tell him who she was, laugh with him about her silly infatuation with him when she and Eliza first spied him at Almack's, describe to him how she and Eliza had decided he'd become much more handsome after they discovered he was a marquess. He'd enjoy a folly like that.

She could never be that girl again, however. She'd become the Vanishing Viscountess, the woman who, hiding in Ireland, had been hunted all through England, the woman who still had a price on her head, a reward her cousin Wexin offered for anyone who could prove she was dead or else bring her back to face her fate.

She walked to the portmanteau and took out their night-clothes, draping them over her arm.

"Will you not come back?" he asked, his voice low.

She glanced at him in surprise. "Come back?"

The corner of his mouth turned up again. "You've caught the affliction."

Her brows knitted. "Affliction?"

He grinned. "The Repeating Blight."

She smiled.

He offered his hand.

She raced forward to take it, dropping the nightclothes on the floor. His fingers closed around her hand and drew her back to where he sat.

"Now where did we leave off?" he whispered, his voice warm again. He brought his gaze to hers.

"I removed your boots," she said in a tone a little too clipped, a little too loud.

"Ah, yes." He placed his hands at her waist.

She stood between his legs. His fingers pressed into her flesh and suddenly those thousand doors blew open in a brisk, hot breeze. She closed her eyes, relishing the sensation again.

He gathered the fabric of her shift in his fingers, inching it up her legs before pulling it off altogether. A moan escaped his lips. She opened her eyes, suddenly nervous.

Corland said she was too tall, too thin, and she feared she would see disappointment on Tanner's face. Instead, his eyes caressed her. He touched her neck and his hand slid down to her collarbone, to her breast. He stroked her as lightly as he had kissed her. Sweet, sweet torture.

He moved over on the bed to make room for her, and she climbed up next to him, reaching for the buttons of his trousers, but he stopped her, holding up a finger that he twirled around and pointed to her legs.

He smiled at her. "Your stockings."

She reached down to remove them, but he held his finger up again. With more sweet torture, he pushed her stockings down her legs, his hands touching her bare skin. She gripped the bed covers to keep from writhing under his touch. When her stockings, too, were tossed aside, his gaze seemed to feast on her.

"You are lovely, Miss—" He started to use the name she'd given him, but cut himself off, and his expression hardened for a moment.

Not wishing to again lose what was building between them, she shifted positions, getting up on her knees. "Now you recline and I will roll your stockings off."

He lay back, but his eyes remained on her. Never before had she been so aware of her nakedness, and never before so relished it.

She removed his stockings and began to unbutton his trousers. His arousal pressed against the fabric. A thrill flashed through her and she daringly let her hand brush against it, wondering if she'd be brazen enough to touch it without the barrier of clothing. His muscles tensed and his breath was ragged.

Marlena had never removed a man's stockings before, certainly not a man's trousers. Corland came to her already undressed, covering himself in only a banyan. Sometimes he had not even troubled himself to remove her nightdress. In those first months of their marriage, though, when she'd been in love with being married, she had not known any better. The belief that Corland loved her had been sufficient to make lovemaking a thrill. She'd relished being touched, being kissed, feeling close to another person. Her body had responded.

Later Corland had used her eager response like a weapon

against her, saying it gave him a disgust of her. Of course, he had no such disgust for the many other women he coupled with. She'd refused him her bed after that discovery, but it mattered little to him.

At this moment, however, she no longer cared if she acted unnaturally wanton. She was consumed with wanting the pleasure a man could give, and she wanted it with Tanner. Perhaps she had always wanted that pleasure from Tanner. Perhaps that had been what her once-girlish infatuation had been all about.

Do you think so, Eliza? she asked silently.

With a surge of energy, she pulled off his trousers.

As she moved from him, he grabbed her arm. "If you leave this bed to fold that garment neatly on to the chair, I vow I will start repeating everything you say."

She glanced back at him, the bubble of laughter tickling her chest. "I was about to do so."

With a flourish, she tossed his trousers into the air, letting them fall to the floor wherever they might.

He smiled. "Come."

She slid closer to him, and in a swift movement he was above her. His legs, rough with hair, pressed against hers. The male part of him also pressed against her. She was seized with an urge to look at it, like he had looked upon her, but he covered her with his body, and she soon forgot anything but the contour of the muscles that rippled beneath his skin, the weight of him, the heat of him.

Tanner raised himself up on his arms, enough for her to breathe and for him to kiss her. There was no gentleness in this kiss, no restraint.

She could not hold back now either, not even if he required it of her. She abandoned herself to kissing him back, taking his tongue inside her mouth, wanting more of him inside her.

She writhed beneath him, and he broke off the kiss. She burned with impatience. He must take her now! *Now.*

He did not. Instead he engaged in the exquisite torture of nibbling on her neck and sliding his lips to her breast. He took her nipple into his mouth, warm and wet and sending shafts of aching need throughout her.

She moaned, arching her back for more. He obliged her, tasting her other breast, tracing her nipple with his tongue, sliding his hand down her body to touch her in her most intimate place.

She gasped with surprise that he would touch like this. Corland had never done so—but soon she moaned at the delicious sensations Tanner's touch created. Suddenly, he slipped a finger inside her, another shock. Another delight. Her release came, rocking her with pleasure, and she clutched at him until the sensations eased.

She'd finished before they'd even started. Disappointment mingled with her satisfaction. "Oh, Tanner," she cried.

He removed his fingers and again held himself over her. "I wish I knew your—" He cut himself off, shaking his head.

He lowered his lips to hers instead, and, to her surprise, her body flared to life again. She ran her hands over his shoulders, his back, his buttocks, as firm as the rest of him. With his knee he urged her legs apart and she trembled with anticipation. In a moment he would enter her. In a moment they would be joined. They would become one.

She held him back, splaying her hands on his chest. He gazed down at her with puzzled eyes.

"Marlena," she rasped, barely able to make the word leave her lips. "My given name is Marlena."

He flashed a smile and kissed her again. "Marlena," he whispered low and deep.

He entered her, and Marlena abandoned thought and

embraced sensation. The air was filled with the scent of him and of their lovemaking. The only sound was their breathing and the caress of their skin as they moved in rhythm. His skin was hot and damp with sweat, and inside her he created feelings more intense than anything she could ever have imagined.

She did not want this to end and yet she rushed with him to its climax, building, building, until from beneath her closed eyes she saw flashes of dancing light. As her pleasure exploded within her with even more intensity than before, she felt him spill his seed inside her, his muscles bunching underneath her fingers.

She felt his muscles relax, felt the weight of him envelop her before he slid off and lay at her side.

"Marlena," he repeated, wrapping his arms around her, clasping her against him.

She melted into him like candle wax under a flame, warm from the passion they shared and from the heat of his body. Tomorrow she would think of how glorious it had been to make love with him, but now she was content to think of nothing but the comforting rhythm of his heartbeat.

When Tanner opened his eyes, she was still asleep next to him, his arm encircling her. He could feel her breath on the skin of his chest: warm, then cool, warm then cool. She felt soft and sweet. Her hair tickled his hand. He grasped a strand between his fingers and toyed with it.

Light shone through the window. They should rise and leave Liverpool as soon as possible. Once Davies realised they were no longer at the Moor's Head where he had last seen them, he would begin to check other inns nearby. They needed to be gone before he reached this one.

It seemed damned odd of Davies to pursue them this far.

For a farmer's son to travel to a city like Liverpool seemed nonsensical all on its own, but it seemed clear his intent was not to steal money, but to abduct Marlena.

Marlena.

She'd given him her name at last, while they made love, a gift that made his emotions surge when he joined with her. It must be her real name, as well, because the name was too unusual to be invented. Something else unique about her.

His ribs began to ache. A change of position would alleviate the discomfort, but he was loathe to wake her, so peaceful in sleep.

He distracted himself from the pain by setting his mind on the problem of Davies's pursuit. It would be foolish to assume Davies would give up now if he had not yet done so and it would be an easy matter for him to discover their direction if they travelled by coach. He could easily catch up to them by hiring a horse—

Tanner almost sat up, but stopped himself lest he woke her.

Hiring a horse.

A horse might travel all manner of routes, but a public coach had a predictable schedule. If he and Marlena—he enjoyed even thinking her name—*rode* on horseback to Edinburgh, they could stray from the coaching roads. It would be nearly impossible to find them. They could change identities whenever they wished, stay at inns in smaller villages.

He grew more excited the more he thought of this. If they owned rather than hired horses, they would be even more difficult to discover.

Tanner frowned. Purchasing a horse cost more money than he could afford. There must be a way…

His arm fell asleep beneath her and his ribs felt like someone was drumming on them from the inside. He tried very gingerly to shift her body, just a mite.

She stirred. "Mmm." Her eyes fluttered open and she looked into his face. And smiled.

He smiled back and suddenly his aches and pains vanished.

She stretched and propped herself up on one arm, glancing towards the window. "It is morning."

"Well into morning," he responded.

"I suppose we should get up." She made no move to do so, however.

He gazed at her, her creamy skin, the swell of her breasts, the deep pink of her nipple. He caressed her neck. "In a moment."

Her eyes darkened. He leaned down and touched his lips to hers. This time she did not restrain herself as she had initially the night before. This time she kissed him back, twining her arms around his neck, pulling him down to her.

His blood raced again and he was instantly hard for her. "Marlena," he murmured against her lips.

She laughed from deep inside her, and found his lips again. He relished this eagerness of hers, a match to his own. She'd surprised him the night before, and pleased him. He was more than ready to be pleased by her again.

Davies waited in a dark corner of the taproom of the Moor's Head, waiting to see the man and woman who called themselves Mr and Mrs Lear come down to breakfast as they'd done the previous morning. The hour was growing later and later and he was beginning to worry.

He'd bungled another attempt to capture her. It was that gentleman's fault. The gentleman always interfered. Davies vowed he would not stop him the next time he had a chance to grab her.

He rose and strolled to the entrance hall where he found

the innkeeper talking with a man Davies had not seen at the inn before. The man was dressed in what Davies would call city clothes and he spoke like a city man, too.

"I have a message for Mr Lear," the man told the innkeeper. "Very important. Where can I find him?"

Davies's ears pricked up at the name Lear.

"I have not seen Mr Lear come below stairs this morning, sir." The innkeeper held out his hand. "I will see he gets the message, if you like."

The man shook his head. "I have to give Mr Lear the message myself. It is not written down. Just tell me what room he is in."

The innkeeper seemed to consider this. With a shrug, he said, "One flight up, three doors on your left."

The man bowed and quickly took the stairs. Davies waited only a moment and then followed him. As Davies reached the top of the stairs, he saw the man trying the doorknob. He had not knocked.

The man opened the door and entered the room. Davies quickened his step. If this man had come for the woman, Davies figured he knew who the man was—the man who had bought the woman's clothes from his mother.

Davies reached the room, and the man came out, almost colliding with him. He appeared furious.

Davies peeked inside the room. It was empty. "They are gone?"

The man looked at him in surprise. "Who are you?"

"Lew Davies."

"Davies…" Recognition dawned on his face. He gave Davies an assessing gaze. "What do you know of them?"

Davies frowned, unsure how much he should say. "I've been watching them. I followed them here from the ship and I know this is their room." Davies decided not to tell the man about his failed attempt to capture the woman. Or that he'd failed twice. "They were here last night."

"Well, they are not here now." The man peered at him. "Why do you follow them?"

"My mam figures there is a reward or you would not pay money for the woman's rags." Davies shrugged.

In a swift movement, the man grabbed his collar and pulled him down so that their faces were an inch apart. "Now you listen here, Davies. I'll brook no interference in this matter. If you value your health, you will stop this and go home to Anglesey to your miserable little farm."

Davies tried to pull away, but this man's grip was too strong. "I'll not go home empty-handed."

The man released him. "I dislike competition. I'm a reasonable man, however. If you give me any useful information to assist me, I'll pay you ten pounds. You must agree to give up this chase, however, or I promise you, if I see you again, you will never return to that farm of yours."

Davies considered this. Ten pounds was pretty good money and he was heartily sick of this chase. "The gentleman with her wore a gold ring with pictures on it."

"What pictures?" the man asked.

Davies rubbed his face. "A stag and an eagle." He thrust out his hand. "Now give me the ten pounds and you'll see no more of me."

The man reached inside his coat and withdrew his purse.

Marlena donned one of her new dresses. Her newly purchased dress, she should say. Although not even as fashionable as the clothing she wore as a governess, the dress was a pleasure to put on after the ill-fitting gown Mrs Davies had begrudgingly given her. And for which Tanner had paid.

She glanced at him standing by the mirror in a shirt not

nearly as fine as the one now packed in the portmanteau with his finely tailored coat. For her sake Tanner was willing to wear baggy trousers and an ill-fitting coat.

She watched him carefully draw the razor down his cheek. Marlena pressed her fingers to her own cheek, remembering how rough his beard had felt against her skin. She sighed, and the mere memory of their lovemaking brought all her senses to life again.

After all the dangers they had endured together, perhaps their lovemaking had been inevitable. Whatever the reason, she would treasure the memory when she reached Edinburgh and must say goodbye to him.

Tanner wiped his face with a towel and turned to her. "I am—unused to making love with ladies' companions." His expression was troubled. "Do—do you know how to care for yourself?"

She did not know what he meant. "Care for myself?"

He averted his eyes. "You know. Prevent a baby."

She had become accustomed to not thinking about this. She waved a dismissive hand. "Do not fear. I am unable to conceive."

She expected him to look relieved. Instead, he looked sympathetic.

Corland had not been sympathetic. After a year of frequent visits to her bedchamber, he'd forced her to have a painful and humiliating examination by a London physician. Afterwards the man put a hand on Corland's shoulder and solemnly pronounced Marlena unable to have children.

Corland had wheeled on her, eyes blazing. "And how am I supposed to beget an heir?" he'd shouted at her, as if the physician's horrible news had not broken her heart.

Tanner dropped the towel on the bureau and walked over to where she stood. He said nothing to her, but lightly touched her arm before crossing to the bed where she had laid out his new-but-old waistcoat and coat, both brown in colour. She took his place at the mirror to pin up her hair.

He was stomping his boots on when he said, "I'll go below and see if they can give me pen and ink and sealing wax." He crossed the room to her and placed a kiss on her neck. "If you can spare me a moment."

She turned and put her arms around him. "Perhaps not."

He leaned down and kissed her, pressing her against him, urging her mouth open with his tongue. She regretted all the clothing they wore, the late hour, the need to hurry out of that inn. All she wanted was to tumble into the bed with him once more.

She managed to release him and draw away. "I will survive your absence if you are not gone too long." He tried to steal another kiss, but she playfully pushed him away. "Go."

Flashing a grin, he walked to the door and removed the chair wedged against it. "Put the chair back." His tone was stern. "And do not answer the door to anyone but me."

She nodded and walked over to him. He gave her another swift kiss before leaving.

After they had made love that morning and she lay in his arms, he told her his new idea of how to safely reach Edinburgh.

On horseback.

They would continue to pretend to be a stable master and his wife, but say they were on a working holiday to discover what horses were bred in whatever part of the country they happened to be at any given moment. He explained that she would have to ride astride, as a stable manager's wife would do, not as a lady in a side saddle.

Marlena had ridden enough in Ireland with Eliza, but she had not ridden astride since a child, climbing on ponies in the paddock, trying hard to keep up with her brother, Niall, and Wexin. Tanner suggested they purchase a pair of trousers for her to wear under her skirts to protect her legs. That idea amused her. She'd often envied her brother and cousin their breeches, when she'd been confined by her skirts.

Tanner's plan to purchase the horses was even more amusing—and daring. He planned to write a note, signed and sealed by the Marquess of Tannerton's signet ring. The letter would authorise his stable manager, the bearer of the letter—Tanner himself—to purchase horses on the marquess's behalf. The money would be transferred from the Liverpool bank. Tanner wrote another letter of reference for "Mr Lear" to show, also signed and sealed by the marquess. With any luck, someone in the horse market of Liverpool would accept the documents. When the letters reached London, his men of business would certainly be puzzled, but they would honour them.

And it would be proof that Tanner had survived the shipwreck and had been in Liverpool. By that time, however, he would likely be on his way back to London.

Within an hour Tanner and Marlena were riding in a hackney coach on their way to a horse market, with no one in the inn wise to their destination. Within three hours, Tanner stood haggling with a horse trader, while Marlena stroked the snout of a sweet bay mare with whom she had fallen in love.

Even though their pace would be slower than if changing horses frequently, the horses needed to have stamina and strength for a cross-country ride. It meant adding more days to the trip than a coach would have taken, but Marlena could not help but look forward to more days—and nights—with Tanner.

As if reading her thoughts, Tanner glanced over at her. She did not dare show how much her heart was set on this horse lest the dealer raise the price. The same dealer also had a strong brown gelding that suited Tanner.

Tanner winked, and she knew the horse would be hers to ride. He followed the man into a room off the stable and Marlena hugged the neck of the horse.

"Dulcea," she whispered the horse's name, "I do believe you will be mine. For a while at least."

A few minutes later Tanner joined her. "It is done." He smiled. "Though my guess is each horse is a good four years older than he told me. No matter, they should do us nicely." Dulcea nudged him with her nose and he patted her neck. "Two forgettable horses." He turned back to Marlena. "Now to the saddle maker. With any luck we should leave Liverpool and our pursuer this very day."

He offered her his hand and she grasped it. Marlena had given up on happiness when Mr Rapp, the Bow Street Runner, arrived at Eliza's graveside, but this trip, alone with Tanner, through the beautiful countryside, swelled her heart with joy.

Chapter Nine

Fia made slow work of gathering the wash from the lines behind the inn. The sun had bleached the bed linens a dazzling white and they flapped in the breeze like an army of flags. It was too fine a day to hurry at her task, a day that almost cheered her.

She pulled one of the bedsheets off the rope strung from one post to another and did battle with a wind determined to prevent her from folding it. The sheet blew over her face for the third time, its scent as fresh as the air around her.

"Would you like some help with that, lass?"

She knew who spoke without seeing him, would have probably sensed his presence even if he'd not spoken. She'd been all too aware of Bram Gunn since his return to Kilrosa.

He caught the end of the sheet and uncovered her face, starting to help her fold the cloth even before she'd answered.

"I can manage this if you have other chores to do." She tried not to look at him, the sun lighting his face and giving reddish glints to his dark hair.

He smiled at her. His two front teeth still overlapped a bit, she noticed. They'd been a distraction every time he'd spoken to her. "If you need help, I've nothin' else to do."

He took the corners of the sheet and walked them over to her, so she could hold them against the corners already in her hands. He was a large man and she felt dwarfed by his size when he came so close. She wondered if the French soldiers he'd fought in the war found him an awesome sight when he charged at them.

Fia shook her head and took the folded ends he offered her. They repeated the process until the sheet was too small for two people. She placed it in the basket and he took the next sheet off the line for her. Somehow the silence between them made Fia too aware of his thick-muscled arms and the lingering scent of the lye soap used to wash the dishes.

"This must seem tame work after the Army," she said.

He smiled, handing her the ends of the sheet. "I prefer it tame. I was fair sick of fighting."

"Uncle Gunn used to say you liked soldiering. He thought you would never come home." She took the ends.

A shadow crossed his face. "Och, I'd had my fill by Waterloo, but the Army took several years t'let me go."

Everyone knew the Scottish regiments saw very hard fighting at Waterloo. Several families around Kilrosa and Parronley lost sons and husbands and brothers to the great battle. It upset her to think Bram, too, might easily have been killed.

He smiled again as they brought the ends of the next sheet together. "And Da thought you would stay in London and marry some fancy footman or shopkeeper."

She glanced away. "London was not what I thought it would be."

They met again and his warm brown eyes were filled with sympathy. "Da also wrote about the business with Miss Parronley. Lady Corland, I mean. It must have been a nasty place for you to be, when she killed him."

She kept her eyes averted. "As they say."

When she looked his way again, his expression was puzzled. She placed the second piece of folded bed linen in the basket and he was ready with another one, the breeze giving him a struggle with it. She grabbed the flapping ends.

He went on, "I must admit, I was glad to hear you'd come home where you have family to look out for you. I thought one of the village boys would have married you by now, though."

She peered at him, thinking he might be fishing for an explanation. Or perhaps Uncle Gunn had already told him she had refused offers of marriage. "Well, I'm not married."

Of all people, she would not wish to tell him why she was not married, that she'd sinned so greatly, sharing Lord Corland's bed, even though it was for fear of being tossed out on the street. Or about how she'd stolen some coins from Lord Corland after he'd finished with her and had fallen asleep. How she'd been putting on her clothes when Lord Wexin came in, dressed so funny. From the dressing room she watched Lord Wexin stab Corland in the neck with a pair of scissors and she'd cried out. Lord Wexin had then tried to stab her with the scissors.

She'd be dead next to Corland if Lady Corland had not come in and fought Lord Wexin off so bravely. Fia had been a terrible coward. She had run away after Wexin threatened to kill her. She'd packed her things and used the coins she'd stolen to travel home to Kilrosa. When the news of the event reached Scotland, Fia learned that everybody thought Lady Corland had killed her husband and Lady Corland had also run away.

Fia had been glad that Lady Corland had escaped, because Fia was still afraid Lord Wexin would kill her if she told anybody what she had seen that night. She did not know if she would have had the courage to tell, even if Lady Corland had not escaped.

Fia did feel a terrible guilt that Lady Corland could not become Baroness Parronley, like she should be. They said that Lord Wexin would inherit Parronley if Lady Corland died. If Wexin came to Parronley, Fia would run away again, but this time she would have no place to go.

"Fia?" Bram stood waiting for her to take the ends of the sheet he held for her.

She snatched the sheet from his hands. "I don't have time for all this talking. I can fold faster on my own. Go to your own chores, Bram."

She expected him to look cross, but his eyes were only tinged with wounding. "Ah, lass," he murmured.

He helped her finish folding the sheet, but turned away when it was done and walked back towards the kitchen door.

Marlena woke in the Carter's Arms, an inn in the lovely Lancashire town they'd reached the previous afternoon. Her muscles felt a bit sore after the ten-mile ride through the countryside, but they did not hurt too badly. She rolled to her side and watched the man lying next to her.

They'd made love again the night before, to her great delight. It had been a languid, leisurely kind of lovemaking, bringing her a night's sleep uninterrupted by nightmares. She smiled, feeling truly rested for the first time since Eliza and the children had taken ill.

Marlena let her gaze fall on Tanner's face, so boyish in repose. She felt a swelling of emotion for this man, so good, so strong, so clever—clever enough to find a way to take her to Edinburgh that no one would think to follow.

He'd purchased a road book and set them on paths where coaches did not travel. The coach from Liverpool went to

Ormskirk, so they journeyed on roads west of Ormskirk, ending up a little closer to Scotland, in this lovely little village of Kirkby, with its redbrick buildings and white stucco inn. They'd had a lovely afternoon of sunshine and crisp breezes, setting a comfortable pace for the horses, all of them becoming more acquainted. She smiled just to think of it.

"Thank you, Tanner," she whispered.

His eyes moved beneath his lids, and she examined the fine lines visible at their corners. The lines deepened when he smiled. He had a strong nose, she thought, but soft cheeks. The beard that shadowed his chin was a bit lighter in colour than his hair, his thick, curly hair, so wayward, its flecks of grey barely visible at his temples. His hair always looked as if someone had just run their fingers through it.

Marlena took a finger and lightly touched one of his curls. *If you could only see him now, Eliza,* she said to herself.

To her surprise, tears stung her eyes. She knew it was because she'd need to say goodbye to him in Edinburgh. He had been so good to her. Would he have been so willing to help her—to make love to her—if he knew she was accused of murder?

He opened his eyes and smiled at her, the lines around his eyes creasing. "Good morning." The lines deepened. "What troubles you?"

She blinked and returned his smile. "Nothing troubles me."

He looked sceptical.

She took a breath. "I suppose I am finding it difficult to believe Davies will not charge into the room or ambush us on the road."

He took a strand of her hair and twirled it around his fingers. "How can he know where we are headed when I do not even know myself?"

She laughed. She loved how he made her laugh when she thought she would never laugh again.

He stretched his muscles, then winced and pressed his side.

She covered his hand with her own. "It still pains you?"

He reached across himself and put his other hand over hers. "Not so much when you touch me."

She slipped her hand from his and stroked his chest, letting her fingers explore the hair peppered there. She returned to the part of his ribcage where there remained a purplish bruise. "Does it hurt still?"

His eyes turned dark. "I would not care if it did."

He pulled her on top of him and kissed her, a long lazy kind of kiss. When it ended she stayed on top of him, liking how his skin felt against hers. She touched his face, tracing where his beard grew.

"Does it hurt to shave?" she asked.

He gave her his appealing half-smile. "Only when I cut myself."

"You could grow a beard like old men sometimes do." She rubbed her finger on his chin.

He pulled her face down to his, scraping his scratchy chin against her. "I could do that. Would you like me to grow a beard?"

She rested her elbows on the mattress next to his ears and fingered his curly hair. "I am certain I cannot tell a marquess what to do."

He laughed. "But you might tell Mr—" He stopped himself. "Who the devil am I today?"

"Adam Timon." She gave him a stern look. "You must remember it."

As they'd ridden through the peaceful countryside the previous day they had discussed using different names each place they went. Tanner suggested using names from Shakespeare. "So I'll have a chance of remembering them," he'd said. He'd made her laugh then, proposing names like Yorik and Coriolanus and Florizel. At least she'd heard of those names. She had never heard of Shakespeare's *Timon of Athens*.

"Adam Timon," he repeated, flashing a smile. He swiftly kissed her, scraping her face with his beard. "May I make love with Mrs Timon, do you suppose?"

"If you promise to remember her name," she retorted.

His lips caressed hers more gently. "I'll remember." He kissed her again and whispered against her mouth, "Marlena."

She felt a flutter inside, glad she'd given him her name, something of her true self. She started to slide off him, to share more of herself with him.

He stopped her. "Stay with me," he murmured.

Her brow wrinkled in confusion, but he soon showed her the purpose of his request, positioning her and entering her this new way. She gasped and quickly realised she must set the rhythm of their lovemaking. She would be responsible for their pleasure this time.

Feeling giddy with the power of it, she moved against him, watching his face.

He pressed his fingers into the flesh of her waist. "Marlena," he groaned.

She watched his passion grow in the changing expressions on his face and felt it in the pressure of his hands and the flexing of his muscles. She was giving him pleasure, giving him herself, as she so ardently wished to do. There was so much she could not share with him, but she could share this pleasure. She could totally share this part of herself.

The need built inside her, as well, and she moved faster

and faster until their pleasure erupted in unison, rocking them both. Marlena abandoned herself to the pulsing release, crying aloud as it reached the peak of intensity.

After the sensation ebbed, she rested on top him, as if she were his blanket. His hand lazily stroked her back.

"We should get up," she murmured.

"We should," he agreed, but he continued to stroke her. "In a minute."

She fully savoured that minute of languor, hating the moment of parting when she finally slid off him. To her delight, he pulled her back, rising over her and delaying their departure a little while longer.

Two hours later they were on the road again, with extra food packed in case they became hungry and a plan to continue north, on any road except the way the public coach would travel. The coach from Liverpool passed through Preston and ended its day at Kendal. Tanner plotted an alternative route, choosing half that distance to see how the horses fared at the end of the day.

Leaving Kirkby, they passed carts and riders and people walking to and from the village. Tanner greeted those who looked at them with curiosity. He was doing quite well at not acting like a marquess. Even so, Marlena could not see how people could not take note of him and remember him, he rode with such confidence and made such an impressive sight.

Marlena feared one of the faces of the people they passed would be Davies, but he could not know where they were bound. He could not know she was the Vanishing Viscountess, although each day passing made it more possible that a newspaper would reach here, reporting that the Vanishing Viscountess had been in a shipwreck and was missing. She was reasonably certain Davies could not read, but he would certainly hear others talking about her being lost at sea.

How many others had died? she wondered. Had Rapp died? She almost dreaded to know.

As they followed a dirt path through the moors, she relaxed. Here it felt as if she and Tanner were the only people in a beautiful world of undulating fields, brown and green and purple from the heather. The air was fragrant with heather and peat and the day was as fine as God could have created.

"It is so lovely," she said, overcome by the beauty of the place.

He smiled at her. "Indeed."

His eyes reflected the green of the hills. She would remember that when their journey was done.

He glanced at her again and began to sing, "Oh the summer time is coming, and the trees are sweetly blooming…"

When he finished the stanza, she laughed. "How is it you know that song?"

He rolled his eyes. "It has been sung at many a *musicale* at which I've had the misfortune to be trapped." He grinned at her and sang the second verse.

A breeze swept through the fields, rippling the colours. Marlena joined him in the chorus. "…all around the blooming heather, Will ye go, Lassie, go…"

This is happiness, she thought. *Look at me, Eliza. I am happy.*

Howard Wexin sat in a comfortable chair in the library of his London townhouse, sipping an excellent brandy he'd managed to procure and gazing absently at the leather-bound volumes filling the mahogany bookshelves that lined the wall. He'd managed quite a nice collection of books, he thought.

The room was elegantly but comfortably furnished. The large black lacquered desk at one end of the room made the tedious business of sorting his papers and reading correspondence almost a pleasure. The comfortable chair in which he sat was upholstered in Chinese brocade, as was the nearby *chaise longue.* The very best of Chinese porcelain and the occasional marble bust of learned men completed the decoration.

Wexin smiled.

His lovely wife, Lydia, was a marvel at choosing the best in décor. Every room of this London townhouse, which her father had purchased for them as a wedding gift, bore the mark of Lydia's excellent taste.

Wexin was grateful, oh so grateful that the Earl of Strathfield had permitted his daughter to marry him. Wexin had possessed equal rank with Strathfield, but Wexin had had no fortune. His father and grandfather had nearly spent the family into ruin. He had not married Lydia three years ago for the extravagant dowry her father offered and he'd fight a duel with any man who said he had. He had married Lydia because he adored her. Nothing could have stopped him from marrying her.

Nothing except her father.

Wexin stared into his brandy glass, remembering how close he had come to incurring Lord Strathfield's disapproval, to losing his lovely Lydia.

He smiled.

The Earl of Strathfield had, in fact, been of great emotional support to Wexin in those difficult days searching for his cousin Marlena to bring her to justice. The earl had even put up some of the money for the reward of her capture—or proof of her death.

That whole sordid affair would soon be over and justice

finally served. After three years Marlena had been found in Ireland. She ought to be on her way to London at this very moment. Ironically, when justice was finally served and dear cousin Marlena hanged, Wexin would become the prosperous new Baron Parronley. Wexin had never expected this good fortune. He'd been way too far down the line of succession.

When, several months ago, news arrived of Niall's death and the death of his sons, Wexin could not believe it. As soon as Marlena was disposed of, Wexin would have both his Lydia and wealth. Life was very, very good.

He took a generous sip of the brandy, relishing its fine taste and comforting warmth as he swallowed.

A knock sounded at the door, and one of the footmen entered. "The mail has come, sir."

Wexin waved his hand. "Place it on the desk, if you will."

The footman bowed and left the room.

Carrying his glass, Wexin rose from his chair and settled in the leather desk chair. He might as well sort the mail now and see if there was anything important, such as a letter from the Bow Street Runner confirming arrival at Holyhead.

On top were two letters for his wife, one from her mother, one from her sister. He smiled at those, knowing they would bring her pleasure. Next was marked Llanfwrog. Odd. He broke the seal and scanned to the signature, his excitement growing. *Arlan Rapp,* the Bow Street Runner.

As Wexin read, however, he shot to his feet. A shipwreck? It was only a bloody short voyage from Dublin. How could there be a shipwreck? She was missing. He looked for the date of the letter. Four days ago.

This was not good news, although, if the Vanishing Viscountess were at the bottom of the Irish Sea, it would save the nasty attention and expense of a trial. He would have to wait longer for the Parronley fortune, in that event, and he greatly needed the funds.

Wexin took a larger gulp of his brandy.

The door opened and his wife, the beautiful Lydia, Countess Wexin, swept in. Her blonde curls were a confection of artful disorder and her morning dress showed enough creamy décolletage for him to feel hungry for her.

"The mail has arrived?" She breezed over to him and planted a kiss on his head. "Is there anything for me, my darling?"

He lifted his face for a proper kiss and pulled her into his lap, pressing his hand against her belly. He hoped she was with child this time. She'd miscarried twice, but perhaps this time the baby would take. He deserved an heir.

He held up the two letters. "Would these be for you, I wonder?"

She snatched them from his hand. "My mother! And my sister!" She slipped off his lap and hurried to the *chaise*. "I must read them straight away."

Her sister remained in Wiltshire at the country home of her wealthy baronet husband. Her mother and father were in Venice, halfway on a Grand Tour.

Wexin gazed fondly at her. "What is the news?"

She waved a quelling hand at him. "Do let me finish, then I will tell you."

He refolded Rapp's letter and placed it in one of the drawers. There was one more letter. He glanced at it and saw that it, too, was from Llanfwrog in Anglesey. He broke the seal. This letter was dated three days ago. There must be news if Rapp wrote again after only one day.

Wexin took a deep breath and read.

"Dash it!" he exclaimed. She was alive. Worse, she had vanished once more.

"What is it, Howard?" Lydia asked.

He looked up. "Nothing. A business matter. Read your mail and do not heed me."

He read the letter again. Rapp had discovered her clothing. She was in the company of a man who'd worn a gold ring and who spoke like a gentleman, and it was known she was travelling north. Rapp said he would follow her and made assurances that he would find her, seize her, and return her to London, but Wexin could not merely sit still and wait. The man had lost her once—who was to say he would not do so again?

Curse her! Damned chit. Marlena had always been an annoyance, even when they were children. She always wanted to do whatever her brother, Niall, did. Niall, like as not, would indulge her and ruin their games.

This whole matter was Corland's fault anyway. The cursed man had not been able to win at cards even when luck stood at his shoulder. It had not been Wexin's fault that Corland resorted to moneylenders who'd been breathing down his neck. It had not been gentlemanly of Corland to call in his vowels, however, money he knew Wexin could not pay, then to threaten to tell the Earl of Strathfield and all the gentlemen of White's Club that Wexin refused to pay his gambling debts.

The Earl of Strathfield might have forgiven Wexin for being the cousin of a murderer, but he would never have forgiven him for not paying debts of honour. If Corland had made good his threat, Strathfield would have refused for his daughter to marry Wexin.

And nothing could have stopped him from marrying Lydia. Nothing.

He just wished he could finish mopping up the mess Corland had created for him. Hang Marlena and be done with the matter.

Wexin covered his mouth with his fist as he rested his elbows on the desk and pondered what to do about his dear cousin Marlena, the Vanishing Viscountess, who ought to vanish for good. He doubted she would go back to Ireland. She was friendless there now. There was only one place he could think of where she would go.

To Parronley. Perhaps she would rally supporters to her cause, and prevent her return to justice here in England. Or perhaps she knew the whereabouts of the maid, the girl who nearly foiled his whole scheme and could foil it still. Unless Wexin found her first.

He glanced over at his wife, her lips moving slightly as she read, breaking into a smile or a frown at whatever the words said on the page. He would still do anything to keep her.

She put down the letter and glanced over at him. "Shall I read them aloud to you?"

He rose and walked over to her, joining her on the *chaise*. After she read her letters he would tell her that important business would take him away from her for a time, though he hated even a day not in her company. If he used a fast coach and changed horses often, it would take four days, five at the most, to reach Parronley. He could not fathom how long it would take to find Marlena.

When he returned to London and the matter was resolved, nothing would ever again threaten to destroy his happiness.

"Read to me, my dearest," he said. "I am all yours."

Chapter Ten

One eventuality for which Tanner had not prepared in his brilliantly conceived plan was for rain. A grave error.

The moors, so serene and beautiful, now were dismal, cold, and wet. The horses, real workers the last three days, were slogging through, but too many of the side roads were like bogs. They'd been forced to stay on the main route, the route the coaches took.

He swivelled around in the saddle to check on Marlena, who followed a little behind him, looking forlorn in her cloak, rain dripping from its hem.

"Let me give you my top coat," he called to her.

She shouted back, "I've said no."

True. She'd refused his top coat at least three times.

"It is as soaked through as my cloak, is it not?" she added. "It would not help."

That was the closest she came to complaining, admitting that help of some sort would be desirable.

They ought to have stopped at the inn in the village they'd just passed, at least longer than the time it took to give the horses some oats and a rest, and themselves something hot to drink next to a warm fire. It had been a coaching inn, however. Some coaches were still on the roads. Even though it was unlikely Davies would find them after so many days and so many miles, Tanner had not been willing to take the chance.

They came to a fork in the road with a signpost bearing the name Pooley Bridge.

Good God. Pooley Bridge.

He had no idea they were near Pooley Bridge.

He turned around to Marlena again. "We'll stop near here."

She followed him unquestioningly as he followed the sign to Pooley Bridge. They soon entered the town, its narrow streets and stone houses familiar. He'd visited only the year before. Then he'd travelled to the area from Northumbria, which was perhaps why he had not realised how near they were. A year ago, after Flynn left him to marry Rose O'Keefe, Tanner had dragged Pomroy along on a tour of all his properties. They'd been gone for weeks.

Had it been only a year? It seemed a lifetime ago that he and Pomroy rode through this town and drank whisky and ale with the farmers and fishermen at the local pub. It even seemed a lifetime ago that Tanner had visited Flynn and Rose in Dublin. A lifetime since he'd stood in the cuddy of the packet ship home, lamenting his useless existence, diverting himself only by watching the woman who now shared his bed.

Sometimes it seemed to Tanner that time began when he and Marlena plunged into the bone-chilling sea. He had been reborn in a manner of speaking, with a new identity and new names each time the sun rose in the sky. Dash it. What was his name today? He had totally forgotten. Lennox, perhaps.

It did not matter.

"That was an inn," Marlena called to him, her tone a tad irritable.

He turned to her. "I saw it. We'll not be stopping there."

She scowled from beneath the drooping hood of her cloak.

"Soon we'll stop," he assured her. "Soon."

The streets were nearly empty of people, and, as he hoped, those caught outside in the rain appeared not to notice that the marquess again rode through their town.

Tanner and Marlena crossed the bridge over River Eamont and were soon in a tree-lined lane. The bright reds, yellows and oranges of the autumn Lake District foliage were muted by the grey curtain of rain.

"Have you made a wrong turn, Tanner?" she called to him.

He brought his horse to a stop and waited for her to come alongside. "Losing faith in me, are you, Marlena?"

She frowned. "I have lost faith in everything these last few hours. Ever since the rain soaked through to my skin."

His brows knitted. "I told you. I will give you my top coat—"

She held up her hand. "Do not even say it. I might snap your head off for it."

He laughed. "Miserable, are we? Do not fret. I promise we shall be warm and dry before you know it."

"We are headed into wilderness, Tanner."

Soon, however, the wilderness opened up, revealing a great expanse of lawn at the end of which was a large stone house, three storeys high.

"Tanner?" Marlena said.

He trotted ahead.

"Tanner," she called again. "This is somebody's house."

He trotted all the way to the front entrance and dismounted.

She followed him. "Tanner, this is somebody's house."

"I know." He extended his hand to help her from her horse.

They climbed the stone steps, and Tanner sounded the knocker on the door, striking it as loudly as he could.

"I greatly dislike this idea," Marlena grumbled. "It was not in our plan to visit houses."

He pounded the knocker again. "Neither was rain."

The two horses drooped their heads and nuzzled the grass, not even bothering to nibble. Tanner knew precisely how they felt. Too weary of being wet and cold to even think of eating.

He sounded the knocker again.

"There is nobody at home." Marlena pulled at his arm. "Let us go back to the village."

"There must be someone home." He pointed towards the roof. "I saw smoke from a chimney."

Finally the door opened a crack.

"Kenney, is that you?" Tanner asked.

The man opened the door wider. "My lord?"

Tanner laughed. "It is indeed. Let us in, man, and have our poor horses tended to. They are as weather-worn as we are."

The man nodded and stepped aside so they could enter.

"Whose house is this?" Marlena whispered as Tanner put his hand on her back and escorted her inside.

He leaned down to her ear. "Mine."

"Oh, dear," said Kenney, looking down at his plain brown breeches and brushing off a coat patched at the sleeves. "Let me assist you. Or should I see to the horses?"

Poor man. This was the shock of his life, the marquess visiting without notice, catching him in his comfortable old clothes instead of livery. "Tell us which room has a fire burning and we shall tend to ourselves. I should like the horses cared for immediately."

Kenney's face creased with wrinkles. "The kitchen has a fire, but that is the only one, my lord."

Tanner took Marlena's arm. "Then we will head for the kitchen, if you will alert the stable. Have them bring the baggage we carried on our saddles as well."

Kenney bowed. "Very good, sir."

Tanner led Marlena through the hall, down a corridor and some stone steps to reach the kitchen. As they came near, he heard the sound of pots rattling.

"Mrs Kenney! Ho there. You have visitors," Tanner called a warning. He did not wish to give her too bad of a fright.

"Oh!" she exclaimed as she turned towards the doorway. "My stars, it is you, my lord. Such a surprise." She eyed Marlena with blatant curiosity. "Good gracious me."

Tanner brought Marlena forward. "Mrs Brown." He put strong emphasis on the *Mrs,* hoping both Mrs Kenney and Marlena would heed his saying of it. A married woman could be excused behaviour for which an unmarried woman would be condemned. "This is Mrs Kenney, wife to Mr Kenney whom you have already met. The Kenneys are the caretakers of the house."

Mrs Kenney curtsied. "Welcome to Dutwood House, Mrs Brown."

Mrs Kenney's curiosity about the unaccompanied woman her employer had brought to his Lake District house was almost palpable. Tanner had no doubt Mr and Mrs Kenney would gossip with the villagers about Marlena after they left, but he'd brook no ill treatment of her while she was here. He trusted the Kenneys were wise enough to realise that.

"Mrs Kenney," he went on. "Mrs Brown is chilled to the bone. May I depend upon you to keep her by the fire and find some dry clothes for her? I will run above stairs and change out of my wet things. I believe I left some clothing here."

Mrs Kenney sprang into action. "Oh, my poor dear. Come here at once."

Mrs Kenney was so genuinely sympathetic, Tanner decided he had nothing to worry about from her. She would treat Marlena well.

The older woman ushered Marlena to the hearth of the large kitchen fireplace and helped her remove her soaking wet cloak. Tanner shrugged out of his top coat and draped it over a chair near the fire. He gave a quick squeeze to Marlena's arm and hurried out, hoping his memory had not failed him and he'd left some clothing in the bedchamber there.

Fia had nothing to do but look out of the window of the inn and watch the rain pouring down. Visitors were few, scattered at tables, merely passing time until the rain stopped.

She did not much relish being idle. It was so much better to be busy. Being busy gave her no time to think.

Someone walked up behind her. She could feel who it was. Bram.

"It is a nasty day." He stood next to her.

She had hardly spoken to Bram these last few days, ever since he'd helped her bring in the washing and made her think on things she'd rather not think on. Worse than that, he had hardly spoken to her.

"Yes," she managed to reply.

It was a puzzle to her why she could feel the heat of him, even though he merely stood next to her. She could feel his breathing and sometimes she even fancied she could hear the beating of his heart. Fia worked around numbers of men every day. The taproom was a favourite place for men to gather, but she never felt the presence of any of those men this acutely.

With everything so quiet, she was even more sensitive to Bram, whose presence seemed big enough to fill the whole room, rather than just the space by her side.

He rocked on his heels, holding his hands behind his back. "The only thing rain is good for is to give us a rest."

She turned to him. "Surely rain is good for crops."

He smiled. "That is true."

She wished he would not smile. His smile made things flutter inside her. She turned back to the window. "I'd rather be working than standing here doin' nothing."

"Bram!" her uncle called from across the room. He was sitting with his feet up on a chair, passing the rainy interlude in conversation with Reverend Bell. "If you've a mind, the glasses could use a bit of wiping."

"Enough restin', I gather." Bram nodded to his father and smiled at Fia. "Come help me, lass."

What could she say? She'd already told him she did not like to be idle.

Bram smiled down at her with his warm brown eyes. "It will give you something to do."

She lifted one shoulder and moved a chair aside so she could go to the bar without walking next to him.

He stepped behind the wooden counter over which his father served the drinks and handed her a cloth, then a glass. She wiped it and gave it back to him to put back on the shelf.

"I have been troubled by something." Bram handed her another glass.

He expected a response. Since he was not looking at her, it was easier for her to oblige. "By what?" She wiped another glass and gave it back to him.

He took it from her hand. "I must apologise to you. The other day when we were out of doors in the fine weather folding sheets, you might have thought I was prying into your troubles."

Her heart raced. "I have no troubles." She reached for a glass and made the mistake of looking into his eyes.

"As you say, lass." He gazed back at her, and she felt something melt inside her. "All the same, I am sorry. I did not mean to distress you."

She snatched the glass from his hand. "I was not distressed."

She wiped with extra vigour and thrust it back at him. He accepted it with annoying calmness. In silence they finished all the glasses on one shelf and started on those on the next.

He finally spoke again. "It is said Lyall and Erroll are vying for your hand."

She handed another wiped glass to him. "Losh, they are mere lads. I do not heed them."

"They are not much younger than you are, surely," he went on. "You are twenty-one, if I'm doing the sums correctly."

She did not miss that he remembered her age. "And they are eighteen. It is a big difference."

"So a man and a woman must be the same age? To marry, that is."

"I did not say that."

"Och, but I think you did say that. You said—"

She interrupted him. "I meant only that a lad of eighteen is too young, when the lass is three years older."

"What if the lass is younger than the man? Is that different to you?" He took a glass from her hand and gave her another one.

"It would be different, aye." She wiped.

He inclined his head towards the vicar. "So if Reverend Bell sought your hand, that would be all right, then?"

She handed the glass back to him. "I'll not be marrying Reverend Bell and he's not wanting me, anyway."

He winked at her. "I was talking about age. Making a point, you might say."

She turned away from him. "My marrying or not marrying is not a matter for you to concern yourself over."

He touched her shoulder. "Come," he said in a soft voice. "I was merely talkin'. I did not mean to poke at you."

"I was just talkin', as well," she mumbled. She took another glass from his hand.

They continued their work again, but this odd awareness of him was worse when they were silent. She smelled the soap of the scullery on him, as well as the smoke of the kitchen fire. She felt each shift of his feet, each move of his muscles. He did not seem a man to be inside a house, even on a rainy day. She could easily imagine him in shirtsleeves, striding through the fields, rain plastering the cloth to his chest, parting his hair into wet curls—

She frowned and wiped twice as hard. She hated being at leisure to think.

"You—you are so much talkin' of marrying," she said, her voice accusing, even though the problem was inside her own head. "Maybe you are thinking of marrying. Maybe you have your eye on some lass here in Kilrosa or in Parronley, now you are done with soldiering."

His expression sobered and his fingers brushed hers as she handed him the glass. "The time is not quite right. I must wait a wee bit more."

She blinked up at him in confusion, not catching any sense to his words. His expression unsettled her so much it felt like her insides had coiled into knots. She wanted to be at peace, not to feel, but just to work and forget.

Ever since Bram had returned home, her peace had fled and she'd started thinking again about Lady Corland and Lord Corland and that horrible night. She again felt that same sick fear she'd felt for months after she ran away from London. It was as if Bram somehow made her numbness go away and now she must feel everything inside her.

"What is it, Fia?" He stepped towards her and put a concerned hand upon her arm. "You look so distressed."

She pulled away. "It is nothing, Bram. Give me another glass. Let us finish this task. I've—I've decided to mop the floor after this."

His eyes continued to gaze upon her with concern, but they continued through the shelves until all the glassware was clean.

At the coaching inn in Penrith, Arlan Rapp sat nursing his ale, talking across the table from a local man. He'd asked the man if he'd seen a gentleman and lady passing through.

The man rubbed his chin. "A well-looking woman?"

Rapp nodded.

"Saw a fellow in Clifton travelling on horseback with a well-looking woman." He took a gulp of ale. "The man was no gentleman, though. Tall fellow. Just a man and wife travelling, seemed like."

"On horseback, you say?" Rapp lifted his eyebrows.

"That is so."

Rapp drummed his fingers on the table.

Several towns before someone had spoken of a tall man and a pretty woman. No horses had been mentioned, however. Horses explained a great deal.

In Liverpool Rapp had discovered that the elusive Mr and Mrs Lear had fled the Moor's Head and stayed at a different inn. They had made enquiries about ships to Glasgow, but had not booked passage. Even though the Viscountess and her companion had purchased seats on the public coach to Kendal, they had not used them.

Rapp knew deep in his gut that the Viscountess was headed to Scotland. He had to follow that belief. Trust that he would find her.

He lifted his tankard to his lips.

They were on horseback.

He'd assumed they had hired a private coach. He'd been wrong, but now at least he was on their trail. If he did not find the Viscountess on the road, he would certainly locate her in Parronley. He would pen another letter to Wexin, appraising him of his progress. He'd sent a letter from Liverpool, but this time he could be even more confident he would apprehend her.

He gazed out of the window where the rain continued unabated. Wherever they were at the moment, they would not travel further this night. Suddenly the bed in the room he'd let at the inn sounded very appealing.

He stood and threw some coins on the table. "I thank you for your information and bid you goodnight. Have more refreshment on me."

Chapter Eleven

Mrs Kenney brought Marlena a nice linen shift and the very softest wool dress her fingers had ever touched. The kitchen fire had warmed her enough that she could step into the scullery for a good wash before donning the dry clothing. She simply went without her corset, which was still too wet, but that was not so awful a thing.

Tanner returned to the kitchen, dressed in plain, comfortable clothes that Marlena imagined were intended for hunting.

"What have you that we might eat, Mrs Kenney?" Tanner asked.

"Some soup is all, m'lord." Her forehead wrinkled in worry.

Tanner smiled at the woman. "Soup sounds splendid." He turned to Marlena. "Does soup not sound splendid to you, Mrs Brown?"

"I should like nothing better," Marlena responded truthfully.

During their meal he entertained her and Mrs Kenney with tales of his visit last year with Pomroy, including a more detailed telling of the beard-growing competition. Marlena was full of admiration for him. He eased Mrs Kenney's distress at being totally unprepared for the arrival of her employer, by showing her that everything she did pleased him. And he eased Marlena's own discomfort, for surely the Kenneys thought her to be Tanner's mistress.

Marlena and Tanner left the kitchen when Mr Kenney reported that fires were built in other rooms prepared for their use. Tanner showed Marlena to a wainscoted drawing room with furniture built for comfort rather than fashion.

She settled herself on a large sofa facing the fire and wrapped a blanket around her for added warmth. Mrs Kenney brought them tea.

Tanner gave her an uncertain look. "Do you mind if I leave you for a moment? There must be a bottle of brandy in this house somewhere that Pomroy and I overlooked."

"Go," she said. "I shall be very happy by this fire with my cup of tea."

While he was gone she sipped her tea and allowed herself the luxury of thinking of nothing at all but the glow of the peat fire, the hiss of moisture escaping it, and the lovely scent that hearkened her back to childhood.

He strode into the room. "Found a bottle!" He lifted it into the air.

"Do you plan to drink your way through this rainstorm the way you and Pomroy did the last time you were here?"

He sighed in mock dismay. "I fear not. There is just this one bottle of brandy and no more than three bottles of wine. I shall save those for our dinners."

He opened the bottle, poured a glass and lifted it to his lips. His eyes closed in satisfaction. "Ah. I have missed this."

He never requested brandy at the small village inns where they'd stayed. To even inquire about brandy would have signalled him a gentleman in disguise.

"Are you not enjoying our trip, Lord Tannerton?"

"Not enjoying it?" He rolled his eyes. "Sleeping at inns that have been the very essence of mediocrity, eating the blandest food England has to offer, being required to recall which blasted name I possess each day—not to mention getting soaked through to the skin—what was there not to enjoy?"

She laughed, but then sobered at the honesty in his words. "Do you regret your insistence on accompanying me?"

He strolled over to the sofa, brandy glass still in hand. Brushing a curl off her forehead, he murmured, "There have been some compensations."

The mere tips of his fingers aroused her senses. Until the rain, their days on the road had been filled with breathtaking vistas and picturesque little villages. Their nights had been filled with lovemaking even more remarkable, more than adequate compensation for the discomfort they endured.

She moved over on the sofa and patted its cushioned seat. "Sit with me."

He lowered himself into the seat and wrapped an arm around her shoulders. Marlena nestled against him, savouring the scent of him mingling with the scent of burning peat.

"You must have had a more enjoyable time with your friend Pomroy," she murmured. "Staying at the finest inns, drinking the best brandy, and eating fine food."

He kissed the top of her head. "Good God, no!" He shuddered. "Pomroy and I were heartily sick of each other by the time our stay was complete." He tapped her on the nose. "Some advice for you. Do not embark on a long journey in the sole company of another person, no matter how great a friend."

She sat up and stared at him. "Is that not what you and I are about?"

The Harlequin Reader Service — Here's how it works:

Accepting your 2 free books and 2 free gifts (gifts valued at approximately $10.00) places you under no obligation to buy anything. You may keep the books and gifts and return the shipping statement marked "cancel." If you do not cancel, about a month later we'll send you 6 additional books and bill you just $4.94 each in the U.S. or $5.49 each in Canada, plus 25¢ shipping and handling per book and applicable taxes if any.* That's the complete price and — compared to cover prices of $5.99 each in the U.S. and $6.99 each in Canada — it's quite a bargain! You may cancel at any time, but if you choose to continue, every month we'll send you 6 more books, which you may either purchase at the discount price or return to us and cancel your subscription.

*Terms and prices subject to change without notice. Sales tax applicable in N.Y. Canadian residents will be charged applicable provincial taxes and GST. Credit or debit balances in a customer's account(s) may be offset by any other outstanding balance owed by or to the customer. Please allow 4 to 6 weeks for delivery. Offer available while quantities last.

NO POSTAGE
NECESSARY
IF MAILED
IN THE
UNITED STATES

BUSINESS REPLY MAIL
FIRST-CLASS MAIL   PERMIT NO. 717   BUFFALO, NY

POSTAGE WILL BE PAID BY ADDRESSEE

HARLEQUIN READER SERVICE
3010 WALDEN AVE
PO BOX 1867
BUFFALO NY 14240-9952

If offer card is missing write to: Harlequin Reader Service, 3010 Walden Ave., P.O. Box 1867, Buffalo NY 14240-1867

Get FREE BOOKS and
FREE GIFTS when you play the...

LAS VEGAS
GAME

*Just scratch off
the gold box with a coin.
Then check below to see
the gifts you get!*

YES! I have scratched off the gold box. Please send me my **2 FREE BOOKS** and **2 FREE GIFTS** for which I qualify. I understand that I am under no obligation to purchase any books as explained on the back of this card.

49 HDL ENVS   **246 HDL EN2S**

FIRST NAME   LAST NAME

ADDRESS

APT.#   CITY

STATE/ PROV.   ZIP/POSTAL CODE   (H-H-01/08)

7	**7**	**7**	Worth TWO FREE BOOKS plus TWO BONUS Mystery Gifts!
🍒	🍒	🍒	Worth TWO FREE BOOKS!
🔔	🔔	♣	TRY AGAIN!

www.eHarlequin.com

Offer limited to one per household and not valid to current subscribers of Harlequin® Historical. All orders subject to approval.

Your Privacy - Harlequin Books is committed to protecting your privacy. Our privacy policy is available online at www.eHarlequin.com or upon request from the Harlequin Reader Service. From time to time we make our lists of customers available to reputable third parties who may have a product or service of interest to you. If you would prefer for us not to share your name and address, please check here.☐

▼ **DETACH AND MAIL CARD TODAY!** ▼

© 2007 HARLEQUIN ENTERPRISES LTD.
® and ™ are trademarks owned and used by the trademark owner and/or its licensee.

He gave a chagrined smile. "Forgive me. I must have sounded gravely insulting."

She settled back against his chest. "You may indeed become heartily sick of me by the time we part."

He did not respond for a while, but tightened his arm around her. "I think not."

She knew she could never tire of his company. He made the morning worth waking for and filled the nights with exquisite pleasure. When she was forced to part from him, her world would turn as grey and dismal as this relentless rain.

Marlena wanted him to think of her as she was now, although she supposed he would eventually read accounts of the Vanishing Viscountess, who drowned in the Irish Sea. He would learn her true identity then. Would he believe she was a murderess? She would never have the chance to know.

Edinburgh should be no more than two or three days' ride now. In two or three days Marlena would vanish for good. She nestled closer to him, wishing the rain would never stop and they would never have to leave this place.

"How many houses do you have?" she asked him, just wanting to hear him talk, to feel his voice rumble in his chest as her ear rested against it.

"Let me see." He took a sip of brandy and she heard him swallow. "Six, I believe. Seven if you count the townhouse in London. I have my properties written down somewhere."

"Seven houses," she whispered. "Did you live in one of them over the others?"

"At Tannerton Hall, almost exclusively."

She and Eliza had managed to get their hands on *The Berkshire Guide: An Account of Its Ancient and Present State* from the lending library and they had all but memorised the entry describing Tannerton Hall as one of the largest and most magnificent houses in the county, the house and gardens designed by William Kent. She was certain she could still recite the description of its ponds and cascades and its sham ruins.

"Until I was sent away to school," he added. "Where I met Pomroy."

Marlena remembered her brother Niall leaving for school at age nine, looking very brave and, at the same time, as if he might cry. Tanner might have even known Niall from Eton, but she could never ask.

"You and Pomroy are indeed friends of longstanding." Like she and Eliza had been.

"We are," he agreed, taking another sip of his brandy. "Pomroy and I are too much of a kind."

That was not how she remembered it. Pomroy had always been full of outrageous mischief, frivolous beyond measure. Tanner, she and Eliza realised even then, had been made of something more solid and dependable.

"Useless creatures, Pomroy and I." He finished the contents of his glass.

"Useless?" she asked.

He shrugged. "When you have an elevated title, the people you employ are the ones who have the knowledge and skill to do the work. Not me." The clock sounded the nine o'clock hour. He inclined his head towards it. "Like the clock. The hands are what you see, but it is all those tiny wheels and things inside that truly keep the time."

She felt sad for him, that he could so belittle himself. "So what do you do with your time?"

He stared at his glass. "Play cards, attend the races, show up at country-house parties." He looked over at her and smiled. "I've even been known to attend the opera." Even his smile seemed sad.

He gently eased her away and walked over to the table

where he'd left the bottle. He carried it back to the sofa and poured himself another glass. Marlena reached for her tea and finished the last of it.

He lifted the bottle to her. "Do you desire a glass? I am quite willing to share."

She shook her head. The wine from their dinner had been enough to make her eyelids heavy. She did not desire to fall asleep when she could spend her time with him.

He sat down next to her and she snuggled beside him again, taking his free hand into her own. "I think your hands are very nice."

He gave a low laugh and squeezed her fingers. "When they are against your skin, they do seem to be of some use."

She sat up and faced him. "Do not speak of yourself as useless when you have done so much for me."

He drew her back against him. "My finest moment, perhaps. Dashing from the privy to rescue you. Devising a means of escape that neglects to take into account the likelihood of rain—"

She put her fingers on his lips. "Stop this. I will have no more of it."

He grasped her hand and placed a kiss on her palm. "Very well, if you do not wish to hear me enumerate my many faults, there is no recourse but to talk about you."

The very last topic of conversation she would have chosen.

He went on, "For a start, where did you live as a child?"

She leaned against him again, not answering him. Her heart wanted him to know her, wanted them both to share all their experiences, their hopes, their dreams. She'd once wanted the same with Corland, but he used her girlish confidences to mock her later. Tanner was Tanner—he was not Corland and could never be, but there was little Marlena could tell Tanner without divulging herself to be the Vanishing Viscountess, pursued by a man Tanner once called a friend.

"I grew up in Scotland," she finally said. "And I, too, went off to school."

"Where in Scotland?" he asked.

She hesitated. "The Lowlands."

He shook his head in seeming exasperation. "Where did you attend school, then?"

"England."

He edged her away, placing his hands on her shoulders so she faced him. "Tell me more, Marlena."

She could not look at him. "It is enough."

He blew out a breath. "Tell me something. Anything. How did you get to be a lady's companion? How did you wind up in Ireland?"

She glanced away, trying to recall the details in the novel she and Eliza had read. "I—I was orphaned and had to make my own way. The school found me the position."

His eyes continued to watch her with scepticism. "Why Ireland?"

For this answer, she could only think of the truth. "When—when I ran away, I went to a friend who took me to Ireland to hide."

His eyes grew dark. "What sort of friend?"

She was puzzled. "I do not understand."

A muscle flexed in his cheek. "A gentleman friend? The man who…introduced you to lovemaking, perhaps?"

"Oh!" She realised why he might suppose this. The fiction she had told him about herself had not included a way to explain her experience in lovemaking. "No, it was not a gentleman. A school friend."

He nestled her against him again. "Then who was the man who—"

She told the truth. "A man who thought women in his employ must serve him in all ways." That described Corland very well.

"The son?" Tanner's arm flexed. "The man accusing you of theft?"

She did not say a word to counter the conclusion to which he'd leapt.

"That bloody bounder."

Yes, he had been. She hated allowing Tanner to believe something untrue.

Tanner must have known her husband. Gentlemen gathered at the same clubs and gaming hells in London. Marlena suspected Corland would have been very charming to a wealthy marquess. Her husband had been quite a charming man when he chose to be, to all appearances a fine fellow, in the same way everyone had thought Wexin to be a fine fellow. Tanner cared about her, she knew. He might believe in her innocence.

She still could not tell him the truth, however. If she told him the truth and he believed her, he might insist on clearing her name. She feared he would only earn the noose for himself if he admitted helping her, an accused murderess.

He twisted around to face her again. "Tell me who this man is. I will avenge you for it. I will make certain you need never fear his despicable wrath another moment."

Yes, he would risk his life for her, she had no doubt.

She put her arms around his neck and snuggled into his lap. "There is no need to avenge me. Soon he shall think me dead and it will all be over."

He held her face in his palms. "It will not be over for me until I know this enemy."

"If I named names," she said truthfully, "no good would come of it."

He released her and rose to his feet. "Do you have so little faith in me?" He picked up his glass and finished his second brandy. "I do not care if you are a jewel thief or not. Let me help you. You do not need to go to Edinburgh—"

"No." She put her legs up on the sofa and hugged her knees. "No," she repeated.

Tanner rubbed a hand through his hair, staring at her. He turned and reached for the brandy bottle again. He could fix this for her. He longed to fix it for her. Pummel that bounder into a bloody pulp for what he'd done to her. That was a task he would perform with pleasure.

At least he could get rid of the charges against her. Why would she not allow him to do so?

He poured himself more of the brown liquid and took a gulp, hoping the brandy would burn some calmness into his chest.

It did not work.

He looked down at her. "Tell me enough for me to help you," he asked again. "Tell me the name of this man and I will make certain he is laid so low he'd dare not lift a finger against you. You would not need to hide. You could—" He cut himself short.

He'd been about to say that she could come back to London with him. She could marry him. He could see that she was protected and cosseted for ever.

It had not been clear to him until this moment. He wanted to marry her. *Her,* not one of the fine, unblemished girls at Almack's who circled him like vultures, waiting for the instant he decided to give up bachelorhood. This was the moment and this was the woman to whom he wanted to give his hand.

He lowered himself down in front of her, his hands on her knees. "Tell me all if it, Marlena. Do not keep secrets from me. Do not decide I cannot help you."

She turned her head away.

He stood again and reached for his brandy, resisting the impulse to smash the glass and the bottle into the fireplace, to flare into flames.

"It grows late." It wasn't long past nine. In London the entertainments would just be starting, but he was suddenly bone weary. "I believe I shall go to bed." He turned to her. "Do you wish me to escort you to your bedchamber, or do you stay here longer?" His voice, so devoid of expression, sounded as if it came from someone else's lips.

Her eyes were huge when she looked up at him. "I shall retire now."

She unfolded herself and stood in her stocking feet. He imagined her feet would be cold on the wooden floors until the riding boots he'd purchased for her and her own pair of half-boots dried. How long before their clothing dried and the rains stopped? How long before he must let her go?

Tanner imagined their clothing was laid out to dry somewhere in the house. He'd told Mr Kenney to open only the rooms they might use. He had readied the drawing room, a dining room and two bedchambers.

Tanner took a candle from the drawing room, its small flame lighting only a few feet around them. The dark wainscoting faded into black as they walked in silence up the stairway. At the top a sconce lit the hall leading to the bedchambers, set side by side. An ancestor and his wife must have slept in the rooms Kenney had chosen. There was a connecting doorway in between. Mr and Mrs Kenney had made the correct assumption about Tanner and his 'Mrs Brown.' They simply had chosen the wrong night.

He walked her to her door. "You have your own bed," he said, still in this voice that did not feel like his own.

"Yes." She went inside, closing the door behind her.

Tanner leaned his forehead against the doorjamb, his mind
and stomach churning with emotion.

If she did not allow him to help her, he would have to let
her go, to say goodbye, to lose her into whatever name and
life she disappeared when he delivered her to Edinburgh. He
might never be able to find her again.

He pushed himself away from the wall and walked to the
next door, the bedchamber designated for the lord of the
house. When he entered, he saw that a lamp burned on a table.
Tanner blew out the candle he held in his hand and set it
down, looking around the room. Mr and Mrs Kenney had
done a fine job of making the house ready and comfortable
for them. He'd see they were well rewarded.

He'd been keeping a tally of those people along the way
who had helped them or even merely been kind. They'd all
be rewarded.

His purse was on the bureau. He walked over to it and
poured out the coins. Not too many remained.

Perhaps Mr Kenney would be willing to loan the marquess
a little spending money.

Tanner dropped the purse, still damp from the rain. He
removed his coat and waistcoat, and kicked off his shoes.
After washing, he put on the silk banyon Kenney had unearthed from some trunk. The garment still smelled of cedar.
He strode to the door connecting his room with Marlena's,
the silk robe billowing as he moved.

She might turn him away, but that would be preferable
to her feeling that he had turned her away. His time with her
was too precious to squander on a selfish need to have
matters his own way.

He opened the door.

She sat at the dressing table in a white nightdress, turning
around at the sound of his entrance. As he walked slowly

towards her, she turned back to the mirror and brushed her hair.

He took the brush from her hand and did the job himself. From the light of a lamp, her hair looked black as midnight, pouring over her shoulders like liquid night, falling in soft waves and feeling like silk beneath his fingers.

She stared at him in the mirror.

He gave a wan smile. "As a lady's maid, am I coming up to snuff?"

A ghost of a smile appeared on her lips. "I shall have to make do with you."

He leaned down and planted a kiss on the top of her head. "I perform other duties as well."

Her eyes darkened. "Such as?"

He squatted down, turning her chair towards him. "Such as apologising." He wrinkled his brow. "I am not precisely certain for what I am apologising. Not for wanting you to confide in me. Not for wanting to make things right for you." He stroked her neck with his thumb. "For making you think I did not want you, perhaps. That was dishonest of me."

She clasped his hand. "Tanner…" she began, her face pinched in distress.

He made her look into his eyes. "If you wish to sleep alone, I will return to my bed." He could not help but add, "My cold and lonely bed…"

She laughed and rose from the chair, pulling him up with her. "I am certain we both have had enough of being cold."

He lifted her into his arms, his banyan falling open as he did so. She slipped her hands up his bare chest to wrap around his neck. He placed her upon the bed linens and threw off the robe, letting it float to the carpeted floor.

She reached for him and he obliged her, climbing on the bed next to her and wrapping her in an embrace all at once.

His kiss was hungry, needful, as if he'd already experienced what it would be like to lose her.

She pulled up her nightdress and he broke off the kiss only long enough to tug the garment over her head and toss it away. She was beneath him, warm and soft and already pressing against him, urging him to enter her, to take her fast.

He thrust himself into her as if he too felt the need to hurry. Gentleness was forgotten as he took her as fast as she demanded and as hard as he wanted. She met him with each stroke, nails digging into the flesh of his back, uttering sounds from deep in her throat. He, too, could not remain quiet, his growls melding with hers in a strange duet, a song they both seemed powerless to silence.

He drove her faster and faster—or was she driving him? He did not know. They were like one person, not separate, not alone, not lost to each other.

Sensation rose, higher and higher, more and more intense. Thought vanished and sheer need took over, and still he moved with her, feeling the same growing crescendo inside her.

He felt her release vibrate and pulse around him, her cry ringing in his ear as his own release came, his own cry, his own symphony of pleasure.

It took a while for the sensation to ebb enough for him to collapse beside her. Though no longer connected to her in the most intimate way, he still felt they were one.

He wanted to crow with masculine delight at it, this feeling of belonging to another person, being a part of her.

"Now that is better," he murmured into her ear, tasting it with his tongue.

"Better than what?" she asked, squirming under his lips, her hands exploring his flesh.

He rose on one elbow. "Than being a damned fool." He

lowered his mouth to her lips and tasted them again with more leisure. She pressed herself against his leg. Her fingers played in his hair.

With some rationality restored, Tanner decided it was far preferable to enjoy the time they had together than to rage at its impending end. Besides, he still had a few days to change her mind. She would not be rid of him so easily.

If he accomplished nothing else in his life, he was determined to accomplish this: making Marlena his marchioness, his wife.

He settled next to her, holding her close. "Do you know what, Miss Brown?"

She wrapped a leg over his. "What, Lord Tannerton?"

"I am in a puzzle."

"A puzzle?" Her fingers were now twirling the hairs on his chest.

Dear God. It did not take much from her to arouse him again. He almost could not talk. "That bout of lovemaking was quite...pleasurable—"

"But?" Her hand was now splayed on his stomach.

"Mmm, uh, it has also been very nice to proceed at a leisurely pace." He rubbed his thumb on her arm, hardly parity with what she was doing to him.

"And?" Her hand slipped lower.

"I—mmm—was about to suggest we try it slowly and—ah—debate which we prefer later."

"Very well." She touched him, circled him with her hand.

Other women had touched him so, but the jolt of emotion that accompanied the sensations she created was totally unique.

He lay on his back and flung his arms over his head, savouring each daring touch.

Suddenly she stopped and rolled away from him. "You must think me terribly wanton."

He turned to her, touching her on the shoulder. She curled up in a ball.

"What is it, Marlena?" he whispered.

"I was being too—too bold, too dissolute, too trollopy."

A laugh escaped him. "Trollopy?"

She rolled over to face him. "Is that not a word?"

He pulled her into his arms, his face level with hers. "I like you trollopy," he murmured. "In fact, I did not think your wantonness terrible in the least."

She blinked. "You did not?"

He kissed her on the forehead. "I was rather enjoying how…trollopy you were behaving."

She laughed. "Are you ever serious? I do not know what to think."

He searched deep into her eyes. "I am entirely serious, Marlena. Your enjoyment, your boldness, is a delight."

She regarded him a long time. "Then I should like to delight you more."

It took Wexin two days before he had made all the arrangements to travel to Parronley. He hired three men to accompany him, men who could be trusted to do what he wanted if he paid them enough. He'd hired them before, when he'd first searched for Marlena and that maid. Even though the men had not found either of them, he'd paid them well and they were more than willing to work for him once more, even to perform his ultimate wish, if he desired them to. He had a fast post-chaise ready to transport him and a coachman who thought they could reach Parronley in four days.

Perhaps he would find the deed done already. Perhaps the Bow Street Runner had already recaptured Marlena. All the better. One thing he knew, Marlena would never escape again.

His valet made a final tug on his neckcloth, brushed the fabric of his fine coat and declared him ready to attend the opera. He and Lydia were to go in the company of friends, including two gentlemen who wanted his support in a bill they would present in the Lords.

Soon, he thought with a rush of excitement. *Very soon my worries will be over.*

He nodded to his valet and crossed the room to his wife's door.

He knocked and opened it. "Are you ready, my dear?"

Her maid was fastening a garnet necklace around her neck. "One moment, Howard."

The maid stepped back. "There, ma'am."

Lydia fussed with the jewels. "Thank you, Nancy." She stood and turned to her admiring husband. "I am quite ready now."

"You look ravishing," he said.

The maid held out her velvet cloak. Wexin took it and draped it over his arm. "Let us go then, my dear."

She held his arm down the marble staircase. "I do wish you would not go off on business tomorrow, Howard. I shall miss you so."

He patted her hand. "And I shall miss you."

They reached the hall where the butler bowed and said, "The carriage is waiting, sir."

Wexin took his hat and gloves from the man and put them on.

"Then allow me to accompany you," Lydia persisted. "I should like to go with you.

He turned to assist her into her cloak. "I would not dream of putting you through something so tedious." He smiled. "I assure you, I will return very soon."

Her beautiful eyes were tinged with unhappiness.

He patted her on the hand again. "Do not look so sad. I shall bring you a gift."

She frowned. "I do not want a gift. I want to be with you."

"Ah, but it shall be a great gift." He smiled. If only she knew how great a gift he planned to give her. He planned, after all, to secure their future together.

Chapter Twelve

Marlena woke to the sound of rain pattering against the window glass. For a moment she thought it was still night, it was so dark in the room, but she could spy a very grey morning through a gap in the curtains.

Tanner was not next to her. She sat up and combed her fingers through her tangled hair.

"Good morning." Tanner stood in the doorway connecting his bedchamber to hers. He rested against the doorframe, dressed in the coat and trousers he'd worn the night before.

"You are dressed already," she said.

He smiled and crossed the room to her, leaning down to give her a warm kiss.

He murmured against her lips, "I could easily undress again."

She was tempted and laughed. "What time is it?"

"Eleven."

"Eleven!" She grabbed her nightdress and put it on. "I had no idea it was so late! Why did you not wake me?"

He sat on the bed. "To what purpose? It was my pleasure to let you sleep as long as you wished."

She slipped off the bed and padded over to the water pitcher and bowl to splash water on her face. "I am not used to staying in bed so long."

Marlena had not slept this late since Corland had been alive and she'd had so little to do.

He walked over to her and hugged her from behind. "Shall I act the lady's maid this morning?"

She reached up and stroked his hair. "I do not know a lady's maid who acts as you do."

He stilled. "Did you once have a lady's maid, Marlena?"

She wished she had not spoken. It was becoming more and more difficult to lie to him about herself, especially when Tanner knew her more intimately than anyone else ever had.

"I did have a lady's maid." She averted her gaze.

The muscles of his arms flexed as if he were surprised that she answered him. They stilled again as if he were thinking of asking her another question about herself.

She turned to him. "Perhaps you can sit on the bed? You make a particularly distracting lady's maid. I will tell you when I need you."

He nuzzled her neck before complying.

It was erotic in its own way to have him watch her wash up and dress. True to his promise, he assisted her in tying the laces on her dress, brushed the tangles from her hair, and, when she was ready, he escorted her below stairs for a simple breakfast of fresh bread, cheese and coddled eggs.

"What did you do while I was sleeping?" she asked as they ate.

His brows came together. "I wrote a letter to London. News of my being aboard the wrecked ship should be reaching my people by now, as well as the documents for the horse purchase." He pierced a piece of egg with his fork and smiled. "My cousin Algernon will be delighted I did not drown. He would have apoplexy if he thought he must become the marquess."

Marlena could not recall ever meeting Tanner's cousin, but she could too easily imagine how those close to Tanner would grieve his loss. "Of course you must let them know you are alive."

He became serious again. "By the time the letter reaches my secretary, you shall be…settled. You need not fear. No one will question my decision to visit one of my properties."

His concern for her brought an ache to her heart. No man had ever cared so much for her. No man had ever put her needs above all else.

For all her initial protests that she could make this journey alone, she knew now she could not have done it without him. She not only owed him her life—she owed him her freedom. The thought of parting from him became ever more unbearable.

He took a sip of tea. "Kenney will carry the letter into the village as soon as the rain clears."

Marlena could imagine Mr and Mrs Kenney telling their friends in the village that the marquess had brought a woman with him. She was confident they would never realize her true identity. Even if they read of the shipwreck, Tanner had said nothing to them about being on the ship. They would never know enough to connect Tanner with the Vanishing Viscountess.

Tanner would know, however. Marlena's appetite fled.

He cleaned his plate and leaned in his chair, balancing it on its two back legs. "What shall we do today?"

She half-expected the chair to slip out from under him, but he seemed heedless of the possibility. "Whatever you wish. I confess it will feel odd to be inside instead of travelling." To be at leisure instead of running.

He smiled. "Let us go on a treasure hunt."

"A treasure hunt?"

He lowered the chair again, to her relief. "We'll explore the house. My grandfather was fond of this house. I can recall visiting him here. Let us see what treasures he and my grandmother left behind. We may discover something useful for our trip."

By mid-afternoon they were in the attic, digging through big wooden chests. Tanner had discovered a lovely wool shawl, now draped around Marlena's shoulders. He also unearthed a gentleman's white wig and coat of bright green silk.

He put both on. "These might have been my grandfather's, although I can well remember my father in wig and lace." He posed for her. "How do I look?"

She giggled. "Quite foppish, actually."

He grinned and knelt down to rummage through the cedar-lined trunk.

"How old were you when your father died?" she asked.

He looked up. "Nineteen."

"So young?" She tried to imagine him that young having such an important title thrust upon him.

He shrugged. "He was thrown from his horse."

"And your mother?"

He pulled the wig off his head and busied himself with the contents of the trunk. "I was about ten. She died in childbirth."

She knew he did not have any brothers or sisters so he had lost his whole family, just as she had.

He sat back and fixed his gaze on her. "And your parents?"

She stared at him for a moment, then told the truth. "My— my mother died of childbirth fever. My father died much later. He was struck by lightning."

"Struck by lightning?"

She nodded. "I confess to having a fear of storms ever since."

His eyes filled with sympathy and he reached across the trunk to stroke her cheek. "And have you any family left?"

Tears stung her eyes as an image of her brother and her sweet little nephews formed in her mind. She shook her head.

"Then we are alike, you and I. Alone," he murmured.

The ache in Marlena's heart returned as their gazes held.

Tanner withdrew his hand and returned to the chest. Marlena peeked inside at more bright-coloured brocades that Tanner folded over as he searched deeper.

"I do not think pink silk is the thing to wear while travelling, do you?" He glanced up at her, his usual good humour returning—except for a remaining hint of emotion in his eyes.

She smiled. "Perhaps not."

He felt along the sides and the bottom and pulled out a flat wooden box. "Here's something."

He opened the hinged lid. Inside were lovely ladies' handkerchiefs of white linen and lace.

"You must have these." He said this in the most casual of voices.

She lifted one and unfolded it. "They are beautiful."

He gazed at her, one corner of his mouth lifting into a wistful smile.

He looked down at the box again. "There is something else." He unfolded one of the handkerchiefs to reveal a lady's ring.

He placed it in Marlena's hand.

"Oh, my!" She held it up to the light of their lamp.

It was a delicate sapphire ring, its glittering blue stone encircled in tiny gold leaves and flowers. "It is so lovely."

She handed it back to him, but he would not take it. "Try it on."

She slipped it on the ring finger of her right hand and it fitted her as if made for her. She held her hand so he could see how pretty it was.

He smiled. "It must have been my grandmother's."

Marlena admired it a moment more before she began pulling it off.

He stopped her with his hand. "Wear it. I want you to have it."

"But it is a family piece," she protested.

He waved a quelling hand. "I want you to have it."

She gazed down it again. "I shall treasure it always."

They turned their attention back to the trunk and then to the next trunk and the next, eventually selecting two old top coats that might prove useful on the journey, as well as the lace handkerchief and Tanner's grandmother's sapphire ring. When they were finished it was nearly time for dinner.

That evening when they sat in the drawing room, Tanner read *Timon of Athens* from a copy of the Shakespeare play he'd discovered in the library. Marlena relaxed by the fire, listening to his deep, expressive voice, the woollen shawl wrapped around her shoulders, the sapphire ring sparkling in the firelight. She wished the rain would never end. She wished she could stay right where she was, with Tanner, for ever.

As she did every Sunday, Fia accompanied her Uncle Gunn and Aunt Priss to the old stone church that had stood between Parronley and Kilrosa for over two hundred years. Bram, of course, was also one of the party, and it was only natural that he walked next to Fia. Even though the sun shone, the roads were still muddy, and Bram took hold of Fia's arm when the ruts in the road made walking difficult.

Fia followed her aunt and uncle to their usual pew, filing

in after them. Bram sat next to Fia, looming over her like he always did. She picked up the prayer book and opened it.

Soon the service began, and Reverend Bell recited the Ten Commandments, the congregation responding in unison. When the reverend came to *Thou shalt not commit adultery,* Fia closed her eyes.

"Lord, have mercy upon us, and incline our hearts to keep this law," she answered along with the others. She hoped God knew how fervently she meant what she said.

Sometimes Fia felt as if she did not belong in the church with all these good people. Still, the sound of their collective voices in prayer, the light filtering through the coloured glass of the windows, the smell of wood and stone and people, all gave her comfort.

Reverend Bell began his sermon, speaking on the virtue of moderation. Fia had to stifle a smile at his choice of topic, this man who spent so much time drinking immoderately in the taproom of the Black Agnes. She made the mistake of glancing at Bram, whose twinkling eyes reflected her amusement.

When the last amens were spoken, the congregation filed out of the church and back into the sunshine. Most lingered to greet Reverend Bell and the elders, as well as to pass time with their neighbours. Fia drifted off to the edge of the group to wait for Uncle Gunn and Aunt Priss, who were as busy chatting as were the others. Pretty Jean Skinner waylaid Bram and now held him captive with her flirting and her silly talk.

Fia glanced away and took another step back. Lyall and Erroll gave her a friendly nod as they walked by, but, as she had predicted, their affections had been transferred elsewhere, to the Brookston sisters, who giggled at every word they said. For once, though, Fia wished they would pay her such attentions, so that perhaps she could be distracted from this odd pain in her chest from watching Bram with Jean.

To her shock Fia felt tears stinging her eyes. She blinked several times, but the tears kept forming anyway. She was also finding it hard to breathe without shuddering. If anyone noticed, what would she ever say? How could she explain?

"Aunt Priss," she called out, hoping she was too far away for her aunt to see anything amiss. "I'm startin' for home."

Her aunt nodded and waved and Fia spun on her heels, trying her best not to look like she was in a big hurry.

As soon as she reached the top of the hill, she turned off the road. Her aunt and uncle would visit with their friends for at least half an hour. She could take the time to collect herself before she walked back to the inn and began working. She did not want to start bawling while she was working. That would be nearly as bad as bawling outside church. Somebody would ask her what was wrong, and she didn't know the answer to that question.

She took the path that led up another hill, climbing to the top where a castle once stood. It was naught but a pile of old stones now, but she liked the place. She climbed up on one of the stones, warmed by the sun, and sat cross-legged, gazing down at Parronley House in the distance.

Seeing the fine house made her think of the lady who ought to be living there now. Everybody knew Lady Corland was now Baroness Parronley, since her brother and his little boys died. It was Fia's fault that the Baroness could not return to her house. If Fia had not sinned with Lord Corland, maybe all the awful things would not have happened.

If only Fia had not left Kilrosa. If only she'd stayed and waited and heeded the scriptures and remained a virtuous girl, she might be worthy to marry a good man.

She did not try to stop the tears. She had not cried for over two years now and she had thought all her tears were gone.

But then Bram came home and now she felt like spilling tears every day. Seeing him with Jean had done it this time.

Some day Jean or some other good, decent girl would marry Bram in that very church where Fia sat next to him this day. Maybe if Fia cried out all her tears now, she would have no more to shed when Bram married.

Fia rocked back and forth, arms wrapped around herself, keening with grief. That day Lord Corland died, it was like she had died, too, and Lady Corland—Baroness Parronley. She and Baroness Parronley might as well be dead.

"What is this, lass? Why are you weeping?"

She jumped and snapped her head up to see Bram walking towards her. She turned away from him, but he soon was standing in front of her.

"Are you ailing?" he asked.

She took a shuddering breath and shook her head.

His hand touched her arm. "Fia lass, tell me what is wrong."

She wiped her eyes with her fingers. "I came here to be alone, Bram."

His hand fell away. "I saw you leave the church and somethin' told me to follow. You don't do weeping like this without reason. If something is so wrong, let me aid you."

She lifted her face to him and stared into his eyes. "You cannot help me." She glanced away. "There's nothing to help me."

He climbed up on the stone and sat beside her. She moved away, but could not go far or she'd fall off.

He stared out on to the valley below. "You were just a wee lass when I left for war, Fia. Twelve years old, but already the bonniest lass I knew. Bright-eyed and lively and full of wanting to know everything. You were the daughter Mam Priss prayed for." He shifted his position. "What happened in London to change you?"

She tried to shrug him off. "You were gone, Bram. You do not know that anything changed me but time."

He lifted his hand, but dropped it again. "Mam Priss said you came back different. And you came back after Miss Parronley killed her husband."

She twisted away from him. "She'd be Baroness Parronley."

"Baroness, then." He peered at her. "Does it have to do with the murder, then?"

She jumped off the rock. "You all talk a great deal."

She started running down the hill but he caught her from behind and spun her around. She tried to swing a fist at him and to pull away, but he held her fast.

"Let me go, Bram," she cried, struggling, but unable to dislodge his large hand around her arm.

He pulled her against him and wrapped his arms around her, engulfing her with his huge warm body. "I will hold you 'til you tell me, lass. I promise to tell no other, but let me know what disturbs you and I'll not bother you over it again."

"Are you forcing me, Bram Gunn?" she mumbled into his chest.

"Ay, I am indeed." He murmured, holding her closer. "Now commence with talking."

"First you have to let me go," she said.

"Say something that is not blather and I'll think on it."

She could never tell him how her heart seemed to cleave in two pieces when he smiled at Jean Skinner. That would be too shaming, but, in the shelter of his strong arms and warm body, she thought it might be safe to tell him about that terrible night. She wanted to tell Bram, who seemed so strong he could carry anything, including this burden she had carried alone for so long.

"I'll do it. I'll do it," she said. "Give me room to breathe."

He loosened his hold on her only a bit.

"Lady Corland did not kill her husband," she began.

His brows rose.

"I was there, Bram." She felt herself turn cold as she remembered it. "I saw it all."

He took her hand and walked her back to sit upon the rock, settling next to her. "Tell me of it, lass."

She took a breath. "I was in the room—in—in Lord Corland's bedchamber."

Fia glanced at Bram, expecting to see his lips purse in disapproval. Instead, he merely nodded for her to go on.

"A man entered the room. He did not see me, but I saw him. He—he was dressed oddly. In Lady Corland's robe. I knew it because it had a lace trim." She swallowed. "The—the man walked over to the bed and leaned over. At first I thought he was going to kiss Lord Corland, but instead—instead…" She faltered.

"Who was the fellow?" he asked mildly.

She turned to face him. "Lord Wexin."

"Lord Wexin?" His eyes widened.

She nodded. "Lady Corland's cousin. The man who inherits Parronley if she is dead." She glanced away again. "He—he—pulled out scissors and—and stabbed Lord Corland in the throat." Her fingers flexed and her hand jabbed as if it were she holding the weapon.

He covered her hand with his own.

Her voice rose higher in pitch and the words poured out. "I guess I screamed, because he came after me then, but Lady Corland ran into the room and stopped him from stabbing me and I thought he would kill her, too. Instead he cried out for help, like it wasn't him doing the stabbing. He—he put the scissors in Lady Corland's hand and the robe, too—it was all full of blood—and then he told me he would kill me if I told anyone what I saw."

Bram's arm tightened across her shoulder.

She pulled away and looked him in the eye. "I ran away then, Bram. I ran and didn't stop until I reached Kilrosa."

"No one can blame you for running, Fia." His expression remained open and accepting.

She felt waves of guilt, however. "You don't understand, Bram. I—I left Lady Corland with him blaming it all on her. It is said she ran away—but what if he found her and killed her, too?"

He took her hand between his two strong ones. "Now, lass. That did not happen. If it did, he would come claiming Parronley, now, wouldn't he?"

His hands felt warm and rough with calluses, but so gentle and calming.

He made her look him in the eye. "Now, y'see, you have nothing to worry over."

Her breathing slowed. Her muscles relaxed, as if she'd indeed passed the weight on to his shoulders and off hers.

His eyes were warm and comforting. "Nothin' will hurt you, Fia. Nothin'. I'll see to it." He paused a moment. "I will take care of you, Fia. For always."

"What are you saying, Bram?" she whispered, feeling the blood drain from her face.

He averted his gaze and his cheeks turned pink. "I'm asking to court you, Fia."

She pulled her hand away. "No!"

The baffled and wounded expression on his face nearly broke her heart.

"You do not understand, Bram." She shook her head. He tried to turn his face away, but she held his chin and looked into his eyes. "Do you not wonder why I was in Lord Corland's room?"

He seemed to look at her very deeply. "You were in Lord Corland's bed."

Her jaw dropped. He spoke the truth like it was nothing.

He smiled wanly. "You were out in the world alone, lass, in a gentleman's house. The world is a treacherous place, I've learned, a place full of temptation—"

"Temptation? It wasn't temptation, Bram." She blew out a breath.

He responded in a quiet voice. "I meant only that I'd not judge you for whatever happened."

She slipped off the rock and stood before him. "I went willingly enough, Bram. I did not want to lose my employment, which he said I would and that no one would hire me again. I did not have any money. I'd seen enough of London to know what happened to girls with no money, and I didn't want that to happen to me. So I bedded him and stole his money so I could get home." She backed away, adding, "Reverend Bell's sermons say I'm not fit to be married, and I'll not pretend I am."

She spun around and started walking down the hill, but she did not make it far before Bram fell in beside her. They walked in silence.

When they were halfway back to Kilrosa he spoke. "War makes a man do terrible things, Fia."

She darted a glance at him, not knowing why he was speaking.

He went on. "A soldier's job is killin'. The commandment says, 'Thou shalt not kill.'"

Fia frowned, puzzled as to why he was telling her this.

He stopped walking and gazed into the distance. "Some of those Frenchies were no more than lads, but I killed them. I can still see their faces, some of them—" He bowed his head and fell silent. When he lifted it again, he looked directly at her. "So I'll not judge what another person does to stay alive, in either body or soul."

He reached for her hands and she allowed him to take them. She lifted her face to his, her breath stolen by the tenderness in his expression. He glanced around, but they were alone on that stretch of road. Very slowly, he leaned down to her and placed his lips on hers.

Chapter Thirteen

Tanner and Marlena spent three wonderful days in Dutwood House. The rain had ceased after their first full day there, but it took time for the land to dry enough for them to venture back on their journey.

Tanner had been delighted to provide her with a chance to rest, to heal her horse-weary legs and his sore ribs. She was able to sleep as late as she wished each morning. All that was required of them was to decide what card game to play, what book to read aloud to each other.

Their time together at Dutwood gave Tanner a taste of what life with her would offer. He was a man easily bored, but all their forced leisure had not brought him even a moment of tedium. Everything they had done had delighted him, mind and body.

Because he'd shared the time with her.

They had ventured out of doors the previous day, donning old boots and trudging through the woods to the lake and back again. The fresh crisp air had put roses in Marlena's cheeks and her blue eyes glittered as brightly as the sapphire in the ring she wore beneath her glove.

Now the idyll was over, but Tanner was resolved that it would not be over for ever.

Mrs Kenney sent them off with a hearty breakfast, knapsacks full of bread and cheese, and laundered, dry clothing. The clean air and bright sun made for an exhilarating morning and the horses at least seemed to relish the return to their journey.

Rather than backtrack to Penrith and the Pooley Bridge, Tanner decided they should travel north through Greystoke, threading their way along minor roads to return to the coaching road near Calthwaite.

Still on his property, their horses climbed a hill below which was the Greystoke road. The valley was alive with colour, the trees even more vibrant with yellow and gold than before the rain.

Tanner glanced at Marlena. She made a lovely picture on the bay mare, with all the bearing of a marchioness, even if riding astride like a farmer's daughter.

"It is lovely here." She gazed out over the fields ahead, lying before them like square patches on a peasant's quilt. Marlena swung around to look behind her where Dutwood House still peeked through the trees.

She sighed. "I shall miss this place."

As would Tanner. Dutwood House was perhaps the most humble and rustic of his properties, but it very lately had become his favourite, because he'd shared it with her.

"By God," he exclaimed suddenly, inadvertently pulling on his horse's reins. "I have an idea." The horse danced in confusion until Tanner got him back under control. "Why not live at Dutwood? You need not go to Edinburgh. You could wait here. You would be Mrs Brown, whom I allowed to live in my house—"

"No, Tanner." Her expression turned stony. "I could not."

"But you could," he insisted, the plan rising fully formed into his head. He would leave her here and return to London. He'd set about discovering her identity and the identity of the man who was her enemy—her seducer. It should not be too difficult. How many lady's companions were accused of theft? Whose father had died of a lightning strike? When he'd cleared her name, he would travel back to Dutwood and return with her as his wife.

"What better place to hide away?" he persisted.

She brought her horse nose to tail with his. "No, Tanner. I've involved you in my troubles enough. You already take too much of a risk merely escorting me to Edinburgh."

He waved a dismissive hand. "You take the risk too seriously."

"I assure you I do not." She spoke quietly.

He signalled his horse to start down the hill, not looking back, but hearing her following him.

When he reached the bottom of the hill, she called to him. "Tanner?"

He turned and waited for her to catch up.

She brought her horse alongside his and reached over to grasp his arm. She made him look into her pain-filled eyes.

"Being with you has been the happiest time in my life." She lowered her head. "But I must leave you in Edinburgh."

He leaned towards her, and with a small, desperate sound in her throat, she closed the distance to put her lips on his. He kissed her back, pouring his emotions into the touch of his lips, trying to show her he would not give her up so easily.

When they finally broke apart, he managed to smile at her. "I shall endeavour to make our last days together as pleasant as possible."

"Yes." Her smile was as forced as his. "It is a lovely day and there is so much beauty to see."

He gazed at her. "So much beauty."

He vowed he would not distress her further, that he would do his best to make her laugh, anything to keep the pain from her eyes.

But he would not give her up so easily.

"Shall we avoid the main coaching route again?" he asked. "These roads seem dry enough."

"It will be safer, will it not?" she responded. "And it will make our trip longer."

He smiled.

They rode at a leisurely pace, stopping by crystalline streams to refresh the horses while they ate Mrs Kenney's bread and cheese and drank the one last bottle of wine from the Dutwood House cellar. As the afternoon wore on, they approached a little village, not far from Carlisle and near the border to Scotland.

Tanner halted his horse and looked down at the village. "If there is a half-decent inn here, I suggest we stay."

"It looks large enough for an inn," Marlena said. "And as sweet a place as Cumberland could offer."

The houses were grey stone and white stucco, in neat rows on the main street and fanning off to the side. An old stone church stood at one end of the town. Thin wisps of smoke came from the chimneys.

As they rode in, Tanner turned to her. "Who are we today, by the way?"

She laughed. "Mr and Mrs Antony."

"Antony," he repeated. "Antony… I have lost the habit of being someone else."

They found the inn, a small but cosy place. Tanner dismounted and held his hand out to help Marlena from her horse. They found the innkeeper inside and arranged for a room.

"Would you care for refreshment?" the innkeeper asked. "We are serving a mutton stew."

"Excellent," Tanner replied. "I need to see to the horses. Is there somewhere my wife could sit undisturbed until I return?"

"There is a private room off the taproom. She is welcome to wait for you there."

Tanner raised his brows to Marlena.

"I think that sounds lovely," she said. "Especially if I might have some tea."

"Indeed, ma'am." The innkeeper led her to the taproom and Tanner walked outside.

He gathered their baggage and placed it right inside the inn's doorway. Then he led the horses to stables kept by the village's smithy.

From the entrance, he could see the smithy talking to another man with a horse. Tanner waited at the door.

"I am looking for someone," Tanner heard the man say to the smithy. "A man and woman."

Tanner stilled.

"They were on horseback. Have they passed through here?"

"Not my stable. You can ask at the inn," the smithy said. "What is the name, in case they show up here?"

The man cleared his throat. "That is the thing. They are not travelling under their own names. The woman is a fugitive. There is a reward for her capture. If you assist me—"

Tanner did not wait to hear more. He backed up the horses, who whinnied in protest at not getting their expected bag of oats. He pulled them back to the inn and ran inside finding the innkeeper in the hall.

"Where is my wife?" Tanner demanded.

The innkeeper looked alarmed. "This way." He led Tanner through the taproom to a small private parlour.

Tanner wasted no time. "We leave now." He threw some coins on the table.

Marlena's eyes grew large with fright, but she followed him, running ahead to the horses while Tanner grabbed their luggage.

She was already seated on her horse. Tanner tossed her one of their bags.

"Go," he said, mounting at the same time.

From behind him, Tanner heard a shout. "That is them! Stop them!"

They took off at a gallop, too fast to be stopped. When they were clear of the town, they slowed the horses, but not to the leisurely pace of that morning. Tanner kept them moving north, keeping an eye on the position of the sun. When the road bent too far in another direction, he led them off the road and over the countryside. He pushed the horses as much as he dared, aware that the animals were tiring and the day advancing. Already the sun was low in the sky and the foliage leeched of vibrant colour. They must stop soon.

Over the crest of a hill, Tanner spied a river wending its way through the valley. Its banks were thick with trees and foliage.

"We'll stop by the river," he called to Marlena.

They descended the hill and followed the river along its banks until Tanner found a sheltered spot where it would be easy for the horses to drink. Tanner's gelding dipped his muzzle in the water even before Tanner dismounted. Tanner helped Marlena from the mare, and, while the horses drank, he fetched the road book and the satchel containing the leftover cheese, bread, and wine. He led Marlena to the shelter of a nearby tree.

"Eat something," he said.

She nodded and pulled out a piece of bread, handing the satchel back to him. "Are we in Scotland now?"

"I believe so." He opened the road book, straining his eyes in the waning daylight. "This must be the River Esk. I think I know about where we are." He closed the book again. "I had better tend to the horses."

Once the horses had enough water, Tanner led them to a patch of grass. They immediately gnawed at the green blades. Taking a cloth from one of the bags, Tanner wiped the sweat off his horse.

Marlena joined him. "Is there another cloth?"

He pulled one from the bag and handed it to her. She tended to her horse, eyeing Tanner cautiously as she worked.

They had barely spoken during the hard ride from the village, but she must realise he was consumed with questions, questions that invaded his mind as he rode, blocked only by the more pressing need to see her to safety.

"We will not reach an inn tonight." Tanner would ask his questions later, after they had settled themselves. "We must stay here. Build a fire."

She made no complaint about spending the night outdoors. She did not grumble that she would be cold or whine that she was hungry and thirsty.

"I'll collect firewood," she said instead.

Tanner removed the bags from the horse's saddles and loosened their girths. Marlena cleared an area for the fire while Tanner walked upstream to a place where the water flowed swiftly. He filled the water skins he'd had the presence of mind to toss in their bags before leaving Dutwood. In a still part of the river he spied some large fish nibbling at the underwater plants, mere shadows in the waning light.

He walked back to Marlena, who had gathered some rocks from the river's edge and was placing them in a circle.

"Give me a hairpin."

She reached under her bonnet and pulled a pin from her hair. "What is it for?"

He picked up a stone and sharpened one end. "To hook a fish. I just need something colourful for bait."

"I'll find something." She rummaged through one of the bags and pulled out a tiny piece of ribbon. "Will this do?"

"It will."

He hated the loss of ease between them and feared he might never find it again.

Tanner walked back to the fish-filled pool and uncoiled a length of string. He tied the improvised hook on one end and stuck the piece of ribbon on it before dropping it into the water.

He used to fish like this when a boy wandering around Tannerton, bothering the gameskeeper enough times that the man eventually took him under his wing and taught him all manner of useful things. Tanner had nearly forgotten them.

At the small pool he and a big fat fellow of a fish sparred until the fish finally took the bait in its mouth. Tanner jerked up on the string and his fish threshed noisily in the water until he pulled him out.

When he returned to Marlena, she had stacked thick pieces of wood with plenty of tinder underneath.

"You've built outdoor fires before," he commented.

"Yes," she admitted.

He opened his tinderbox and struck a flame.

He roasted the fish, which they ate with their fingers, remaining silent. It was obvious to Tanner that Marlena had hidden something from him about herself, something so important a reward was on her head and a Bow Street Runner was pursuing her.

After he ate, Tanner rose to check on the horses, safely

tethered nearby. When he returned, the sun was no more than a glow on the horizon, but the fire burned brightly. Marlena still sat by the fire, hugging her knees and wrapped in his grandmother's woollen shawl.

He sat near her.

She spoke, breaking their long silence. "It was Rapp, wasn't it?"

Tanner nodded.

She stared into the fire. "I thought Davies was pursuing us, but it was Rapp. Rapp knows I am alive."

He fixed his gaze on her. "There is a reward on your head, as well. I heard him speak of it. Do not tell me it is due to the theft of a few jewels."

Marlena lowered her head to her knees, then turned to gaze at him. The flames of the campfire illuminated his handsome face, filled with anger and confusion and pain. She took a deep, ragged breath, aching with the knowledge that everything had changed.

Rapp knew she was alive.

"Answer me," Tanner demanded.

She swallowed and averted her gaze, not knowing how much to tell him. She quickly glanced back. "Did Rapp see you? Did he see your face?"

He looked puzzled. "I do not think so, but—"

"That's good," she whispered, more to herself than to him.

"You did not answer me," he accused, his voice turning deeper, rougher.

There was only one way to convince him that matters had changed. She must tell him the truth. "I am an accused murderer."

His brows rose.

She fought for courage to continue. "I tell you this much only to impress upon you how serious this is. There is no fixing this, Tanner. They mean to see me hanged—you, too, if you are discovered helping me." She searched his face to see if he comprehended. "It is not too late for you. Rapp still does not know who you are."

He waved his hand. "Never mind that. Who are you supposed to have murdered?"

Marlena gave him a direct gaze. "My husband."

He gaped. "Husband!"

She turned her face away. "Yes."

He laughed drily. "So your tale of being a lady's companion accused of theft—that was a lie?" It was more a statement than a question.

She nodded.

"And this man who supposedly seduced you..." He glared at her.

It seemed too difficult to explain that she had partially told him the truth. She had described Corland. "A lie, Tanner. It was all a lie." She bowed her head.

His hand closed into a fist. "You were *married*?" He put a biting emphasis on the word *married*. "You were not some lady's companion at the mercy of her employer's son—" He broke off as if he was too angry to form words. Tanner rose to his feet and paced next to her.

She looked up at him. "Tanner, you must see I did not know you at first. I could not tell you I was an accused murderer. You were a marquess and, as such, how could I know you would not turn me in? The shipwreck gave me a chance to be free. I could not allow anything to jeopardise that chance."

He was too tall for the glow of the campfire to reach his face. She could not see his expression, but she could feel his emotion. "I was not always a stranger, Marlena, not after we shared a bed."

She glanced away.

He persisted, his voice low and pained. "A husband, Marlena. How can you justify not telling me you had been married? Married."

His words were like a sharp sword. "Tanner, I regret—" She covered her face with her hands, before lifting her head to him again. "I ought to have informed you of the danger I placed you in."

"The danger?" He scoffed.

"It was wrong of me."

He pulled off his hat and swept a hand through his hair. "Do you think I care of that?" He paced again, then leaned down to her, grabbing her chin in his hand. "When we made love, Marlena—you should have told me a husband preceded me. Who was he? Am I to know that?"

She pulled away from his grasp. "No."

He straightened, his face in shadow again. "No?"

Marlena rose to her knees. "I will not tell you. Not now. Not when Rapp knows I am alive."

"I fail to see what that has to do with it." He placed his hands on his hips.

"We must separate. Rapp will pursue me, do you not see that? If he or anyone discovers you have been seen with me—" She broke off again, sitting back on her legs. "Your ignorance of me may offer some protection. You shall be able to protest that I duped you—which I did—and you had no idea whom you assisted."

He stared down at her. "Do *you* not see that I am not speaking of Rapp, but of you and me and what I thought was real between us?"

She wrapped her arms around her waist. Wounding him so much cut her up inside like a thousand knife blades.

He folded his arms across his chest, almost a mirror image of her. "We are close to Edinburgh. Two, three days at the most. I will take you to Edinburgh and that will be the end of it."

He was mistaken. The end had already come.

He turned from her and strode over to where they had placed their bags. He returned to toss one of them at her.

She caught it and clutched it to her breast.

"It will be cold tonight," he said in a flat voice. "Cover up as much as possible."

He turned and walked away, the darkness covering him. Marlena fingered the sapphire ring he had given her before opening the bag to do as he'd bid.

After he returned to the campfire, Marlena feigned being asleep. She watched him through slitted eyelids as he settled by the fire, making a pillow of one of the bags and covering himself with a top coat.

She watched him thrash around in search of a comfortable position. When he settled the campfire illuminated his face. When the furrows in his brow eased and the rigidity of his jaw slackened, his features took on a boyish vulnerability. She knew he had finally fallen asleep.

Marlena had watched him until the fire dwindled to embers and dawn glowed through the trees. She now rose carefully, trying not to make a sound.

She rolled the extra top coat they'd brought with them from Dutwood House and stuffed it in the bag. With one last long look at him, she mouthed, "Goodbye." Forcing herself to turn away, she carried the bag to Dulcea.

The horse nickered in greeting.

"Shhhhh," she whispered.

She slung the bag on the horse's back and tightened the girth. Tanner's horse became interested in this project and nudged her with his muzzle. She turned and stroked the gelding's neck.

"Take good care of him," she whispered, rubbing her cheek against the horse's coarse hair.

The animal snorted and nodded as if understanding her command.

She untied the reins of the mare and led her away on foot, mounting only when she was at some distance. She followed the river, which led her north as she needed to travel, pushing the horse to walk as fast as possible over the uneven ground.

When the sun rose in the sky and melted the mist, she stopped to remove Tanner's grandmother's shawl from under her cloak, holding it against her for a moment, as if embracing Tanner again. She folded it and put it in the bag. Dulcea put her nose in the clear water of the river and drank. Marlena then led the horse to a little glade where she nibbled some grass.

The land around Marlena looked like the hills of home. The Scottish air even smelled like home. What she would give to see Parronley again, to have the comfort of familiar old faces, to feel home once more. Likely no one would remember her there; thirteen years had passed, and she had changed so much. She doubted anyone could find the young carefree girl she'd been at age twelve in her face now. She did not even speak the same as she once did. She'd lost her Scottish burr like she had lost everything else of her life in Scotland.

Marlena turned around in her saddle to gaze back from where she'd come, from where she had left Tanner. Was he awake now? Perhaps when he found her gone, he would curse her so much he would turn south and make his way back into the safe life of the Marquess of Tannerton.

She remounted her horse and threaded her way upriver. The River Esk flowed near Parronley, she remembered. All she need do was follow the river, then watch for signs pointing to Edinburgh to the east. She stayed on the natural terrain, although it slowed her pace. Sometimes she'd glimpse the road and be tempted to use it. Then a carriage or a cart or a rider would pass by, and she'd shrink back to the river bank again.

Try as she might to think only of the land ahead of her, Tanner invaded her thoughts. She tried not to imagine how he must despise her, not only for lying to him, but also for sneaking away while he slept.

When the sun grew high in the sky, she selected a spot for her and the horse to drink from the river. After they were refreshed, she walked the mare up a hill to get her bearings. The horse nibbled on the grass, but Marlena had brought with her only one small piece of bread and two smaller chunks of cheese, leaving the remainder for Tanner. She nibbled on one piece of cheese, careful to eat only half.

At the crest of the hill, Marlena saw that the river led into a town. Within the town the river broke into two branches. Which branch was the River Esk? The sun was now directly overhead, so she could not tell which way was north. Worst of all, it appeared she had no choice but to ride down and cross the bridge. She could not avoid being seen.

She sank to the ground, resting while Dulcea ate her fill. The town bustled with activity. Perhaps the number of people would protect her. She could attempt to merge with them unnoticed as she passed through.

She led the horse back down the hill and continued to follow the river bank until she found a good place to join the road when no horse or vehicle was in sight. Soon, however, she was among several other riders, carts and pedestrians. A sign indicated the town's name was Langholm, a name that only dimly rang in her memory, a market town, perhaps. Its stone-and-stucco buildings reminded her of Parronley, as did the hills rising around it like the frame around a painting.

As she entered the town the smell of roasting meat and baking bread wafted from the shops and inns. Her hunger increased, but she was determined to save her meagre stash of food for the night. One establishment she passed smelled of cooking fish, reminding her of Tanner's fish dinner the night before.

Trying to look as if she belonged with the flow of traffic, she rode closer and closer to the bridge. The sun seemed to hover over her left shoulder now, and the bridge seemed to lead her north. Her nerves calmed, even though seeing children dashing through the streets, shopworkers standing in doorways, farmers driving their carts, all made her feel very alone.

I'll become used to it, won't I, Eliza? she said to herself. *I'll become used to being alone.* Used to being without Tanner.

She passed the parish church and prayed God would keep her safe. And keep Tanner safe. It comforted her somewhat that Eliza would be looking down in heaven watching out for her. *Watch over Tanner, too, Eliza,* she begged.

The bridge was very near now and Marlena's heart beat faster. Her ordeal was almost over and it had been astonishingly easy. When she reached the bridge, she breathed a sigh of relief. She crossed, already searching for a place where she might leave the road again.

Out of the corner of her eye she saw a horse come from behind her. The horse rode so close she felt it brush Dulcea. When the horse's muzzle came level with Dulcea's shoulder, Marlena spied a man's arm reaching towards her.

She signalled Dulcea to take off at a gallop, hearing a voice behind her. "Halt, my lady."

She did not look back. She galloped past a farm cart and some pedestrians who jumped to the side at her sudden approach. She could hear horse's hooves behind her in pursuit.

He caught up to her at an empty dip in the road, a place where no one could see a man accosting a lone woman, no chance someone would come to her aid. Rapp tried to grab her horse's bridle. She jerked the horse's head away from him and Dulcea reared and gnashed her teeth.

Rapp backed his horse away. "Give it up," he demanded. "I have you now."

"No!" she cried.

Dulcea reared again.

Suddenly there was the pounding hooves of another horse. A lone horseman bore down on them.

Tanner!

He reached them in an instant, looking more like a bandit than a rescuer. His face was covered by a cloth and he advanced on Rapp, not slowing his pace, and knocked Rapp from his saddle with one swing of his arm. Rapp's horse skittered away.

"I'll get you," Rapp cried, jumping to his feet, his fist in the air.

Tanner turned to Marlena. "Come on," he cried, as Rapp went for his horse.

Marlena set Dulcea into a gallop again, Tanner riding at her side. They galloped away from Langholm. When the road rose high they looked behind and saw that Rapp was following, although his form was a mere speck in the distance. When the road dipped again, Tanner turned them off through a break in the trees.

"This way," he called.

They rode to a place where the trees and brush cloaked

them, slowing their tiring horses to a walk. Soon they reached the banks of a narrow stream, shallow enough that the rocks beneath the water were clearly visible.

"The horses must rest." Tanner dismounted and only then pulled off the cloth that masked his face. "Let them drink here."

He walked over to her and held out his hands to assist her from her horse. She put hers on his shoulders, and he grabbed her waist, holding her until her feet reached the ground. He still did not release her.

Looking into her eyes, he said, "Stay here. I am going to obscure our trail."

She nodded and he moved off, grabbing a small branch to carry with him. She held the reins of the horses by the river-bank, pulling their heads away when it seemed as if they were drinking too fast.

Her emotions were in turmoil. Her heart had leapt into her throat when she had seen him coming to her rescue. She wanted only to touch him, hold him, taste his lips. At the same time she felt as if she had doomed him to a terrible fate.

For if Rapp knew she was alive and correctly guessed that she had been headed towards Scotland, Wexin also knew this and Wexin was twice the danger Rapp was.

Marlena's heart beat faster when she heard Tanner return, leaves swishing as he approached. He walked with his head down. The dear, rumpled hat the innkeeper in Cemaes had given him obscured his face. As he came close he lifted his head, his expression thunderous as if he were holding back a maelstorm of anger. After glaring at her, he walked upstream a little way, disappearing around a bend.

When he came back he walked over to her. "How are the horses?"

"They seem to be settling," she replied, almost unable to breathe. "I did not let them drink too much all at once."

He nodded in approval.

"Tanner—" she began.

He held up a hand, and could scarcely look at her. "How did you intend to find your way to Edinburgh without even a map?" he snapped.

"I was going to follow the river. The River Esk flows near Edinburgh."

He shook his head. "That is a different River Esk."

Her eyes widened in surprise. She had no idea there could be two River Esks in Scotland. She might have been wandering the countryside for days without food or money.

"Enough of this foolishness." He gave her a level look. "I'll see you to Edinburgh. I'll see you there safely, but you stay with me. I'll not have your life on my conscience as well."

She opened her mouth to ask him what he meant, but he turned away from her, looking upstream.

"We ride in the water," he said. "Even if Rapp finds where we left the road, there is a chance we can still throw him off."

He helped her to remount and she rode her horse into the stream. He mounted and did the same, but rode his horse across to the other bank and then he made the horse back up into the water.

A clever ploy. The sort of trick Niall would have played on Wexin when they were gambolling over Parronley as boys.

They stayed in the stream for as long as they could, but the rocks underneath were slippery and difficult for the horses to walk upon. Tanner led them to the far bank of the stream and in a moment they were back to a landscape of rolling, grassy hills.

Tanner dismounted. "The horses need to feed."

She slipped off her horse before he could assist her.

He walked up to the crest of the hill, his very stride conveying an aura of command, of power. She watched him, as hungry for his smile, his laughter, as she was for food. Her stomach hurt and she pressed her hand to it.

When he returned he said. "There is nothing to be seen to give me any bearings. I think we should stay off the roads and ride north as best we can."

"Tanner—"

He fixed his gaze on her. "I am remaining with you."

She nodded, her throat tight. His words had an axe-hard edge.

She had assumed the pain she caused him would drive him away. Instead he had come after her, rescuing her once again, saving her life one more time.

He'd done more than save her life, however; he had made her want to live again.

After Corland was killed, Marlena's way of life died, too, then her family died—Niall and his dear little sons. Then Eliza. Everything Marlena thought worth living for had gone. Seeing Tanner again on the ship from Ireland rekindled those days when life had been full of dancing, and dreams and happiness. She'd briefly found happiness again at Tanner's side.

He glanced over at the horses. "We'll let them eat as much as they want, then we'll start off again."

He avoided sitting with Marlena, but rather paced to and fro, looking out on the valley, perhaps expecting Rapp to appear below. When Tanner and Marlena mounted their horses and rode again, their pace was slow over the hilly terrain.

In spite of her worries, Marlena was awed by the Scottish landscape, so unexpected and yet familiar at the same time. The hills retained a hint of the vibrant green they wore in summer, but had donned browns and oranges and purples as well.

She had forgotten how much she loved this land.

"Oh, hell," Tanner muttered.

She glanced towards him.

He pointed to the horizon where black clouds formed a line, like an army ready to attack.

"Rain," he said. "We had better find some shelter."

There was not much shelter to discover in the wilderness, however. When they came to the crest of yet another hill, the ruins of a castle came into view. They headed for it as the first of the raindrops started to fall and the roll of thunder sounded in the distance.

"If we are fortunate, it will have a roof," Tanner said as they approached the huge crumbling building, its brownish-grey stone walls whispering of days long gone.

"There is thunder, Tanner."

The stone was the same colour as Parronley, Marlena noticed, trying to distract herself from the approaching thunderstorm.

There was, indeed, a room large enough for the horses, sheltered on three sides with enough of a roof to keep the rain away. One tower of the castle remained intact, its stone staircase circling up to the battlements from which arrows once flew and vats of hot oil were poured on invaders.

They took the bags and saddles and blankets off the horses and carried them to the staircase of the tower.

"No fire tonight," Tanner said as he dropped the bag on the stairs.

"No fish, either," Marlena responded, trying to disguise her fear of the building storm.

He turned to her with concern. "You must be hungry."

She opened her bag. "I have some cheese and bread saved. We can share it." She broke it apart and gave the larger piece to Tanner. He took out a skin that he'd filled with water and handed it to her. With old stone walls surrounding them, they ate and drank in silence while the heavens opened up and lightning flashed, followed seconds later by a loud clap of thunder.

"Put on as many clothes as you can," Tanner told her. "I will check on the horses." He was no more than a silhouette against the tower's threshold.

"Tanner—" Marlena began, wanting to ask him not to leave her alone with the thunder and lightning crashing around them.

He turned away and began to walk out.

"Wait!" She felt like she could not breathe.

He looked over his shoulder.

"The storm…" She took a breath.

"I'll return. Stay here." His eyes bore into her. "No more leaving, Marlena."

"No more leaving," she repeated.

Fia looked up when the door of the taproom opened, and Lyall and Erroll Gibb entered, in mid-conversation, hair dripping from the rain.

"Och, no harm will come to them," Lyall said to his brother. "You are worried for naught."

"You know how these Englishmen can be, Lyall." Erroll nodded to Reverend Bell who sat over in a corner, his hand wrapped around a glass. "You cannot trust them with your women."

Erroll tripped on the leg of a chair, grabbing it before it fell and making it look as if he'd chosen it to sit upon.

Lyall flopped down in the chair opposite him. "There's naught we can do about it."

Fia walked over to them. "I hope you both wiped your boots before tracking mud in here."

Lyall smiled up at her. "That we did, Fia, so hold your scold."

He gave her that besotted stare, and she worried that perhaps his affections had not been attached to one of the Brookston girls, after all.

"What will you be having?" she asked them both.

"Ale," replied a disquieted Erroll.

"Ale," agreed his brother.

"Ale it is." She nodded, but Erroll blocked her way with his arm before she could be off to the tap.

"Tell us, Fia." His brows knitted together so tightly they looked as if they were only one jagged line across his forehead. "You worked in London, in a fancy house—"

She felt a knot grow in her stomach. "It was long ago."

"Ay, but—" Erroll swallowed as if he had difficulty bringing out the right words to speak. "We were wonderin' what it was like. What the English laird of the place was like."

She felt blood drain from her face.

He went on. "I mean, could ye trust the man?"

Fia struggled to find her voice. "What reason do you have for asking me the question?"

Lyall reached over and whacked his brother on the shoulder. "You idiot! You know what happened where Fia was. Miss Parronley-that-was and all that." He looked at her in apology for his brother. "Don't mind him, Fia. He's daft."

Her knees shook.

Errol tossed his brother a scathing look. He turned back to Fia. "I was just askin' because Mary and Sara Brookston went to work at Parronley and I was worried because—"

She stopped him. "Why did they go to work at Parronley?" The house had been shut up with minimal staff ever since Baron Parronley and his two boys had died, and his poor, grieving wife went home to her parents. Lady Corland was the Baroness, but, of course, no one knew where to find her.

Lyall answered, "Lord Wexin showed up, wantin' to stay there; seeing as he will be the laird there some day, they opened the house and needed girls to help with the cleaning."

Lord Wexin.

The room went dark and the sounds of people talking became like echoes.

Fia had feared this day. She'd hoped it would never come. Parronley House was an old and draughty place that had been neglected for years. Before they died, the young baron and his children only came for summers. With Lady Corland gone and no one in charge, things were in even more disarray. The crofters continued to farm the land, but not much else happened there. Fia hoped Wexin would stay on his own English estate and leave Parronley alone.

"I'll fetch your ale," she mumbled, walking through the maze of tables and chairs by memory.

The only reason for Wexin to come to Parronley would be if he inherited, and if he inherited it meant that Lady Corland was dead.

This likelihood loomed over Fia like a shroud. If Lady Corland were dead, it was Fia's fault. No matter how, no matter where. Her fault for not telling what she saw.

Fia managed to reach the bar where Bram was drawing ale while his father took a rest.

Her vision cleared enough to see Bram look upon her with concern. "What is it, lass?"

She forced her voice to sound unaffected. "Two ales for the Gibb brothers."

He reached over the bar to her. "No, I meant, what is it with you? Are you ill?"

Though her heart was beating a rapid tattoo, she made herself look him in the eye. "I'm not ill. I merely want you to give me two ales."

He paused, still examining her like her sleeve had caught fire or something. He eventually drew two ales from the tap and handed them to her.

She carried them to Lyall and Erroll and did not tarry a moment in case they would start talking again. She went straight to the kitchen and kept walking through to the outside door.

Her aunt was stirring a pot of soup. "Are you ill, Fia? You look pale."

Fia pasted a smile on her face. "I'm in need of air," she said. "The taproom is quiet enough. I'll be only a moment."

She stood in the shelter of the doorway, trying to will herself to stay put and not run into the rain and as far away from Kilrosa and Parronley as she could get. To run like that would only be foolhardy. She needed to pack. She needed her money. She needed a place to go.

Because if Wexin found her here, he would kill her.

Chapter Fourteen

The night was over, the patrons gone, and Fia had somehow made it through. It helped that the rain thinned the numbers in the taproom, and that she became numb, acting like one of those automatons she'd seen in shops in London. Her aunt and uncle were abed, due to rise early and fix the breakfast. Bram was in the kitchen. Fia was alone, wiping the tables. In the solitude, she could think.

Wexin visited Parronley, not Kilrosa. It would be odd of him to come to Kilrosa when Parronley was the closer village. He could have no business here. Kilrosa had no one more important than Laird Hay, whose lands bordered the village and were not nearly as vast as the Parronley lands. She could easily keep out of Wexin's path. He could not possibly stay long.

If Wexin came to live in the area, though, she would have to leave. There would be no other choice to make. Perhaps Erroll and Lyall could find out from the Brookston sisters, if she could think of a way of asking them without raising their curiosity.

Fia wiped the last table and set the chairs up on top of it, so she could mop where the mud had inevitably been tracked in. She turned to go and fetch the mop and bucket and nearly ran into Bram, standing with his arms folded.

She must have numbed herself so well she had not sensed him, but now her heart pounded in her chest and her blood raced through her veins.

"You startled me," she said, her voice too breathless. "I thought you were cleaning the kitchen."

"The kitchen can wait." He merely watched her, his brown eyes looking black in the dim light. "What happened to you tonight?"

She shook her head and started to march past him. "I have no time for your silly questions, Bram. Nothing happened. It was a dull night."

He seized her arm and bent down to her. "Somethin' frightened the blood from your face, lass, and you near to fainted. Tell me."

She tried to pull away. "Do you not have work to do?"

He held fast and stared into her eyes. "Nothin' is more important than you, lass."

She felt as if her knees would give out from under her, but Bram's hands kept her upright.

He flipped a chair off the table and sat her down in it. Then he grabbed another and sat facing her. "Now tell me of it."

"Oh, Bram…" her voice cracked and tears of fear filled her eyes "…Lord Wexin is at Parronley."

His eyes grew wide. "Lord Wexin!"

"Aye." Her body trembled. "I am afraid. He will kill me, Bram. I know he will kill me."

He took her by the hand and gently settled her on his lap, wrapping his strong arms around her. "There now," he murmured in a soothing voice. "No harm will come to you. I will see to it."

She pulled away from him. "You must not go near him,

Bram. Do you hear me? Don't get any foolish ideas. I won't stand for it. I won't."

He held her tight against his chest. "Och, if you keep actin' this way, I'll be thinking you care about me."

"I do care about you, Bram. I couldn't bear it if something happened to you because of me." Her words were spoken into his chest.

He held her and rocked her and she almost felt safe. "I'm afraid his comin' here means something bad. Like he's killed Lady Corland or something. He's never come before." She shuddered.

"What does he know of you, Fia? Would he guess you are here?" he asked.

She shook her head, rubbing her cheek against his apron, which smelled of hops and ferment and comfort. "I do not think he knows my name or anything about me. He would have come for me before if he knew. I thought about this a long time and I figured out that he could not very well ask about me, not without causing people to have questions he would not want to answer."

"Ay," Bram said, the sound rumbling in his chest. "He'd be revealing you were in the room."

"You have no idea how many months it took me to realise that." She sighed. "Bram, I'm worried about why he's here. He's found Lady Corland, is all I can guess. She must be dead."

He brushed the hair from her brow and tucked it back under her cap. "That may not be, lass. I'll invent an errand in Parronley and find out what I can." He gave her an intent look. "But if anyone comes here who frightens you, tell Da you are sick and hide yourself until I come back."

Rain dripped through the roof of the castle ruins, making puddles on the stone floor. Tanner rubbed down the horses and checked their tethers. The two animals seemed content enough in their makeshift stable, munching on the blades of grass that grew up through the cracks in the floor as if they were feasting on troughs of hay. By the time Tanner finished, the scant light had waned and the storm intensified, lighting his way back to the stairwell with flashes of lightning.

When he reached the doorway, he could not see Marlena on the stairs and, for a fleeting moment, feared she had run off again.

"I did what you said." Her tremulous voice floated down from above and he could just make out her shape sitting several stair steps up from the open doorway.

"What I said?" he repeated, remembering how when he'd repeated things before it had led to lovemaking.

"I put on as many clothes as I could," she said. "And I took out some clothes for you, as well." She lifted some dark garment to show him.

Lightning flashed and she gasped, clutching the garment to her as the thunder followed.

He hurried up the steps. "The storm will pass soon."

She handed him the coat. "I know."

He removed his top coat and put the coat she'd given him on top of the one he already wore.

"I moved everything up here. It is not so damp and is more sheltered from the wind." The shaking of her voice was unmistakable.

He sat beside her and covered them both with his top coat. She had placed their bags on higher steps to act as pillows, and the horse blankets beneath them as the cushions for their stone settee.

Lightning flashed again and she flinched.

He put his arm around her. "We're safe enough here."

She laughed softly. "It is silly of me to be afraid."

He drew her closer, needing her as much as she needed his comfort.

His anger had fled, but a knot of fear still lingered. She'd come so close to being captured, and he no longer knew if his fortune and influence could save her.

Tanner closed his eyes and again saw Marlena battling the Bow Street Runner, who nearly had her in his grasp. His blood still burned with the thought of that man's hands upon her.

When Tanner woke that morning to find her gone, he'd been frantic with worry and enraged at himself for not anticipating her flight. With luck, guesswork and prayer he had followed her trail and finally caught a glimpse of her in the crowded streets of Langholm. He'd seen Rapp as well and he'd feared they were too far ahead for him to catch them up in time.

The storm quieted, the lightning faded, and the thunder seemed to roll away. Tanner felt Marlena relax and she seemed to melt against him.

When he'd embarked on this adventure, his intention had always been to save her, to give back a life, to atone for those lives that were lost because of him. He had not expected to fall in love with her.

Tanner had pretty much despaired of falling in love. The respectable women he met never captured his interest, and his string of mistresses quickly bored him. Both sets of women were more enamoured of his money than of him.

Marlena, on the other hand, had refused the help his money could offer her.

"Are you warm enough?" she asked.

"Yes," he responded in a quiet voice. "Sleep if you can, Marlena. With luck we will reach Edinburgh tomorrow."

The darkness and the silence did not help him fall asleep,

however. He felt her warmth, heard her breathing, smelled the scent that was uniquely hers. He couldn't shift his position for fear of disturbing her sleep.

"Tanner?" Her voice drifted through the darkness. "What did you mean when you said you did not want my life on your conscience *as well*."

He paused before answering. "That I will see you safe to Edinburgh, is what I meant."

She shifted, moving even closer to him. "No, you said *as well*. What did you mean, *as well?* Do you have a person's life on your conscience?"

He paused again, considering how to answer. "I did not kill anyone, if that is what you mean, but I caused the deaths of three people."

"How did you do that?" She asked the question in a soft voice, an accepting voice.

"Arrogance," he replied. She might as well know the sort of man he was. "Let us say, I coveted a prize so much, and fancied myself so clever, that I never thought my adversary would kill to win."

She touched his leg. "Then was it not your adversary who caused the deaths?"

The sensation sent need flashing through him. "I do not hold the man blameless," he admitted. "But neither am I absolved. Had I not decided to rub his nose in my superiority, he might be alive and the two others as well." It was surprisingly difficult to admit this to her. "They died because I cared only about winning."

She threaded her arm around his and leaned her cheek on his shoulder. "If only we could know what was to happen, we could decide very well then, could we not?"

He could only think how good it felt having her so near again.

"You are the best man I have ever known," she rasped.

He held her tightly. *There is no fixing this,* she'd said the night before. They would part in Edinburgh, but in his heart she would always be his marchioness.

"When I bring you to safety, I might deserve a piece of that regard," he said.

She groped in the darkness until she found his face. Holding his head in her hands, she guided him to her, missing his lips at first.

When she found his mouth, he pulled her on top of him. Into the kiss he poured all his terror at almost seeing her captured and his grief at losing her for good.

Marlena contented herself with kissing him, being held by him, touching him. It was like a gift.

She wished this castle still had its old bedchambers with big, old beds made of dark wood. Parronley used to have musty unused rooms where Marlena had pretended she was a maiden sought after by knights in chain mail and armour.

She sighed. Tanner possessed more chivalry than all the knights gathered at King Arthur's Round Table. Tears stung her eyes. She squeezed them shut, determined to defer the grief of losing him until after she sent him away.

Marlena had awoken several times during the night, each time savouring anew the bittersweet joy of feeling engulfed by him, of relishing the scent of him, of being soothed by the even cadence of his breathing. When she opened her eyes and saw light peeking through the cracks in the wall, her spirits plummeted.

He must have heard her stir, because he woke, too. His eyes were even more intense in the growing light, tinged with the same sadness that tore her apart inside.

"We must rise. Be on our way," he said.

But he made no move to leave. Instead he held her in a long, warm, sheltering embrace, and she wanted nothing more than to remain for ever in his strong arms, a place of safety, refuge. Love.

Inevitably they had to depart. After they shed their extra clothing, Marlena repacked the bags. Tanner saddled the horses. Their two stalwart steeds seemed none the worse for spending a damp night in the castle and were even eager to continue the journey. Too soon Marlena and Tanner left the castle behind and headed north once more.

The ground, still wet from the rain, made their progress difficult. Marlena ought to have rued the slow pace, but instead it raised her selfish hopes for one more night with Tanner.

Tanner turned to her. "We should chance stopping at a village. Give the horses something proper to eat and ourselves as well." He smiled at her. "Unless you are not hungry."

She smiled back. "I am famished." Her smile quickly fled. "But what of Rapp? Dare we stop?"

His brows knit. "If we stay in this remote area, the chance of Rapp coming to the same village at the same time seems unlikely. We need food." He patted his horse's neck. "All of us." He gave her a reassuring gaze. "Let us look for a road to follow."

They found a path that wound around a hill and followed it, hoping it led to a road. The morning wore on without them finding a village.

"Will we make Edinburgh today, do you think?" Marlena asked at one point.

"I believe so," he said in a flat voice.

They fell silent, plodding along to the next hill, still no road in sight. The path widened enough for them to ride side by side.

Tanner looked over at her. "What happens when we reach Edinbugh, Marlena?"

She darted a glance at him, but quickly looked away. "We must part."

After a pause, he spoke again. "Am I to simply leave you, or is there someone waiting for you, someone to help you?"

She could barely look at him. "There is an old teacher from my school…" It was, she hoped, the last falsehood she would tell him. She knew no one in Edinburgh, but, then, she was counting on no one in Edinburgh knowing her.

His pained expression told her that he'd recognised her lie.

She changed the subject. "What of you, Tanner? Will you have enough money to get back to London?"

He frowned. "When I become the Marquess again, I will be able to get funds easily enough."

She was relieved, not wishing him to endure any more hardship on her behalf.

He spoke again. "I have been thinking. Before we part, we must set up a way for me to send you money—"

She broke in. "No, Tanner. You must not be connected to me ever again."

"I will not leave you destitute and alone." His horse jumped forward at his sharp tone.

"I will get by, Tanner," she called after him.

He increased his pace and she fell far enough behind to make further discussion impossible. Soon the terrain required all their attention as they climbed higher and higher to the crest of a hill. Marlena felt a *frisson* of nerves travel up her spine as they climbed, but she knew of no reason why.

When they reached the crest, he stopped and waited for her. As she caught up to him, Marlena scanned the vista. Low clouds gave a dreamlike appearance to the valley below until a sudden breeze swept them away.

In the distance was the sea and before it sat a great house
built of brownish-grey stone complete with turrets and towers
and pointed rooftops. The house, once hazy from her long
absence, was now all too clear in her vision.

Parronley House.

Each room, each view, every walkway in the garden,
every furrow in the parkland, every rock in the cliffs beyond
the house, rushed into her mind. Again, she and Niall ran
through the rooms, frolicked in the garden, jumped from the
cliffs into the deep pools of water in the sea.

"No," she cried, backing her horse away from the sight.

Tanner looked around him. "What?"

She caught herself and shook her head. "Nothing, Tanner.
The house looked like a place where ghosts might dwell."

There was truth to that. Too many ghosts would inhabit
this place, if only in her memory—her parents, her brother,
the life she had left behind...

The living demons were who she must fear the most,
however. She and Tanner had come directly to the place Rapp
would think to look for her. *Parronley.*

Marlena pointed to her left. "I—I thought I spied a road
over that way. Just a glimpse."

She knew there was a road there, a road that led away from
Parronley, a road that could lead them on to Edinburgh, only
about ten miles away. They must reach Edinburgh now. She
would push him on.

At the bottom of the hill, exactly where she said it would
be, was the road. When they reached it, the sun was high, near
noon for certain. They came upon a signpost Marlena knew
would be there. Kilrosa one way; Parronley the other. While
her nerves jangled so severely she thought he would notice,
he stopped to consult the map.

He pointed to Kilrosa. "This way."

She breathed a sigh of relief.

"We must stop at this next village," he said. "The horses are tiring and we all need food."

She wanted to tell him she was not tired. She was not hungry. She wanted to beg him to go on to Edinburgh.

They no sooner rode past the road sign when Tanner's horse began to falter. "Deuce," he said. "My horse has thrown a shoe."

Marlena's panic escalated. More delay.

Tanner dismounted and lifted the horse's hoof. "He needs a new shoe for certain. I hope he has not injured his leg. The village should not be too far."

About five miles away, Marlena recalled.

Five excruciating miles. Tanner had to lead his horse on foot and their progress seemed snail-like. Marlena expected every minute that Rapp would descend upon them.

She hoped no one in Kilrosa would recognise her. Surely her appearance had changed dramatically, and no one would look for that little girl in this plainly dressed woman with dirt splattered on her skirt and mud caking her boots. None of them, she hoped, would be expecting the Baroness Parronley in this disguise.

They came upon the church, which was just as she remembered it, made of the same stone as Parronley House. The buildings of Kilrosa would be made of that stone as well, so different from the buildings of London. Or Bath. Or Kent, where Corland's estate was located. So many memories came flooding back, of riding with Niall over these same hills, walking these same roads to the church on fine-weather days.

The village was soon ahead and it too sparked memories of the handful of times she visited it as a child. Parronley had been closer to her father's estate than Kilrosa and there had been few reasons to travel the extra miles to visit it. Still, as they entered Kilrosa, its winding main road with shops and the inn and smithy were familiar.

"Let us first find a stable and a smithy," Tanner said.

Marlena could have taken him directly to the stable, suddenly remembering one of the rare times her father allowed her and Niall to ride with him on some errand in the village. The local laird's property was nearby, she recalled, and her father had met the man in the local inn.

At the stable, a man approached them. Marlena held her breath, but to her relief, he showed no sign of recognising her.

"Good day to you," Tanner said to the man. "Is this your stable?"

"It is," the man said.

Tanner offered the man a handshake. "We've been travelling and my horse has thrown a shoe."

"Let me have a look at the fellow." The stableman lifted the horse's leg and examined its hoof. He rubbed his hands over the leg. "He's strained it, but he's not lame. You are lucky. I'll fetch the smithy and we'll tend to him, but you'd better rest the horse a day or two."

Marlena turned her head away as she dismounted, feeling as if every drop of blood had drained from her face.

She heard Tanner ask, "Is there an inn here?"

The man pointed to it, but Marlena could have pointed to it as well. "The Black Agnes. Not many folks come to stay there." He shifted from one foot to another. "Folks more often stay at Parronley, over yonder." He inclined his head in that direction. "When folks had business with the baron when he was alive. Poor devil. Not so much now."

"The baron?" Tanner asked conversationally.

Marlena thought Tanner must have known Niall as Baron Parronley once, from school or in London.

"Died of fever some time back, his boys with him." The

man patted Tanner's horse. "Aye. Parronley has seen its share of troubles. There's worse—"

Marlena broke in. "I do apologise for interrupting, but I should like to go to the inn now." She had no wish for the stableman to go on about the sad tale of the baroness who killed her husband.

Tanner gave her a sympathetic glance, and took the bags from their saddles. "We'll be at the inn if you need to reach us," he told the man. "I'll check with you later, in any event."

The man peered at him. "English, are ye?"

Tanner laughed. "Yes. We are."

Marlena started to walk away. "May we go, please?"

Tanner bid goodbye to the man and caught up to Marlena. "You must be hungry."

"As must you." She hurried towards the inn.

They entered, but found no one in the hallway. Tanner stepped into the taproom and returned with a smiling older gentleman who looked so perfectly like an innkeeper Marlena could not tell if she had seen him before. She kept her face averted just in case.

"Sorry for not seeing ye come in," the innkeeper said. "My name is Gunn."

"Pleased to meet you, Mr Gunn." Tanner shook his hand. "Are you filled with guests or do you have a room for us?"

Perhaps Tanner's question was his way to check if Rapp could be staying at the inn. Marlena knew that if Rapp were this close—and she greatly feared he would be—he would stay in Parronley.

Gunn laughed. "As it is, you are our only guests. I'll show you the room, but I'd be obliged if you would sign the book for me."

Marlena relaxed a little bit. The Black Agnes in Kilrosa seemed safe enough for the moment.

Mr Gunn dipped a pen in ink and handed it to Tanner. Marlena glanced over to see what named he signed, so she would know who they were this day. *Adam Henry and wife*, after all the Henries in Shakespeare's plays.

She stared at his signature. *Adam Henry and wife.*

Under Scottish law a couple only needed only to declare themselves as man and wife in front of a witness to be legally wed. She and Tanner would be considered married the same as if they had been two impetuous lovers eloping to Gretna Green.

She would never claim to be Tanner's wife, except in her own heart. She touched the sapphire ring he had given her at Dutwood House. She would think of it as her wedding ring.

Mr Gunn took them up the stairs. "You can put your bags in the room and I'll start a fire."

"Can we get a meal in the taproom?" Tanner asked. "We have been on the road since morning."

"You may indeed," Gunn replied.

"May I have water to wash with first?" Marlena asked.

"And we had better change our clothes." Tanner added. "Is there someone who can brush the dirt of the road off them?"

Mr Gunn smiled. "You do have a wee bit o' mud on you, haven't you? I'll bring water directly and we'll launder what can be washed and also tend to the rest."

As soon as Gunn left, Tanner turned to Marlena, putting his hands on her shoulders. "Is anything amiss, Marlena? You've not said much since my horse lost a shoe."

Since seeing Parronley House, she thought. "I am tired and sore and hungry, that is all."

He kneaded her shoulders and wrapped his arms around her. "We may be forced to rest here a day or so, if my horse requires it. Would you mind very much?"

She hoped he didn't feel her tremble. She feared Rapp was in Parronley, or would be shortly. He might take it into his head to look for them in Kilrosa. If he found Tanner with her, Tanner would lose his chance to escape.

"I cannot like you being seen with me, Tanner, not with Rapp about."

He put his arms around her and held her against his chest. "We will take care." He pulled away. "Let us change into clean clothes so they can launder these."

They changed out of their mud-spattered clothing and Marlena sat on the bed to wait for the water.

Tanner touched her face. "I will go down to the taproom and discreetly inquire if anyone has seen Rapp." He gave her a reassuring smile. "Do you wish for me to come back up to fetch you?"

She caught his hand and held it to her cheek. "I'll come down to the taproom. Have them bring you your food as soon as you are ready."

When he opened the door to leave, he turned to her. "I do not regret that we must stay together longer."

After he left, Marlena lay down on the bed, exhausted from the ride and the worry. She closed her eyes and even her hunger could not prevent her from falling half-asleep.

A knock came at the door. "Your water, ma'am."

"Come in." Marlena sat up and rubbed her eyes.

The girl carried the water pitcher and some towels to a small table near the fireplace.

"Thank you so much." Marlena stood.

At that same moment the girl turned towards her and Marlena saw her face.

Fia Small.

Marlena gasped.

The girl's face went white. "Lady Corland."

The last Marlena had seen of Fia Small had been when Corland lay dead in a pool of blood, and her cousin had thrust the murder weapon into her hand.

Chapter Fifteen

The ale felt cool on Tanner's throat and greatly welcome. Gunn had reassured him that no stranger had been in the town for days. He could relax with a pint while he waited for Marlena. He'd built up a powerful thirst on that stretch of road. How long had it been since he'd walked five miles? Since he'd walked anywhere, come to think of it? His feet had held up tolerably well!. Thanks to his bootmaker, he suspected. Hoby's cobbling skills were unsurpassed.

Gunn brought him a plate of bread and cheese and Tanner tore off a piece of bread and chewed on it.

He thought of strolling past Hoby's boot shop on St James's Street, of popping into Locke's for a new hat, of spending the afternoon at White's with other bored aristocrats.

He lifted the tankard to his lips and washed down the bread. The time he'd spent with Marlena meant so much more to him, even with all its discomforts.

A large man in an apron walked out of the kitchen, stopped abruptly and looked around.

The man turned to Gunn. "Where's Fia?"

The innkeeper inclined his head in Tanner's direction. "We have guests. Fia's tending to the room."

The young man swung around and stared at Tanner, suspicion and challenge in his eyes.

"Well, go ask the man if he desires another ale." Gunn made a shooing gesture with his hands.

The large man approached Tanner with a less-than-friendly demeanour. "Do you want more?"

Tanner looked up at him. "I do." He handed the man the tankard.

The man reached for it, looking directly into Tanner's face. Both his hand and his jaw dropped. "M'lord, what are you doin' here?"

Tanner looked around to see if anyone heard, but there was only one other patron in the taproom and he was sitting off in a corner his hands wrapped around a glass. Mr Gunn was busy behind the bar.

"You've taken me for someone else," Tanner said quickly.

"Nay, I have not." The big man's voice was still full of wonder. "You are the Marquess of Tannerton. I'd know you anywhere."

This man couldn't be more than thirty years, was definitely Scots, by his accent. He looked as if he'd stepped out from that Morier painting Tanner had seen once, the painting of the Battle of Culloden, hardly England's finest hour. Where the devil would he have met the fellow?

Tanner peered at him. "How is it you think you know me?"

"I was there, m'lord," the man said with reverence. "In Brussels after the battle. I saw what you did for the lads. No man worked harder for them than you, sir." He bowed.

Tanner glanced around again. "For God's sake, sit down, and keep your voice low."

The man sat, but stiff as the ramrod he'd probably carried in the battle.

"You were a soldier?" Tanner remembered the wagons of men that poured into Brussels after the battle. Men bleeding, missing limbs or eyes or entire faces, some crying for their mothers, some stoically helping others.

"71st Infantry," the man said.

The 71st helped send Napoleon's Imperial Guard packing, Tanner recalled. "What is your name?"

"Bram Gunn. This is my father's inn." He stood up abruptly. "I'll fetch your ale."

Tanner watched him carefully to see if he'd tell his father the Marquess of Tannerton sat in their inn looking more like a crofter than a marquess, but young Gunn only asked his father to draw another tankard of ale. Tanner blew out a relieved breath.

When Gunn brought the ale, Tanner again gestured for him to sit. The man stared at Tanner, his eyes wide, sitting as stiffly as if he'd been in Wellington's presence.

Tanner took a sip. "You are perhaps wondering why I do not at the moment look like a marquess."

Gunn nodded.

Tanner decided to tell the truth—but not all of it. The elder Gunn sauntered into the kitchen and the other patron was nodding off. No one would overhear.

"I am with a lady," he told young Bram. "She is in some danger, and I am escorting her to a safe place. I do not wish to call attention to myself." He gazed at the former soldier, trying to gauge his reaction. "Hence the clothing."

Gunn's eyes narrowed and he tilted his head slightly. "My father said our guests were a man and his wife. Would that be you and the lady?"

Taken a bit aback by the man's reaction, Tanner took another sip. "That is our disguise, yes."

Gunn leaned forward. "You are in Scotland, m'lord. Did you not know that if you say you are man and wife in Scotland, you are married?"

Tanner took a huge gulp. He ought to have remembered that fact. "It is all part of the ploy," he managed.

Tanner had inadvertently been granted his wish—to make Marlena his marchioness. The irony was painful, but marriage to Marlena pleased Tanner very much.

"So long as you know it," Gunn said.

Tanner gave him a direct look. "It is very important to me that this whole matter, who I am, who I am with, is not spoken of to anyone. May I trust you to say nothing of it?"

Gunn met his eye with a serious and determined look. "I'd do anything you ask, m'lord. Some of the lads you helped were like my brothers."

Tanner smiled at him. "First thing is to call me Henry, not m'lord. I am Mr Henry here, accompanied by Mrs Henry."

Gumm grinned back. "I'll do my best, m'l—Henry."

The door opened with a bang, and both Tanner and Gunn looked over. A well-dressed man swept in.

"Is there no one in this village?" The man spun around.

Hell, thought Tanner. He knew this man.

Wexin.

Who would have thought there could be two people who knew him in this tiny village completely surrounded by Scottish hills?

In his younger days, Tanner and Pomroy made the rounds of London's gaming hells with Wexin and others, but Wexin and his cronies gambled too recklessly for Tanner and Pomroy's tastes and the association ended. Tanner knew Wexin had married Strathfield's daughter when Tanner had still been in Brussels. He'd seen them from time to time at London social events.

Gunn stood up and the man came closer.

"I need the direction to Laird Hay." His head jerked back when he saw Tanner. "Good God, what are you doing here, Tanner?"

Tanner stood and inclined his head towards Gunn. "Passing time with Bram here. We knew each other in Brussels." He extended his hand to Wexin. "I might ask the same of you, Wexin."

Bram stepped back suddenly and knocked over a chair.

Wexin gave the young man a look of disgust and turned back to Tanner. "Business. At Parronley, you know."

Tanner did not know, but he had the feeling he ought to have known.

Wexin went on. "I am invited to dine at Laird Hay's and I do not know the direction." He snapped his neck again and looked Tanner up and down. "Why do you dress like a ruffian?"

Bram spoke up. "His lordship is wearin' clothes I found for him, sir, until his are cleaned and dry."

Tanner smiled. "I was caught in the rain. Everything I owned got wet." He fingered the cloth of his coat. "These garments are remarkably comfortable."

Wexin gave a sniff of disgust.

Bram glared at him. "If ye be seeking the laird, you must ride the main road out of town, about one mile. Follow the first fork you come to in the road and it will lead you to Laird Hay."

Wexin's brows lifted. "About a mile, you say?"

Bram nodded.

Tanner pulled out a chair. "Have a drink with us. The ale is quite nice, I assure you. Bram was about to get us both another pint."

Wexin's nose rose in the air. "I am expected at the laird's. When do you leave this godforsaken village?"

"Early on the morrow," Tanner said. "Too bad you cannot stay. I wanted to hear all the London news. How is your lovely wife, by the way?"

"She is well. I am anxious to return to her." Wexin's voice softened.

"Then I shall see you back in London," Tanner said. "Or have you and Lady Wexin retired to the country?"

"We remain in London." Wexin looked impatiently towards the door. "I must beg your leave."

Tanner waved his hand. "By all means. I would be grateful if you would refrain from informing Laird Hay of my presence here. I should like to avoid the delay of a dinner invitation."

Wexin sighed. "As would I. But I must be on my way. Do forgive me."

"Indeed. Good to see you." Tanner sat down again as Wexin left.

Bram stared at the man's back until he was out the door.

"Thank you, Bram." Tanner blew out a breath. "You saved my hide."

Bram watched Wexin through the window as he mounted his horse and rode away. "Is he a friend of yours?" Bram asked.

Tanner shook his head. "Not a friend. Merely someone I know." He peered at Bram. "Why?"

"I do not like the man," Bram replied.

Marlena rushed over as the maid's eyes rolled back in her head. She caught the girl before she fell and eased her across to a chair.

Fia bent over, her head in her hands. "I thought you were dead, m'lady. I was sure of it, because—"

Marlena spoke at the same time. "I feared you were dead, too. I feared he'd found you." She touched the girl's shoulder.

Fia sat up, some colour returning to her face. "I've been here in Kilrosa. I was a year here before I stopped being afraid he'd come. And now—"

"I am so glad." Marlena crouched down so her face was even with Fia's. She took the girl's hands in her own. "I am so relieved. I wanted you to be safe and not try to tell anyone what happened."

Fia's eyes widened. "You do not mind I did not tell what I saw?"

Marlena squeezed her hands. "He would have killed you."

Fia shuddered. "You will not tell anyone about me. Please?"

"No," she reassured. "I promise."

Fia looked at her. "Where did you go, m'lady? They were searching for you everywhere."

"A friend took me to Ireland to be her children's governess. But her brother came and recognised me. I—I had to leave there."

"Oh, m'lady, you had to be a governess?" The girl looked horrified.

"It was a happy time," Marlena reassured her. "Really."

Fia's eyes were still wide. "Why did you come here? This is not a safe place for you."

"We did not mean to come here. We wound up too far east." Marlena clamped her mouth shut before she revealed too much. It was better not to speak of her final destination.

"M'lady, are ye married again?"

Yes, Marlena thought. *To Tanner.* "There is a man helping me."

"But if you stay the night with him—"

Marlena knew. The marriage would be consummated.

They heard a horse outside and someone shouting in the street below. Fia's chair was right next to the window. She opened the curtain and peered out.

With a gasp, Fia drew back, her fist in her mouth as if to keep from screaming.

"What is it, Fia?" Marlena opened the curtain, but all she saw was a man's figure entering the inn.

"It is him." The girl rose from the chair and backed away. "Him."

Marlena crossed over to her. "Who?"

"Lord Wexin!" Fia's voice cracked and she trembled all over.

Marlena froze.

She had expected Rapp, not Wexin. He must have come to find her. Marlena dashed to the fireplace and grabbed the poker for a weapon. She stood by the door and listened, fearing to hear his footsteps approaching.

The next sound they heard was not footsteps on the stairs, but horse's hooves again.

Fia ran to the window. "He's riding away!"

Marlena released the breath she'd been holding and leaned against the door.

Fia turned to her. "When I heard he had come to Parronley, I thought it meant you were dead."

"It means he is looking for me, I fear." Marlena's mind was racing. What should she say to Tanner? Wexin must never know Tanner was here with her, but what if he'd seen Tanner here?

"If he finds me—" Fia's voice broke.

A knock on the door made them both jump. "Fia! Are ye in there?"

"It is Bram," Fia said.

Tanner's voice also came through the door. "Marlena?"

She hurriedly put the poker back by the fireplace.

Tanner opened the door, and a large man pushed past him to rush to Fia's side. "I've something to tell you, lass."

"I know…" she glanced to the window "…we saw him, but, Bram, you will never guess." She extended her arm towards Marlena. "This is Lady Corland!"

Fia's Bram bowed. "My lady."

"I do not wish it to be known—" Marlena began.

Tanner turned to her. "Lady Corland?"

His eyes scanned her and her heart thumped painfully in her chest. She could just feel him searching his mind for where the name fitted into the puzzle.

His glance slid to Fia and her Bram. "I would like to be alone with her."

Bram bowed. "Of course, m'lord."

Tanner's expression did not change. "Take care, Bram. Say no more than that we are Mr and Mrs Henry. To anyone."

Bram glanced to Fia and back to Tanner. "May I tell Fia, m'lord? The lass has a right to know."

Tanner's gaze turned to Fia. "She knows more than I do, I believe," he murmured. He nodded, looking back at Bram. "No one else, Bram. This lady's—" he shot a glance to Marlena "—*Lady Corland's* well-being depends upon it." He spoke the name with venom. "Corland," he repeated in a near-whisper.

"Ay, you have my word—Mr Henry." Bram took Fia by the arm and whisked her from the room.

Marlena braced herself as Tanner faced her, not speaking. His expression told her he had put the facts together.

He knew.

He walked over to the window and looked out. "What was it the newspapers called you?" His voice was flat, devoid of humour, devoid of any emotion.

She felt sick inside. "The Vanishing Viscountess."

"That was it. *The Vanishing Viscountess.*" He nodded, still gazing into the street where Wexin had ridden off. "I was in Belgium, I believe. We were busy with other matters at the time."

A few weeks after her story reached the newspapers, the battle of Waterloo took over everyone's attention. That horrible news had erased her from the printed page, and she'd been largely forgotten.

"But I do recall a newspaper reaching us." He turned back to her. "Lord Corland was murdered in his bed, as I recall."

She straightened her spine. "He was."

He turned away. "Corland was your husband."

A shaft of pain pierced her heart. "I did not kill him," she added helplessly. "But you must see why I did not tell you."

He spun around again. "I do not see that at all, Marlena. Did you think I would not believe you?"

She straightened her spine. "You would not have believed me at first. Corland. Wexin. You knew those men. You would not have believed me."

His brows came together and he stared towards the window. "What has Wexin to do with it?"

"Wexin killed Corland. He placed the blame on me."

"Wexin?" He glanced back at her in surprise.

"He is very dangerous, Tanner." She spoke in an even tone. "He would kill you if he knew you were with me."

His expression turned sceptical. "Wexin?"

She took a breath and released it. "I knew you would not believe me. I would not have believed it myself if I had not seen what he'd done. I still have no idea why he did it. Wexin and Corland were friends, but Wexin—my cousin—set it up to look as if I had killed my husband." She shivered. "He is searching for me, Tanner."

He continued to gaze at her. "Why would Wexin search here?"

She gave a wry smile. "He assumed I would flee to Parronley."

His brows came together again. "Why?"

"It is my home, Tanner." She glanced away from him, seeing the house and land once again in her mind. "I spent my childhood in Parronley. When…" her voice faltered "…when my brother—you knew Niall, I think—and my two little nephews died, I became the heir. The title was such it could pass to daughters as well as sons."

"You are the Baroness?"

She shrugged. "I could not claim the title, of course, but, yes, the Baroness Parronley."

He pressed his fingers to his temple. "I do remember your brother. I remember reading about his death." His eyes, however, were filled with anger, not sympathy. "You had better tell me the whole now, Marlena. I would be obliged if you would trust me with the truth."

She told him all of it. Of coming upon Wexin dressed in her robe, holding her scissors, wiping Corland's blood on her clothing. Of seeing Corland, eyes staring, throat cut.

She told him how Wexin called for help and how servants came running. How when they waited for a magistrate, she escaped and ran to Eliza, who gave her refuge.

She told him everything except about Fia, because she had promised the girl not to reveal her part in it.

Tanner listened, but she could not read his stony expression. He stood still, taking in all she said.

As she spoke, she heard how ludicrous her version of the story sounded. Who would believe it? She'd always known Wexin had set up a brilliant plot against her.

When she finished, Tanner said nothing and still did not

move. She could not bear any longer to watch him and she turned to lean on the nearby table, where the jug of water waited for her.

"You do not believe me," she whispered into the tense silence.

He lifted a hand as if to silence her. "That is not it, Marlena." He backed away from her. "I need to be alone. I'll send food up to you. Stay in the room. Do not leave."

Before she could say a word, he was gone.

Marlena sank on to the nearest chair. She buried her head in her hands.

Chapter Sixteen

"You must tell what you know, lass." Bram held Fia's hands in his big strong ones.

Fia looked away. She hated Bram knowing how weak and cowardly she was.

They stood in the yard behind the inn. It was chilly outside, but she'd hardly felt anything since they'd left Lady Corland's room.

Lady Corland had found a strong man to protect her. A Marquess must be a grand man indeed. She did not need Fia to help her. Bram was strong, too, and he said he'd protect Fia, but she was still afraid.

"Think on it," Bram went on. "She's been hiding all this time, and so have you. You can go to the laird and tell him the truth. You'd both be free then."

She shook her head. "You do not know what Wexin can do, Bram. We'd have to go to London, and Wexin would kill us before we got there."

"I'd go with you, Fia. Naught would happen to you." He brushed a hand through her hair.

She pulled away. "Then he would kill you, too, Bram, and that would be worse!"

The door opened and Fia's aunt appeared in the doorway. "What're you two doin' out here? There's people wanting food and drink inside."

"We'll come now, Mam," Bram said.

Aunt Priss went back inside, the door slamming behind her.

"Come, lass, we must work." Bram held out his hand.

Fia hung back. "I want to go to my sister's house tomorrow, Bram. Will you take me? He won't chance to find me there."

Her sister was married to one of the laird's crofters. If Fia hid there, Wexin would not happen upon her as he almost had today. Bram could come fetch her when Wexin went away again.

Bram frowned. "If I can't change your mind, lass…"

They walked inside, passing through the kitchen, where Aunt Priss handed Bram a tray. "Some food and tea for the guest upstairs, Bram. Will you take it to her?" She turned to Fia. "There's people waiting in the taproom. What's got into you, Fia?"

"I'm sorry, Aunt Priss," she replied. "I forgot the time."

Bram, carrying the tray, followed Fia as she hurried into the taproom.

As soon as they crossed that threshold, Lord Tannerton stopped them. "Is that food for her?" he asked.

Bram nodded. "Aye."

The marquess glanced around and leaned forward, a fierce look in his eyes. "Will you betray her? Will you tell the magistrate that she is here?"

"Tell the laird? No!" cried Fia. "Don't say such a thing, m'lord."

"Call him Mr Henry, Fia," Bram corrected. "You have our vow. We'll not betray Lady Parr—we'll not betray her."

Tannerton nodded, but he blocked their way again. "Why? Tell me why you won't betray her."

"She did not do it," said Fia.

"You believe her?" Tannerton looked from one to the other.

Fia had been certain Lady Corland would tell the marquess about her seeing the murder and now it seemed as if she hadn't.

Bram gave her a glance. He turned to the marquess. "We believe her, sir."

Fia felt tears well in her eyes. Bram could have told the marquess right then about her seeing what really happened. He didn't, even though he thought the marquess was a very great man because of what he'd done in Brussels.

"Do ye not believe her, sir?" Fia asked the marquess.

"Of course I do," he answered sharply. His voice softened. "I merely wondered if I was the only one."

He thanked them again for agreeing to keep Marlena's secret and he returned to a table where a tankard of ale waited for him.

Fia reached for the tray in Bram's hands. "Will you let me take this to her? Will you care for the patrons 'til I'm back?"

"If you like." He gave her the tray.

Fia carried it up the flight of stairs and knocked on the door to Lady Corland's room. "It is Fia, ma'am."

Lady Corland opened it.

"Some food for you, ma'am." She set the tray on the table.

The lady looked pale and upset, and Fia felt a wave of guilt for not wanting to try to help her by telling the laird what she'd seen so long ago. She could not do it. She was so afraid inside she thought she might break in pieces.

"You didn't tell the marquess about me," Fia said.

Lady Corland looked at her in surprise. "I promised you."

"I thank you." Fia hung her head. "I—I want to go away. Is it all right with you, m'lady? Is it all right I don't tell what I know?"

The lady gave her a soft look. "It would be very dangerous to tell what you know, Fia. With my—my friend's help, I can go into hiding again. Then we both will be safe."

"Where will you be going, m'lady?" What place would be safe for her? Wexin was a rich man. He could go anywhere to find her.

Lady Corland's expression turned serious. "I'll not tell you, Fia. I don't want you to have the burden of knowing it, but you are not to worry. Eventually Lord Wexin will leave Parronley. You should be safe to live your life here with your young man."

Fia felt her face go hot. "Och, Bram is not my young man."

"Isn't he?" The lady smiled.

Fia was too embarrassed to answer. She glanced towards the door. "I'd best be seeing to the patrons."

"I understand."

"You can place the tray in the hall if you'd like it to be out of your way." Fia shuffled her feet. "I'll fetch it later."

"I will do that."

Fia walked to the door and opened it. "If I don't see you again, I wish you fare well."

"I wish you fare well, too."

Fia smiled because her ladyship spoke the words just like a Scotswoman. Fia hurried out of the room and down the stairs.

The first patrons Fia saw in the taproom were Erroll and Lyall Gibb. "Ho, you, Fia. We heard you had a guest in the inn. The man over there? Who is he?"

She remembered what the marquess asked of her. "He's

somebody who got lost. What other reason has a stranger to come to Kilrosa?"

She glanced over at Bram who was working the tap at the moment. He had an approving look on his face.

"Now what do you want to drink?" she asked the Gibb brothers.

Tanner swayed a bit as he took the first step on the stairway. He grasped the banister to steady himself. Perhaps he should not have switched to whisky. Damned good drink, however.

He reached the room and entered with a clatter. Night had fallen. He'd intended not to wake her. He glanced to the bed, but it was empty.

Damnation. Had she run again?

He steadied himself on the edge of the bed, but he really wanted to pound his fist into the wall. Suddenly from the corner of his eye he saw something move.

She stood up from a chair near the fire.

Her hair was loose and flowed down to her shoulders. She wore the nightdress that the wife of that first innkeeper had given to her. After their nights together, he knew the feel of the cloth and the feel of her beneath it.

"You are still awake?" Idiotic thing for him to say. Of course she was.

"I rested some." Her voice floated across the room as if on the wings of angels.

He was waxing poetic. Must be jug-bitten.

"Sleeping is difficult," she added.

Her scent seemed to fill the room, the scent of soap and something indefinable, like a rare flower.

There he went again. Poetic. "Have you been in the room all this time?"

"I went below stairs to the necessary," she said.

He frowned. "All alone?"

"I was careful," she replied.

He winced with guilt. He should have checked on her; should have seen if she needed him. "I would have gone with you. Why did you not come to get me in the taproom?"

"I thought you did not want me there."

He wanted her wherever he was. Wanting her had consumed his thoughts while he'd been consuming multiple glasses of whisky. "I would not have minded."

He felt himself listing to the side, and grabbed hold of the bedpost. "Did you have enough to eat?"

"I did, thank you."

Blast it. He hated the caution in her voice. He desired hearing her voice filled with the same passion that burned inside him. That passion for her had remained constant even when faced with her unbelievable story.

No matter how preposterous her story, he believed her. He'd spent days with her. He'd lain with her. He *knew* her, knew the woman she was, no matter what name she went by, what story she told.

She should have trusted him. After that first time of love-making, she should have told him who she was—that she had been married. Blast the idea of protecting him.

"I knew Corland," he told her, as if she could follow the direction of his mind.

She lowered her head. "I presumed you knew him."

Tanner's throat went suddenly dry. "Did you love him, Marlena?"

She glanced up. "I thought I loved him at first. He was very charming."

"He was a damned fellow," Tanner said.

She met his gaze. "He—he was not unlike the man I invented in my tale for you."

Tanner gave a disgusted laugh. "The fictional jewel thief?"

She nodded.

"At least some of what you told me was true." He advanced towards her. "Corland was a bounder and debaucher. Did you not think I would understand—?" He stopped short of touching her.

She interrupted him. "Understand why I would kill him, do you mean?" She spun away from him.

He put his hands on her shoulders and turned her to face him. "You cannot think I do not believe you."

She avoided looking at him.

He lifted her chin with one hand. "I cannot abide thinking of you married to Corland, of your being in his bed—" He needed to brace himself on her shoulder.

"Tanner," she said breathlessly.

He shook his head. "You should have trusted me, Marlena. You've made me bring you to the place of greatest danger to you. Wexin is not five miles away."

She said nothing, merely looked into his eyes.

He released her, lifting both hands before placing one of them on the table for balance.

Did she think he would never discover she was the Vanishing Viscountess? During his stay in the taproom, he realised the crime made no difference to him. He could not leave her merely because it was not theft, but a murder charge on her head. He'd move all the mountains of Scotland to keep her from the hangman's noose. To protect her from Wexin.

"Wexin." He spat out the name. "The cursed villain! Why the devil did he wish to kill Corland in the first place? He gambled unwisely, but otherwise I would not have thought him capable of such tresh—treachery."

He swayed and lowered himself carefully into the chair next to him.

She sat on the opposite chair. "Are you drunk, Tanner?"

He tried to give her a composed look. "Merely a trifle disguised."

A smile teased at the corner of her mouth.

He smiled in return, but forced himself to at least look sober. "I was thinking we should go to France."

"France?" She sat up straighter.

He leaned on the table. "Instead of Edinburgh. Although we'll have to go to Edinburgh, I think, to get passage to France. The thing is, Wexin cannot get to you in France. You cannot be arrested in a different country. I should think Wexin would give it up with me protecting you."

"Wait." She touched his hand. "What do you mean *we* should go to France?"

His hand tingled at her touch, the sensation spreading through him. "I would not send you there alone," he managed to respond.

"Tanner—"

His mind was clear, even if the alcohol made him a trifle unsteady. He knew what must be done, what he wanted above all things.

"I worked this out, Marlena." He met her gaze soberly. "I'm not needed here. There is nothing for me to do but pursue pleasure. Gambling. Hunting. Other sport." Words were failing him and he wanted to make her understand." He winced. "The last time I amused myself, three people wound up dead—"

"The responsibility for that was not yours," she protested.

He waved a hand. "It was. No escaping truth. Thing is, I can help you. Have helped you. Might as well keep helping you—"

"Tanner, traveling with me to Paris will take time. Weeks, maybe. The more time you spend with me, the more risk there is of being connected with me and accused of helping me escape."

He laughed softly. "You do not know what I am trying to say. I would take you to Paris and stay with you. Live with you."

"No." She rose from the chair. "You cannot mean this."

"Of course I mean it."

"Tanner, you are a marquess." She gaped at him.

He wanted to pull her on to his lap and show her he was a man first, before a marquess.

She stepped away from him. "You cannot leave your responsibilities."

He waved his hand again. "That is just it. I can. I have hired a legion of workers who do an excellent job running the whole lot. That is my point, Marlena. *I* am not needed. My affairs have been set up to run well. For two generations the set-up has worked to perfection. I am the least important person in keeping them running well." He stood. "Oh, perhaps I may be needed for a signature or two, but documents can be couriered to me. You would be safe. We could have a life together." He touched her face, gently. "What do you say, Marlena?"

"Oh, Tanner." She wrapped her arms around his neck.

He seized her in his arms and captured her lips, kissing her with more hunger than when they'd gone without food. She was all softness, all curves, and his hands glided over her body, relishing where he touched, longing to feel her bare skin.

She pushed his coat over his shoulders and pulled on the sleeves until the garment fell to the floor. He wanted to laugh for joy, because she wanted him, too. She had thought of undressing him at the same moment he had thought of undressing her.

They were like two sides of a coin, he realised. Parts of the same whole, making no sense unless they were together. He wanted to show her, make her understand that they belonged together.

That he could not live without her.

This revelation had come to him in the taproom. *He could not live without her.*

She unbuttoned his waistcoat, and he shrugged out of it, pulling the shirttails out of his trousers next. Her delicate hands worked the buttons on the fall of his trousers, tantalising him, making him yearn for her fingers to touch where he was now so powerfully aroused for her.

Her fingers skimmed that part of him and again he had the fancy that they thought with one mind.

"Your boots," she murmured, urgency in her voice.

Damn the boots, he thought, not wanting to stop for such practicality as removing his boots. She knelt before him to pull them off, and his trousers after them. Her hands stroked his thighs as if wanting to come closer.

"Marlena," he rasped, unable to wait.

He pulled her on top of him, his hands under her nightdress, finding her breasts, feeling her nipples harden for him.

She moaned. "Can we do it now, Tanner? Here."

One mind, he thought. One passion. Never had he been with a woman so attuned to him. Never had he felt so complete as when joining with her.

"You and I can do whatever we wish." He felt more powerful with her than with all the trappings his title afforded him.

He positioned her on to him, entering her there on the chair. The moment of joining accelerated his joy and his need of her. They even moved as one, in perfect rhythm, their need growing in unison. He closed his eyes and let himself be lost in her, to relish this belonging to one person. To feel that this, above all else, gave meaning to his life.

They were as one in their moment of satisfaction, as well. He felt the release of his seed, the culmination of his pleasure at the same moment he felt her pulse against him. Their voices cried out together, and their last writhing of ecstasy came as if they were one.

He'd long abandoned the idea of leaving her in some god-awful place in Edinburgh without the intention of freeing her and coming back to her. Now he realised he did not want to leave her at all. It would be like leaving all that gave his life meaning.

He held her quietly on his lap for a few minutes until the reality of cramped muscles set in.

"I'm taking you to bed," he murmured into her ear.

She slid off his lap and pulled him to her as soon as her feet touched the floor. A kiss joined them once more, a uniting kiss.

He picked her up into his arms and carried her to the bed where they quickly disposed of her nightdress and his shirt and joined each other, skin to skin, under the covers. To his delight their passion rapidly rose again.

Afterwards she lay in his arms, and he savoured the smoothness of her skin against his.

He turned his head and kissed her on the temple. "You know what this means, do you not?" he said to her, his voice tinged with the joy that permeated every part of him.

"Mmm, what?" she murmured sleepily.

"We are married." He grinned and turned to her for a quick taste of her mouth. "We are in Scotland, claiming to be husband and wife, and we have just consummated our union." He swept a hand through her now tangled hair. "We are married."

"Married." She sighed.

In spite of all his drink, he lay awake while she drifted to sleep, his mind spinning with plans to reach Edinburgh. They would have to hide there somehow until he was able to access his funds and get enough money to set themselves up in France. He'd like them to be married properly, by clergy, if possible, but he could not feel more married to her than he did at this moment.

Soon he would be able to shower her with everything his wealth could provide her. He fell asleep, thinking of jewels and dresses and shoes and trinkets, every luxury he wanted to buy her.

Lord Wexin returned to Parronley in the dark after a deadly tedious meal with Laird Hay. He did learn a bit about how landowners were increasing their profits here in Scotland, by forcing out the crofters so there would be more land for sheep. The wool industry seemed to be doing quite well.

He frowned as he left the horse to a stable boy and found his way up the dark path to the great mausoleum of a house that smelled of years of being closed up. He could do nothing here until he inherited, and, unless Rapp located Marlena, that might never happen. He needed her to be found. Needed even more for her to be dead. Why the devil could she not have drowned in that shipwreck and her body wash up on shore? Everything would have been so easy that way.

He entered the house and found the elderly butler napping in a chair in the hall.

"Here, man!" Wexin said loudly. "Take my things."

The man woke with a snort and struggled arthritically to his feet. "M'lord," he mumbled, taking his hat and gloves and catching the top coat that was thrown into his arms. "Begging you pardon, m'lord, but a man arrived while you were out."

"A man?" Wexin raised his brows.

"Ay, sir," the old man said. "He said you would wish to see him this night. A Mr Rapp, sir."

"Why did you not say it was Rapp in the first place?" Wexin snapped.

The butler shrugged. "He waits in an anteroom near the kitchen."

"Is the drawing room lit with candles and a fire as I instructed?" Wexin demanded.

The butler bowed. "Ay, m'lord."

"Then bring me some brandy and have Rapp attend me there."

Wexin made his way across the hall, his heels clicking on the stone floor. The drawing room had none of the elegance and fine taste that his lovely Lydia had brought to their London townhouse, but he supposed it would do for the likes of Rapp.

A few minutes later Wexin was settled with a tolerable bottle of brandy. The butler announced Rapp, who strode in.

Wexin waited for the butler to close the door and for the man's receding footsteps to be heard.

"How did you know I was here?" Wexin demanded.

Rapp responded, "Your arrival was spoken of in Parronley. I am staying at the inn there."

Wexin waved an impatient hand. "Well, what is your report?

Rapp straightened. "I have seen her travelling in the company of a man. I am convinced she is coming here."

"You saw her and did not capture her?" Wexin huffed.

Two spots of colour tinged Rapp's cheeks. "She managed to elude me. Once in Liverpool. Once on the road outside Langholm, but I am confident she will not elude me a third time."

Wexin gave a sardonic laugh. "One woman managed to elude you twice? Three times if we count your losing her in the shipwreck?" He should have hired a more ruthless man to escort his cousin back to London, one who would have seen that a shipwreck ended her life.

"The man in her company came to her aid," explained Rapp.

Wexin glared. "And who is this man?"

Rapp pressed his lips together before speaking. "I have not seen his face. They change names at every stop. He may wear a signet ring, however."

"A signet ring?" Wexin's excitement grew. "Do you know the seal?"

Rapp lifted his chin. "Only that it included a stag and an eagle."

Tannerton's seal!

Wexin took a sip of brandy to disguise a smile. How many other gentlemen with a stag and eagle on their crest would be rusticating in this god-forsaken part of Scotland? It had to be Tannerton, and Marlena was with him. Wexin's hand trembled. He had been so close to her this very day.

He retained his composure. "This is all you have for me? That she travels in this direction with a man wearing a ring? I could have guessed as much."

Well, he would not have guessed she'd have a man with her, let alone a marquess, but it did make sense that she could not have come this far all alone.

"They travelled on horseback," Rapp responded, an edge in his voice. "That made it more difficult to follow their progress. They have largely remained off the coaching and toll roads."

Wexin waved a hand. "Go. You are dismissed. I'll have no further need of your services. Return to Bow Street and wherever else the deuce you belong."

Rapp frowned. "What of my pay, sir?"

Wexin eyed him with disdain. "No prisoner. No pay." He waved a hand. "Be off with you. I cannot abide incompetence and failure. I dare say you can find your way to the village. Do not show your face in this house again."

Rapp took one threatening step towards Wexin, but then he seemed to think better of it. He turned around and walked out, slamming the door behind him.

Wexin released a grin. He'd wait long enough for Rapp to be gone and then he would send for the men he'd brought with him from London, men who would not let a woman and a pampered marquess defeat them so easily.

He raised his glass in a toast. "To you, cousin Marlena. Soon we see each other again. Then you will meet your fate."

Rapp stormed out of the house and back to the stable for his hired horse.

Damned Wexin. He released a whole string of epithets towards this man who had not only cheated him out of his pay, but also the sum of money he'd spent along the road. He would show the ruddy man. There was still a reward waiting in London for the return of the Vanishing Viscountess. Rapp intended to collect that reward and Lord Wexin could go to the devil for all he cared.

Chapter Seventeen

Marlena awoke in Tanner's arms, with the delicious knowledge that each morning from now on she would awaken in the same spot. She'd never dared hope for happiness again, but Tanner had delivered it to her as surely as he had rescued her from the Irish Sea, impossible tasks both.

She ignored the twinges of guilt that teased at her conscience. She'd not asked Tanner to give up his life in England for her. He'd offered it. He wanted it. She pushed away the nagging thought that he would some day regret leaving his duties, his country.

She could not help but worry about the people of Parronley. Perhaps she could assume her title as Baroness when she was in France. Perhaps she could care for her people *in absentia* as Tanner planned to do.

At least they would not be under Wexin's care.

Another fear tugged at her sleeve. Would Wexin come after her even in France? Would she and Tanner still have to constantly look over their shoulders?

His eyes opened and gazed warmly into hers. "Good morning, wife."

She smiled. They were married. Could she really allow herself to believe that dream had come true?

Eliza, she thought. *Am I married to the Marquess of Tannerton?*

"Good morning," she responded.

He gathered her in his arms and kissed her, her body answering with the flushed excitement and yearning he always elicited in her, even in those days when she and Eliza were mooning over him.

She laughed softly. "Did you know you danced with me once, Tanner?"

His face screwed up in disbelief. "I would have remembered."

She touched his mouth with her finger tracing the outline of his lips. "At Lady Erstine's masquerade ball. I was dressed as a maiden from the time of King Arthur with a pointed hat and a flowing veil. And a mask, of course. You never saw my face."

His lips formed into a rueful smile. "I would treasure the memory—if I remembered it."

She laughed again. "I would never expect you to remember me. I was a very forgettable girl in those days, but my friend Eliza and I kept an account of you. We were quite enamoured of you."

"You jest."

She stroked his chin, loving how scratchy his growth of beard felt on her fingertips. "It is true, but a long time ago. A marquess was reaching too high for us. At the end of the season, Corland became my suitor and my brother declared he would make me a good husband."

Tanner's smile disappeared. He took a strand of her hair and twirled it in his fingers. "Your brother ought to have known better."

"Oh, I suppose Corland charmed Niall as thoroughly as he did me."

Tanner's brow furrowed. "Did you have any happiness with Corland, Marlena?"

She stared into his eyes, seeing flecks of brown in their mossy green. "Briefly, when I was too starry-eyed to know better, and Corland still had my money to spend." She cupped her palm against his cheek. "It never felt like this."

His eyes darkened and he placed his lips on hers again, giving her more in one kiss than she'd ever imagined a man could give.

"Marlena," he murmured, tasting of her lips again and again. "Wife."

She was certain of what love meant now. It meant how she felt about this man, how his mere whispering of her name sent shafts of desire through her, how his touch aroused her senses, how his smile filled her with joy.

She rolled on to her back and he covered her, worshipping her with his gaze, soothing her with his hands, thrilling her with his coupling. When he entered her it was all that she could do not to cry out in joy. He was hers. She, a fugitive everywhere else, was at home with him.

He moved with exquisite gentleness, making their passion grow. Though lost to sensation as the pleasure built inside her, one thought remained. She would belong to him like this for ever.

Sparkles of light seemed to dance behind her eyelids as he brought her passion to its peak. She imagined the light passing through her skin, becoming a part of her, belonging to her in a way she would never have to give up.

When she lay again in his arms, sated and safe, her joy turned to contentment.

She must have fallen asleep again, because when she

woke, he was at the basin shaving, wearing only his trousers.

"Why did you not wake me?" she asked. The room was bright with sunlight. The morning well advanced. "It must be late."

He turned. "No need to do so. We have only ten miles to go by the map. An easy ride. I thought I would dress first and let you sleep."

She rose from the bed and retrieved her nightdress from the floor. Slipping it on, she walked over to him and hugged him from behind.

He turned and kissed her, then wiped the soap he left on her face with his thumb. "I think it best you remain in the room while I check on the horses. With any luck my horse will be fit for the journey."

"I do not mind." She loved their simple room in this humble inn. It was the site of her wedding, after all, and it felt safe.

She washed and dressed, finishing just as he was ready to go out of the door. As she started to pin up her hair, he gave her another swift kiss. "I'll be back. Before I head for the stable, I'll arrange for some food to be sent up for us."

After he left, she hurried to the window to watch him walk out of the inn, so tall, so commanding in his masculine stride. She felt as giddy as the girl she'd once been, watching him saunter into a ballroom.

Dare I be so happy, Eliza?

When he was no longer in sight, she finished dressing her hair and covered it with a cap. She straightened the bedcovers, her hand smoothing the linens, remembering how they had become so twisted and tangled with their lovemaking.

She had just finished tidying the room when Fia's Bram brought her breakfast.

He set the tray on the table. Such a big bear of a man, she thought and smiled to herself, remembering Fia's protest about him. They were so obviously besotted with each other.

"How is Fia today, Bram?" she asked.

"Och," replied the large man, "I walked her to her sister's early this morn. That cursed flesher has her in a great fright, y'know. Best she hide for a bit."

Flesher. She had not heard that Scottish term for *butcher* in many years. It was an apt name for Wexin, she thought with a shudder.

"Whatever keeps her safe." She caught Bram's eye. "Wexin is a very dangerous man, Bram. You must be very wary of him, for Fia's sake."

A hard, determined look came over his face. "Aye, I'll keep her safe."

"Good." She smiled.

"Lord Tannerton will see you safe, as well, m'lady. He is a fine man. He'll see you to your destination without that demon finding you." He nodded his head in emphasis.

Marlena regarded him with curiosity. "From where do you know Lord Tannerton, Bram?"

"From Brussels, m'lady."

"Brussels?"

"Ay." He nodded again. "It was after the great battle. I was in the 71st, ma'am, who fought in the battle. After that day I was walkin' into Brussels with the wounded." He pushed up his sleeve and showed her a jagged scar. "I was not bad hurt, but others were dyin'. His lordship carried the lads from the wagons. He found houses to take the lads and tend them and he paid with his own money for the caring of them. Did it all day, m'lady. And the next. And the next."

"Lord Tannerton did that?"

"Aye, ma'am, and there were plenty lords who ran back

to England that day, but not his lordship." His chest puffed out in pride as he spoke. "And then a year later I heard my officers talking that his lordship spoke in Parliament, to help the lads that came back, maimed and unable to work."

Parliament. The House of Lords.

Tanner had neglected to tell her that he had taken his seat in the Lords, but of course he would have done so.

Bram concluded. "Lord Tannerton is a great man."

"Yes," she agreed, her voice suddenly cracking.

Bram glanced to the door. "I'd best be going back to my duties, ma'am, if you are no longer needing me."

"No," she said distractedly. "I do not need you, but I thank you, Bram."

He bowed and strode out of the room.

Marlena grabbed hold of the bedpost, pressing her cheek against the smooth wood. She squeezed her eyes shut.

A great man, Bram had said. Tanner was a great man, a man who organised the care of the wounded at Waterloo. A man who spoke for those men in the House of Lords. He had said nothing to Marlena of this part of his life.

Marlena sank into the chair, but had little appetite for the food in front of her. She absently nibbled on a piece of bread, picturing Tanner's strong arms carrying men from wagons, seeing Tanner heedless of blood staining his clothes, thinking only of what must be done. She thought of him standing in the Lords, among all those important, titled men, his deep masculine voice booming to the far recesses of the room.

He was an important man.

There was another quick knock at the door, and Tanner walked in, a line of worry between his brows.

He smiled at her, though, and crossed the room to her, kissing her upturned face. When he sat down across from her, the worry line remained. "The horse needs another day of rest, the stableman tells me."

"I see," she responded.

He tilted his head. "I tried to barter for another horse, but the man did not think he could procure one before the end of the day."

"Could we walk or take one horse?" she asked.

He shook his head. "It slows us considerably. Should Rapp or Wexin encounter us, we'd have little chance of escaping." He lifted his palm. "I also thought about a carriage, but Bram said this village does not have a coaching inn. We would have to go to Parronley for it." He rubbed his face. "Wexin must be watching the coaching inn."

The fear felt like a hard rock inside her. "When can we leave?"

"Tomorrow, the stableman assures me." He reached across the table and took her hand.

She squeezed his fingers. "We can wait a day, can we not? We can hide in this room. Bram will warn us if anyone comes."

He lifted her hand to his lips. "That is the wisest course, I believe."

She poured his tea and placed some ham and cheese on his plate. She listened with only half an ear as he told her more particulars about the horse and his thoughts of what route they could take to avoid the more travelled roads.

"I spoke to Bram and he will draw us a map." He took a bite of ham.

Her heart began to pound faster. She tried to keep her voice calm. "Bram said he knew you from Waterloo, that you were in Brussels after the battle. He spoke of your heroic work with the wounded."

"Heroic?" He shook his head. "I assure you, I merely helped a little. There was nothing else to do."

What Bram described had been considerable, but Marlena did not argue the point.

"What were you doing in Brussels?" she asked instead.

The newspapers during that time had reported that some of the English had considered Brussels somewhat of a social event, the place to be, until Napoleon decided to be there as well.

"Pure accident, I was there." Tanner took a sip of tea. "I'd been at the Congress of Vienna. Assisting Castlereagh, you know. When he went back to England, I stayed. Helped Wellington for a bit and went on to Brussels when his Grace was called there."

Her jaw dropped. "You were at the Congress of Vienna?"

After Napoleon's first abdication, all the powers of Europe gathered in Vienna to decide the fate of the Continent. If Tanner had been there, someone must have considered his assistance very important indeed—important enough to be a part of deciding the fate of nations.

"Just helping out a bit. Castlereagh talked me into it." He chewed on a piece of bread.

She supposed Wellington had "talked him into" helping him as well. Marlena leaned back in her chair and stared at him. "Goodness, Tanner, what else have you done?"

"Done?" His brows rose. "I did not *do* anything. I merely assisted."

"Why you?" She lifted her cup.

He shrugged. "I suppose the Duke of Clarence suggested my name to Castlereagh."

"The Duke of Clarence!" The King's son. The Prince Regent's brother. She nearly spilled her tea.

"Friend of mine." He pierced another piece of ham with his fork and popped it in his mouth.

Although it seemed as if she could no longer breathe, she coaxed more out of him. He leaned his chair and balanced it

on its back legs as he told her about his activity in the Lords.
His efforts seemed considerable to her, although he spoke of
them as trifles. He shrugged his work off as no more remarkable or important than wagering on a horse race or playing
at cards. Merely another means to relieve boredom.

The more he talked, the tighter the knot grew inside
Marlena, the harder each breath came. It was plain as a
pikestaff that Tanner did not see what was so very evident to
a common man like Bram and to her. Tanner was a man
capable of great achievement, not only because of the title
he bore, but more so because of the man he was. He was
capable of befriending Whigs and Tories alike, princes and
common men, to charm them all with his affable manners,
influence them with the sheer force of his personality.

Marlena swallowed against a rising sense of despair. If
Tanner took her to France, if he remained with her, connected to her, what would happen to all those people he
might have helped, the other men who might perish if he were
not there to assume their burdens?

She choked back a sob.

He let the chair right itself again, peering at her with
concern. "What is it, Marlena?"

"Oh." She blinked away threatening tears. "I suppose I
am afraid."

He reached across the table and grasped her hand. "I'll
make certain no harm comes to you. We'll make it to
Edinbugh and to Paris."

You cannot let him do this, Marlena, the voice of Eliza
seemed to warn.

I know it, she replied inside. *I know it.*

He smiled at her, eyes like a warm caress. "What shall we
do to pass the time today, Marlena, confined to this room as we
are?"

Her heart swelled with love for him, for his ready desire to ease her fears. What frightened her now was more than her capture, however.

She tried to smile back. "I do not know, Tanner."

He rose from his chair, still holding her hand. "I shall think of something."

Wexin waited in the breakfast parlour, finishing his meal, while his lackeys had been dispatched to Kilrosa to discover if Marlena was indeed in residence there. Wexin had roused himself early and called his men to him to apprise them of his suspicions, ordering them to find her without delay. Now he had no choice but to wait for their report.

Wexin hoped his men would not tell him that she had fled already. The thought of her being so close and yet slipping through his fingers would drive him into a real fury. He wanted this business concluded quickly.

He took a deep breath, cautioning himself not to think in such a depressive vein. Marlena was in Kilrosa. He could sense it. All that was required now was a plan to capture her.

It was unfortunate that Tannerton accompanied her. Such a man would be a formidable enemy, one powerful enough to convince others of Marlena's innocence. And Wexin's guilt. Obviously, Tannerton must be killed, but the death of a marquess would arouse a great deal of undesired attention.

Wexin picked up a newspaper fetched for him by a footman the previous day. He supposed it would be several days old, having come from Edinburgh, but he needed the distraction.

A report caught his eye. *Packet Boat Wrecks.*

Wexin half-rose from his chair as he read the report of the boat Marlena had been on. Tannerton must have been on the packet boat, too. He nearly whooped with glee. Rapp said Tannerton and Marlena had been using false names.

Perhaps no one knew that the Marquess was alive. Wexin could dispose of him here in Scotland where no one would be looking. They'd assume he drowned.

The butler entered and Wexin refolded the newspaper quickly. "Well, what is it?" he snapped.

"Your men to see you, m'lord." The old man bowed.

Wexin straightened and gestured at the remnants of his breakfast. "Get rid of this and tell them to come in."

The butler bowed again and stacked up the plates in his hand. He reached for Wexin's tea cup.

"Leave me my tea, you fool." Wexin shooed him away.

Two of his men entered the room. Wexin signalled them to wait until the butler walked away with the dishes.

"What news, then?" Wexin asked, unable to suppress the eagerness in his voice.

Smith, as stout and solid as a powder keg, spoke up. "We've got nothing for certain, m'lord."

Wexin pounded his fist on the table.

The other man, Jones, shorter and leaner, but in a way that made him a good scrapper, broke in, "We are certain the woman is at the inn, m'lord. It is just that no one is talking about her."

"We saw the gentleman, though," Smith added. "He went to the stable. The man has two horses there, so she must be with him."

This sounded promising. "You left someone to watch the inn, I hope."

Jones nodded. "Oh, we did that, sir. Williams is watching the place."

Wexin stifled a laugh. Smith. Jones. Williams. Not real names, he'd wager a pony, but these were the sort of men who would get results, not incompetent asses like Rapp. He was well rid of that fellow.

He frowned again. They would be much too conspicuous, all of them, waiting and watching in the village. He must come up with another plan. "Can they be spotted leaving the village?"

"Unless they leave on foot," Jones replied. "There is only one road in and out."

Wexin leaned forward. "Here is what we do. Two men watch the road, one man watches the inn. We must attempt not to be conspicuous, however." His brow furrowed in thought. "I will accompany you." He would ensure they did not make some stupid mistake.

Smith piped up, "I overheard the stableman talking to the gentleman. One of their horses almost went lame and cannot make the trip until tomorrow. I think they won't go anywhere until then."

"We must assume nothing. We must watch them." Wexin drummed his fingers on the table. "If it were me, I would leave under cover of darkness." He felt energised with excitement. "Just in case, one of you must watch the inn all day; the others, the road, but when darkness falls, the real vigil begins."

Chapter Eighteen

The day with Tanner was a delight. They rarely left the room and did not leave the inn at all. Most of the time they remained in bed, making love or merely talking.

Marlena was hungry to know all about him, asking endless questions about his childhood, his thoughts, his secret wishes. He insisted his only wish was to be with her, but that statement only made tears prick her eyes again.

She soaked up tales of boyhood escapades, various larks that always seemed instigated by his friend, Pomroy, which took Tanner's cleverness to extricate them.

She told him about herself, about living at Parronley and leaving there for school, never to return. She told him about Eliza, how they were school friends and débutantes together. She told how Eliza took her in when she'd run to her, making Marlena a part of her Irish home, keeping her safe until Eliza's brother came to visit. Marlena talked about Eliza and her children becoming ill, and how Marlena tried so hard to keep her dear friend alive. Marlena talked about Niall, about his death, and the death of her nephews. Tanner held her when she finally could cry for them all and for herself.

And for him.

Time hung suspended, giving the illusion they would have all the time in the world to lie abed, talking. Loving. Then in an instant it was night, and desolation replaced the joy of her all-too-brief marriage to the Marquess of Tannerton.

The path she must take stayed in her mind while they talked and made love.

She knew better than to merely run. Tanner would find her and protect her, no matter what. Her only choice was to turn herself in, and he must not be a party to that. She must do it alone and never let it be known that Tanner had helped her.

The prospect of death lost some of its terror, at least. She had lived a lifetime in a few short days, more than some people live if they reach one hundred years. She'd known Tanner. She'd known love.

She wrote a letter to him in snatches, whenever he left the room to get them food, or to check on the horses. What he would think or do when he read it, she did not know.

In the letter she asked for his promise not to reveal that he had helped her, to give her the gift of knowing he would not share her fate.

She explained why she was leaving, to free him to do the good he was destined to do—nay, *obligated* to do with his personality and position. She reminded him of all the people they had met on their journey who needed him to look out for them. The innkeepers and stable boys, the blacksmiths and tavern girls, the caretakers at Dutwood, Bram and Fia, everyone who had helped them. She asked him to care for them in her name.

She wrote that it grieved her to know how much her leaving would wound him, but the more bound she felt to him, the more right it seemed. They had been born to duty, and his duty was to care for those who needed him. She would not allow him to sacrifice those people for her alone.

She closed the letter saying how much she loved him, and how grateful she was to have been his wife.

When they made love for the last time, each caress, each kiss brought pain as well as delight. She savoured every moment of the experience for herself, but there was more to it than that. This lovemaking was like a prayer, a prayer to give him happiness, to help him remember how greatly she loved him.

She lay in his arms afterwards, listening to his heartbeat and to each breath of air he took in. She could feel him drift to sleep as his breathing slowed. It was so tempting to close her eyes and join him in sleep, but she forced herself to remain awake.

She had watched the window, waiting for a glimmer of light. When it came, all too soon, she slipped from his arms and dressed herself. Her bag was already packed with her clothing, each item reminding her of Tanner. When all was ready, she placed the letter on the table where she knew he would see it, and took one long, last look at him, so peacefully unaware, his hair mussed, his handsome face still wearing a hint of a smile.

"I shall love you always, my husband," she whispered so quietly she was not certain she hadn't merely thought the words.

Turning the knob slowly, she opened the door, and walked away from the man she loved.

In the hall of the inn, she paused to don her cloak. As she stepped into the street, she saw a person rushing towards her. Marlena drew back to hide in the shadows.

It was Fia, hurrying to the inn's door as if she were being pursued.

Marlena stepped into the light. "Fia? What is wrong?"

The girl gave a sharp cry. "Lady Corland!"

"Has something happened?" Marlena looked at the girl with worry.

"Och, m'lady." Fia tried to catch her breath. "It is me that's wrong and I could not sleep for it."

"I do not understand." She took Fia's arm and led her away to where their voices would not so easily carry through the inn's windows.

Fia looked at the bag she had slung over her shoulder. "Are you and Lord Tannerton leavin' so early, m'lady? Because you need to hear what I say before you go."

It was too much to explain to the girl. "What is it, Fia?"

"I came to tell Bram I'm goin' to the laird. I'm going to tell Laird Hay what happened that night. I do not know what he can do, but he's the magistrate and I'm going to tell him." Even in the near-darkness, Marlena could see the resolute set of Fia's chin.

She held the girl by the shoulders. "No, Fia. It is too dangerous. Wexin—"

"I'm done with being afraid of Lord Wexin, m'lady," Fia cried. "It is wrong that he can go free and you have to hide." She paused, glancing towards the inn. "I cannot ask Bram to love me if I don't do something to stop this. Bram would do it in my place. I know he would."

"Fia, Bram would love you no matter. It truly is too dangerous." She gave her a little shake.

Fia twisted out of her grasp. "Nae, m'lady. I would not be worthy of his loving me. I woke my sister and told her I was comin' back. I'm asking Bram to take me to the laird. He'll believe us, I know he will. He's a good man, the laird is."

Marlena could hear the blood roaring through her body, ringing in her ears. She did not know if it was fear or excitement. She did not know if they could dare test the truth. Or dare to hope.

"I'm waking Bram for him to take me as soon as it is light. You cannot stop me." She leaned towards Marlena. "You should come with us—Lord Tannerton, too—the laird is sure to do something, if his lordship tells him to."

She gave Fia an agonised glance. "I'll go with you," she told Fia. "But Lord Tannerton must not be part of it. If this does not work, he could hang along with me."

"His lordship would not like you going without him, m'lady," Fia said.

They started to walk back to the door of the inn when two men jumped out of the shadows and seized them, clamping huge hands over their mouths. Marlena felt the point of a knife against her throat.

His breath foul with rotting teeth, the man holding her sneered, "You are coming with us. Do not make a sound or you both will be sliced to bits."

The other man made a high whistle and, as they were dragged behind the building and past the stable, two more men emerged from opposite directions.

One of them whispered, "Do you have her?"

"Take a look," Marlena's captor said, stuffing a dirty handkerchief in her mouth so that she thought she would gag.

The man came closer and peered into her face. He smiled, his teeth glowing white. "My dear cousin."

Wexin.

Her nightmare had come true, and Fia's, as well.

The knife still pointed to her throat, the man bound her hands.

"This other one said something about going to the laird," Fia's captor said.

Wexin turned and strode over to Fia, bound and gagged as well. Wexin gasped and squeezed Fia's face in his hand. "My good fortune is boundless this day." He turned to the men. "Quickly, before someone hears. Let us be off."

The men carried Marlena and Fia over their shoulders and

quickly made their way out of the village. Marlena struggled to keep her wits about her, to look for an opportunity to escape and to free Fia.

The men had hidden horses outside of town. Marlena was thrown over a horse's back and bounced painfully against its withers as its rider put the horse into a gallop. She presumed they headed towards Parronley, to the home she had not been inside for over thirteen years.

She could see little but the horse's shoulder and the ground and she only glimpsed the entrance of Parronley when they passed through the wrought-iron gate and on to its cobbled road. She lifted her head and caught a glimpse of the house in the distance, lit from behind with the glow of dawn.

"This way," called Wexin. "The day grows light. We will lock them away until I decide what to do. Finding the girl puts this entire matter in a new light."

Marlena tried to keep her wits about her to make out which wing of the house the men were taking them, using the lightest part of the sky to tell her which way was east.

One of the men opened a door that creaked on its hinges. She and Fia were carried into pitch blackness.

"We need light," Wexin said.

She had not been able to determine exactly where they were. She had been so long away, and there were so many parts of the house unused even when she lived there.

Finally torches were lit and they were carried down a stone staircase and into what looked like a dungeon.

"In here." Wexin led the men to a room with a stone floor and stone walls and the smell of damp and decades of disuse. He put the torch in an iron bracket on the wall.

She and Fia were dumped on the floor like sacks of flour. The young woman thrashed against her bindings.

Marlena managed to sit up. She glared at Wexin.

He laughed. "I will remove that disgusting cloth from your mouth, my dear cousin. You may remember that no one can hear you in this place." He pulled out the handkerchief and held it in two fingers away from his body, dropping it on the ground. "There you are, my dear. I am certain that feels much better." He turned to the men who had captured them. "You have done an excellent job. Wait for me outside."

While their footsteps receded up the stone stairway, Wexin walked over to Fia. He pulled her hair, and she stopped struggling. Marlena could make out Fia's glaring eyes in the light of the torch. Wexin leaned down into Fia's face.

"It *is* you." His voice was triumphant as he removed Fia's gag. "You change everything, my sweet little maid. Who would have guessed I would find you here with her? I'd hoped you'd landed in a Cheapside brothel and died of the pox, but I could not depend upon it, you realise."

Fia twisted away from him.

"Why does she change everything, Wexin?" Marlena asked, more to take his attention from the girl than anything else.

He turned back to her. "I may be able to take you back to London for your trial and to weep for your wickedness as you walk to the scaffold, after all."

"What had you intended otherwise?" she asked, knowing he was capable of treachery much greater than taking her back for a sham of a trial.

"Well, to kill you, of course." He sauntered over to her. "I thought perhaps you might vanish, once and for all." He put a finger to his cheek. "Although that would delay the wealth of the barony passing to me. No, if you are hanged, then I shall have all of the Parronley lands for raising sheep. I assure you, I am in great need of the revenue that will earn. I just need to get rid of the crofters, but that is the fashion, I hear."

Marlena felt sick. What would happen to Parronley's crofters? Where would they go?

She glared at him. "Perhaps I shall escape again and deny you the pleasure of my death."

He tilted his head. "Believe me, it is no pleasure, cousin Marlena. It is a necessity, however. You and the maid."

She made herself laugh. "You have been so clever, Wexin. I never would have guessed it of you." Perhaps if she kept him talking, Fia could free herself from her bindings. Marlena worked on her own. "I always thought you merely followed in Corland's shadow—"

Wexin grabbed the front of her dress, lifting her off the floor as he put his face into hers. "I follow in no man's shadow." He dropped her back on to the floor. "Least of all your husband's. Corland was a fool and not at all a gentleman."

Marlena could not disagree. She sat up again and tried to keep him talking. "Is that why you killed him? Because he was not a gentleman?"

He laughed. "Yes. Yes. It was." He stared down at her. "Do you know what he threatened to do?"

"Beat you at cards?" she taunted. "Steal your mistress?"

She glanced at Fia and saw her trying to free her hands.

Wexin's eyes flashed. "Worse than that, Marlena. He threatened to call in my vowels." He looked skyward, as if remembering. "He'd gambled even more excessively than usual. He'd gone to the moneylenders and he could not meet their payments. So he called in my debt to him, so he would have money to pay the moneylenders. I did not have it."

Her eyes widened. "You killed Corland because you owed him money?"

He leaned close to her face again. "I killed him because he threatened to spread the word that I reneged on my duties as a gentleman. Lord Strathfield, you know, would look with great disgust upon any man who failed to pay a debt of honour. He'd refuse my offer of marriage to his daughter." He leaned back again. "That was a risk I was not prepared to take."

Marlena shook her head, unable to believe her ears. "You killed Corland because a man might consider you less of a gentleman?"

"That is the right of it." Wexin laughed. "But Corland's life had negligible value."

She tried to rise. "What of my life, Wexin? Did my life have no value? From the start you planned it so I would be blamed."

He sighed and rubbed his palms together. "Now that I do regret, but there was nothing else to do. I could not risk anyone thinking it was *me*, could I? Corland had given you so many reasons to do him in; you were the most logical choice." He turned to Fia again. "All would have been well if this little chit had not shared his bed that night."

He took a step towards Fia, but she lashed out, kicking her bound feet at him. He backed off again.

"I think I must kill you both." Wexin sighed. "I am too impatient to wait for a trial. I merely must ponder the best means of doing so." He sauntered to the door, then turned and touched his forehead. "There is the matter of Lord Tannerton, as well. He must also die."

Marlena went rigid with rage and it was all she could do to disguise it from Wexin. Her death mattered little, but Tanner and Fia must live.

Wexin paused again in the doorway. "I am not a heartless man, Marlena. I shall leave you the torch so you will not have to spend all of your last hours in darkness."

He closed the door behind him and turned a rusty key in the lock.

"My lady," Fia cried from the corner of the room. "Bram will try to stop him and he will get killed, too! We must escape from here."

Tanner, in that delicious moment between sleeping and waking, reached across the bed, expecting to pull Marlena's warm soft body next to his. He felt only cool sheets.

His eyes instantly flew open.

She was gone.

He sat up, heart pounding, knowing he would not find her in the room. "Blast it, Marlena. Why run from me now?"

He continued to swear as he jumped out of bed and reached for his clothes. When he pulled on his shirt, he saw the paper folded on the table. He grabbed it and read.

Forgive me, my love, the letter began.

Forgive her? He'd throttle her for putting herself in so much danger.

He read only far enough to see she was going to the laird. He threw the pages down and finished dressing, pounding his boots on to his feet as he rushed out of the door.

He ran down the stairs and into the taproom, looking for Bram. He needed the man's help.

Bram's stepmother jumped, dropping a spoon into a large pot of porridge. "Mr Henry, ye gave me a fright!"

"Where is your son?" he bellowed, scaring her more.

She placed a hand on her chest. "I do not know."

Tanner caught sight of the door to the back of the building and ran outside that way, rather than retrace his steps through the inn. As he reached the yard, Bram came towards him.

"Have you seen Fia, m'lord?" The man was white-faced. "She's left her sister's house."

"Lady Corland is gone," Tanner said, not answering him.

"Lady Corland!" Bram's stepmother stood in the doorway. "Bram, what is this? The baroness?"

Her stepson said only, "Mam, check if Fia is in the inn and be quick!"

She ran inside. Bram and Tanner followed, falling in step with each other.

"I walked to Fia's sister's house, wantin' to see her." Bram was breathing hard. "She'd left before dawn, her sister said."

"Lady Corland has gone to the laird."

They hurried through the kitchen when Mrs Gunn ran up to them. "Her room is the same as when she left it."

"They've both gone to the laird, then." Bram frowned, pushing his way towards the inn's entrance.

"What is it, Bram?" his mother cried. "Why do you talk of Lady Corland?"

"I cannot explain, Mam," Bram said as he and Tanner reached the door.

"To the stables," Tanner said. "We'll ride."

If Marlena and Fia had taken the horses, he would simply commandeer whatever horse was there. Both horses were there, however, already saddled as Tanner had requested of the stableman the previous day.

"Your steed is right as rain today, sir," the man said.

Good, Tanner thought. He might need to run the horse hard.

He lengthened Marlena's stirrups to fit Bram and within two minutes they were off.

"Show me the way," Tanner said.

As they rode, Tanner told Bram about Marlena's letter.

"I told Fia I would take her to the laird." Bram frowned. "I told her she must tell what she knows."

"What she knows?" Tanner asked.

Bram faced him as they rode. "She witnessed the whole

thing, m'lord. She saw what Wexin did to her lady's husband, and Wexin saw Fia."

"My God." Both women were in danger. "Let us hope they made it safely to the laird's, then."

Why the devil had Marlena left this time? Tanner fought against the pain of her running from him again. He needed first to know she and the maid were safe.

There was no sign of Marlena and Fia on the road. Bram led them to a comfortable country house with a well-tended park and good land around it.

They left the horses at the laird's front door. A footman answered the knock, greeting Bram by name.

"Has Fia Small and another lady come this day?" Bram asked the man.

"Fia?" The footman looked puzzled. "Call upon the laird?"

"Never mind that," Tanner said, striding into the hallway with Bram in his wake. "Tell the laird the Marquess of Tannerton wants to see him immediately.

The footman's eyes widened. "The who?"

"Do it. *Now.*" Tanner barked.

It still seemed like precious minutes passed before they were ushered into a drawing room where an elderly man was still buttoning a brocade waistcoat, a white wig askew on his head.

Tanner strode up to him. "I am Tannerton. We need to know if Lady Corland and Fia Small have called upon you."

The man straightened his wig. "Lady Corland? Do you mean *that* Lady Corland? The murderess?"

"The accused murderess." Tanner tried not to lose patience. "We have reason to believe she and Miss Small intended to call upon you."

"Fia?" The laird shook his head in confusion. "No one has

called this morning, I do not believe." He walked to the door. "Lamont," he said to the footman. "Check with the staff if Fia Small has been here."

He glanced back at Tanner. "You are the *Marquess* of Tannerton?"

"Yes," Tanner replied.

The man's eyes looked uncertain. "May I offer you refreshment?"

Bram spoke up. "We cannot tarry, sir. We need to find them."

Tanner took the laird's arm and leaned close to him. "We may require your assistance. I must apprise you of this whole matter…"

As concisely as possible, he explained Marlena's situation, Fia's involvement and Wexin's treachery.

"Dear heavens." The laird collapsed into a chair. "Wexin dined with me two days ago. He seemed a decent fellow."

Tanner stood over him. "Are you saying you do not believe what I have told you?"

The man lifted his hands. "Oh, dear me, no. Who am I to dispute a marquess?"

"It is true, all of it," Bram put in. "Fia would not tell it false."

The footman returned. "No one has come here this morning."

"M'lord?" Bram turned to Tanner, his face white.

Tanner started for the door. "We are going to Wexin, Laird. I would be obliged if you would mount some men to come after us in case we need assistance."

Laird Hay stood. "I will do it."

Tanner and Bram ran out to the horses and were soon back on the road.

"Parronley is about seven miles, m'lord," Bram told him. He shot Tanner a pained look. "He has them, doesn't he?"

"I fear so."

Tanner prayed they would reach Parronley in time. He had no doubt in his mind that Wexin intended to kill both Marlena and Fia.

God, he prayed. *Do not let me have Marlena's death on my conscience. Save her. Take me, but save her.*

They set a fast pace, but had to slow down as they rode through Kilrosa; its people were now awake and busy and crowding the road.

"Where are ye goin'?" some shouted to Bram.

"I cannot explain now," Bram answered them.

Once out of Kilrosa, they put the horses to a gallop. Over a rise, however, a horseman approached.

Rapp, the Bow Street Runner.

"Whoa, there!" Rapp turned his horse sideways to block the road. "Not so hasty." He held a pistol and aimed it directly at Tanner. "You are not going anywhere."

Chapter Nineteen

Marlena struggled at the ropes that bound her wrists. "We *will* escape, Fia." She looked about their dungeon, trying to fix some memory with it. "Somehow."

The ropes were too tight to free her hands. She moved across to Fia. "See if you can untie me."

Fia wiggled her way closer to Marlena and they sat back to back, Fia trying to loosen the knot. "I cannot do it, m'lady."

"Perhaps I can untie yours," Marlena said. She found the knot and worked at it with her fingers. It would not loosen. "Let me try my teeth."

She manoeuvred herself so that she lay on the stone, her face in reach of Fia's hands. At least she could see the knot this way. It had been knotted several times. She pulled at the top strand with her teeth.

It formed a loop. She tugged at it until the loop loosened more. Quickly she swung around again and was able to get a finger through the loop, pulling one of the rope ends through it. She worked on the rest of the knot, first with her teeth, then with her fingers, until it came undone.

Fia hurried to untie her legs and then she worked on Marlena's bindings. In a moment, they both were free.

"I remember playing in the dungeons," Marlena said. "Niall and I. Wexin, too." She closed her eyes, trying to see it clearly in her memory.

When she was small Wexin had threatened to toss her in one of these rooms and throw away the key if she did not leave him and Niall alone. She later begged Niall to promise never to lock her in. Niall had hugged her and reassured her he would hide a key in all three of the dungeon rooms so she might never be locked in.

Did you hide the key, Niall? Marlena said to herself. *Show me. Please show me.*

She walked around the room, touching the wall, examining it, picking at stones that looked as if they might be dislodged.

"There should be a key hidden in here," she told Fia, who immediately began to search the other wall.

Niall would have made it easy, Marlena thought.

She ran to the door and examined its thick wood. There in a niche between two boards was a key. "Here it is," she cried. She could not pry it out with her fingers. The damp had rusted it and it was well lodged in its hiding place. "We need something to tease it out."

She pulled a hairpin from her hair and used it to pick around the key.

"Can you pry it out?" asked Fia, pacing behind her.

"I will," Marlena responded determinedly.

A sliver of wood broke off, giving Marlena sufficient space to hook the hairpin under the key. She pulled and the key moved enough so that she could grasp its end with her fingers.

It pulled free. "I have it!"

She put the key in the lock and turned, her heart leaping

as the sound echoed in the chamber. Now if the old door would not creak so loud that their captors would hear it, they would be free.

Holding her breath, she pushed on the door. Its creaking sounded as loud as a demon's scream, but no one came.

Marlena turned to Fia. "There might be a guard at the outside door. We will have to go another way."

The dungeons hid a tunnel through the cliffs out to a tiny cove where the water was deep enough and still enough for a boat. It was a secret escape route for the laird should he need to get away by sea. Her old grandfather used to boast that his father had been prepared to use the tunnel to aid in the escape of Bonnie Prince Charlie, had the Prince come to Parronley. Marlena and Niall had been forbidden to play in it, so, naturally, they had explored the tunnel whenever they could.

Marlena grabbed the torch from its bracket on the wall. It was already burning low. "We must hurry."

She led Fia out of their prison chamber and turned away from where light peeped in from the top of a stone stairway.

"This way," she whispered. "There is a tunnel."

"A tunnel." Fia's voice was fearful but resolute.

As if Marlena had been there yesterday, she led Fia to the hidden entrance. Now they need only hope that the tunnel was still clear, that over the years the walls that had remained passable for three centuries had not collapsed. Debris that Marlena dared not try to identify crunched under their feet, and they heard the skittering of tiny animals, rats or mice, probably.

"How much further?" Fia gasped.

"I think not far," Marlena said, although there was nothing but darkness up ahead and the torch was burning out.

"I cannot believe my good fortune," said Rapp, still aiming his pistol at Tanner. "And, in case you decide you must play the odds that I will shoot and miss, I should warn you, this pistol has rifling in the barrel."

The man was reading Tanner's mind. Rifling made the ball shoot straight and true. "Rapp, stand aside and let us through. It is a matter of life and death."

"Life and death? Your life. Your death." Rapp leaned forward in his saddle. "I do not feel inclined to let you go, Mr Lear or whatever your name is. You have been harbouring and abetting my fugitive and I am going to see you pay the consequences. Now, where is she?"

"You ought not to speak to him that way," Bram cried, moving his horse closer.

Rapp gave Bram a fierce glance. "You had better stay where you are, or I will shoot him."

"Don't be daft, man," Bram went on. "It is a marquess you'd be shooting."

Rapp laughed. "Impersonating a peer, are you now? That will get you in more difficulty."

"He *is* a marquess," Bram said.

Tanner started to remove his glove. "I will show you my signet ring, if you wish."

"Bah." Rapp waved the pistol. "What do I know of rings? Besides, you may have stolen it."

Tanner lost all patience. He needed to find Marlena, to stop Wexin. "Listen, Rapp. I *am* the Marquess of Tannerton, and you will put that pistol down now. I need your help, not your interference."

Rapp frowned. "Do not try to trick me. I worked for Tannerton once. I would know—"

Tanner cut him off. "And you never met me, did you? You worked for me a year ago last summer, was it not? What was your task? To go to Brighton to find the whereabouts of Lord Greythorne? Or into the rookery to learn who might have killed two people? Or, perhaps you were one of those guarding the Vauxhall singer? Perhaps you were on duty that night when she and I were abducted from under your noses, but then, if you had been one of those men, you should recognise me now."

Tanner waited, glaring at Rapp, so furious, he felt like playing the odds and charging directly into the man. The ball might not hit a vital part of him. He ought to chance it.

Marlena's life depended upon it.

"Tannerton?" Rapp's arm lowered. He immediately raised it again. "It cannot be. You are not dressed like a marquess."

"Fool," Tanner bellowed. "I was in the shipwreck. Do you not remember me? I remember you. I remember you pushing your prisoner aside so you could take her place in the boat. You left her to die. May you be damned for it!"

Rapp bowed his head. "God help me." He glanced up again, but the pistol swayed in his grip. "You must understand. I have a wife. Children. She would have died anyway."

Tanner advanced on the man, moving his horse in slow, steady steps. "She will die now, if you do not let us through. Wexin has her. Wexin is the real villain. Wexin killed Corland—"

"Wexin?" Rapp's eyes widened.

Tanner nodded. "He made it look as if Lady Corland did it. She is innocent, Rapp. You saved yourself on the packet, leaving an innocent woman to die."

Rapp's face contorted and he let his arm drop completely, his shoulders shaking.

Tanner brought his horse next to Rapp's. "I need your help, Rapp, not useless bawling. Come with us to stop Wexin. Save her life now."

Rapp straightened his spine and nodded. He stuck his

pistol back into his pocket, and turned his horse around. Bram started forward and shouted, "Let us go."

The three men galloped towards Parronley, and Tanner prayed they would not arrive too late.

The butler appeared at the door of the drawing room where Wexin was taking a cup of tea. The old man opened his mouth, but Jones pushed past him.

"Leave us," Wexin told the butler.

Jones watched until the man closed the door. He turned back to Wexin. "They are gone."

"Who is gone?" Wexin asked.

"The women."

"What?" Wexin jumped to his feet, knocking over the small table upon which sat his tea cup. "How could that happen?"

Jones slapped his hands against his sides. "I do not know. Williams went to check on them. The door was open and they were gone."

Wexin's fingers curled into fists. "You were supposed to be guarding them."

"We were," Jones protested. "We sat at the top of the stairs, right outside. They could not have got past us."

"Well, they did get past you, obviously." He started for the door. "We must search for them."

Wexin grabbed his top coat and the two loaded pistols he'd carried with him earlier that morning. He patted a pocket of the coat, feeling the knife he had also carried.

He and Jones hurried outside and around the house to the wing where they had imprisoned the women. Wexin descended the stone stairway and examined the room that ought to have kept them prisoner. Their bindings lay on the stone floor of the dungeon. The torch was gone.

He climbed back up the stairs. When he stepped outside

to where Jones waited for him, Williams came running towards them from across the park.

At still some distance, Williams stopped and shouted, "We've found them!" He pointed in the direction of the cliffs and gestured for them to follow. Wexin ran, with Jones close behind.

The cliffs were nearby. Wexin soon saw Marlena and the girl silhouetted against the sky. They froze when they saw Smith and Williams advancing on them. They turned and ran back towards the edge of the cliff.

Wexin's worries were eased. The cliffs were at least twenty feet high, with nothing but water below. He had them trapped. There was nowhere for them to go.

He laughed in triumph as Williams and Smith caught up with the two women, but Marlena fought off Smith, and Wexin frowned again. If Smith released her, Wexin would have the man's head put on a pike. He wished like the devil that he'd killed the women right away. Their bodies could have rotted in that dungeon for as long as he needed to decide how to dispose of them. When he got his hands on them again, Wexin would not make the mistake a second time.

To his horror, Marlena, her hair loose now in the struggle, dug her fingers into Smith's eyes. Smith screamed and let go, clutching his face. She rushed to her companion and started fighting with Williams.

Wexin quickened his step. "Hurry, Jones. They must not escape."

Williams was teetering near the cliff's edge, trying to hold on to the maid, while Marlena was hitting him and pulling on his clothing. Wexin reached the struggle and, with a surge of strength borne of his anger, seized Marlena by the hair and pulled her off Williams.

"This shall be the end of you, cousin." He caught her in a firm hold.

"You idiot." She struggled. "How many servants do you think are watching from the windows?"

He glanced over at the house where the windows sparkled in the sunlight. Curse her, she was probably correct. If he was being watched, he'd have to keep them alive.

But not for long. Marlena and her maid would never reach London.

Williams now had a good hold on the maid and was dragging her back towards the house.

Wexin, sick of Marlena's nonsense, pulled out his knife and held it against her throat. "Come nicely with me, my dear. You know my skill with a sharp blade."

"I know it well." She ceased her struggling, but stood her ground. "Does your wife know this side of you, Wexin?" she taunted. "Is she as bloodthirsty? Your Lady Macbeth, perhaps?"

He pushed the point of the knife into her skin, drawing blood. He did not care how many servants watched. "Do not speak of my wife!"

At that moment, horses' hooves thundered in his ears. He looked up to see three horsemen advancing upon them. Jones turned and ran, one of the men on horseback turning to pursue him. Another made straight for the maid, and a third headed directly towards him.

Tannerton.

Tanner instantly took in the tableau in front of him, but his gaze was riveted on Wexin, who held Marlena at knife-point close to the edge of the cliff.

When they had ridden up to the house, an elderly manservant had run out and yelled for them to head for the cliffs. They had barely broken speed to do so.

Tanner saw Marlena's hands gripped around Wexin's

wrist, and she managed to break free of Wexin's knife as Tanner approached.

Tanner leapt off his horse, knocking Wexin to the ground, but the momentum sent Tanner rolling dangerously close to the cliff's edge. When he looked up, Wexin was advancing on him, eyes wild with fury.

"Give it up, Wexin," Tanner said, scrambling to his feet. "Your game is over."

Wexin, no longer holding the knife, reached in his coat and pulled out a pistol. He pressed the weapon against Tanner's chest.

"It is your game that is over, Tannerton," Wexin cried. "I will blow a hole through you."

Tanner lifted his arms and glanced over the cliff to see that the sea was a good twenty feet below them. Its waves sounded a steady rhythm, like a battlefield drumbeat. Tanner edged closer to the precipice.

"You will never get away with this," Tanner warned, his voice low with rage at this man bent on destroying Marlena. Tanner's feet were close enough to the edge to knock pebbles over the side.

Wexin's face was red. "I will take you to hell with me, and my cousin, too." He moved the pistol to Tanner's heart and straightened his shoulders.

"No!"

Tanner heard Marlena's cry the same moment she barrelled into him. As a shot pierced the air, Tanner and Marlena flew off the edge of the cliff.

"Mar—" Tanner managed before they hit the icy water and plunged into its depths.

It was as if a nightmare repeated itself. Tanner felt the same bone-numbing cold as the night of the shipwreck, the same disorientation, the same desperate need for air. He thrashed in the water, one hand still gripping Marlena's clothing. He'd be damned if he'd allow the sea to take her now, not after all they had been through. This time, daylight shone through the water like hope. Tanner kicked towards it.

They broke the surface and both gasped for air. Still holding on to her, Tanner swam in the direction of the tiny sliver of beach at the opening of what looked like a cave.

As they stumbled out of the water, Tanner took her in his arms and held her tight against him. "Marlena. We might have been killed."

"No." Her teeth chattered as she spoke. "I knew. Used to swim here. We escaped through the tunnel, Fia and I." She shivered. "So cold."

She made no sense, but Tanner could only think that he might lose her yet if he could not get her warm and dry. He glanced around, searching for a way out.

Wexin leaned over the edge of the cliff. "No! It cannot be!"

Marlena tried to pull away at the sight of him. Tanner covered her with his arms and backed towards the mouth of the cave. There were more shouts from above and the sound of a pistol shot rang through the air.

It is not over yet, thought Tanner.

At that moment, a man in livery, carrying a torch, appeared at the entrance of the cave. "This way," the man said.

Tanner lifted her into his arms. "I'm so cold, Tanner," she murmured. "I'm so cold."

Marlena woke in a familiar place, but one as disorientating as if she'd been transported to Van Diemen's land. She was in the room of her childhood, its walls and furniture the same as the day she had left it.

"Are you feelin' rested, m'lady?" Fia leaned over her, placing a hand on her forehead.

Events came rushing back.

"Tanner?" She sat up.

"Fear not. He is here. Below stairs with the laird and Bram and some others. They are sorting matters out."

"Wexin?"

Fia averted her gaze. "He is dead, ma'am. Shot himself after you and Lord Tanner climbed out of the water."

Marlena put a hand over her mouth, remembering Wexin's face the moment she knew he'd decided to shoot Tanner, the moment she ran and she and Tanner flew off the edge of the cliff.

Her memory was hazy after that. She recalled the icy cold water. She recalled Tanner pulling her on to the beach and carrying her through the tunnel. He'd carried her up the stairs to this room and had undressed her while shouting for dry clothes and blankets.

She looked down at herself. She was wearing an old nightdress that still smelled of cedar. "Are there clothes for me? I want to get up." And find Tanner, she could have added.

"Right here," Fia said. "I'll help you."

Fia helped her don a dress that might have once been her mother's, an old velvet gown in deep green.

"I'll help with your hair," Fia said, sitting her down at her old dressing table where Marlena's maid once plaited her hair and told her stories of Shellycoat and Selkies.

She opened the drawers of the table and found a forgotten ribbon in one and a comb in the other. Fia combed out the tangles in her hair.

"Tell me what happened, Fia."

Fia's brows knit. "Well, after you and Lord Tannerton went off the side, Lord Wexin ran to the edge. Bram was fighting the fellow who had me, and there was another man helping. A Bow Street Runner, Bram said."

"Not Rapp." Marlena's eyes widened.

"I do not know, ma'am, but he was helpin'." Fia worked the comb through a strand of Marlena's hair. "Lord Wexin must have seen ye come out of the water, because he yelled and then he took a pistol to his head and fired it." The girl shuddered. "It was an ugly sight, but I'm glad of it. I'm glad he is dead."

Marlena touched the cut on her neck, a small reminder of her cousin. "Is it over, then, Fia?"

"Aye, it is over and done, and we have naught to worry over. The laird came and I told him everything. Those men helping Wexin were all tied up, and some of the laird's men took them away. Lord Tannerton and the laird and some other men from Kilrosa are all below stairs talking about what is next to be done."

Marlena's cut stood out an angry red against her pale skin. "And you, Fia, were you hurt?"

Fia shook her head. "Nothin' to speak of, ma'am."

"And Bram?"

Fia's face filled with colour. "He is very well, ma'am."

Marlena smiled. "I am glad."

Fia's eyelids fluttered. "I am going to marry Bram, m'lady. He asked me after they took Wexin's body inside. He took me aside and kissed me. He knows all about me and still says he wants to marry me."

Marlena reached up to clasp her hand. "He is a very lucky man to have you."

Fia's face flushed with colour again as she tied the ribbon around Marlena's hair. Marlena slipped her feet into a pair of old silk shoes that must have also been her mother's. She and Fia walked down the stairway to the hall of Parronley House, another familiar site.

An elderly man approached her, bowing deeply. "Baroness."

"Forbes!" She recognised the old butler and threw her arms around him. "It is so good to see you."

When she let go of him, she saw tears in his eyes.

"It is good to see you, my lady." His voice was thick with emotion.

"Where are they?" she asked him.

"The drawing room, ma'am." He led the way, stepping inside the room first. "The Baroness Parronley," he announced.

A murmur went through the room as the gentlemen stood. Marlena caught a glimpse of Rapp, who averted his face from her. She would ask about Rapp later. When Bram stepped forward to take Fia's hand, Marlena smiled inside.

Then her gaze found Tanner.

He stood at the far end of the room, the apex of the group. The clothes he wore were old fashioned and even more ill fitting than those they had purchased in Liverpool, but, still, he had the air of command. The other men showed deference to his authority.

The other men bowed and addressed her as Baroness as she crossed the room. Tanner's gaze followed her progress, his expression a mixture of both tension and relief. As she reached him, his eyes glowed, warming her more than a blazing fire could do.

His arms opened to her and she stepped into his embrace.

"Gentlemen," she heard Tanner say, his voice deep and full of emotion, "may I present you to the Marchioness of Tannerton." His arms tightened around her. "My wife."

Heedless of their audience, Marlena wrapped her arms around his neck. "My husband," she murmured before his lips closed on hers.

Home, again. To stay.

Epilogue

Tanner stepped out of the Palace of Westminster, weary of sitting all day listening to the debates, tired to death of looking at the red walls, red chairs, red carpet. He was heartily sick of red. The bland beige of the buildings in the street was a welcome relief.

He chatted with Lords Heronvale and Bathurst. Lord Levenhorne walked by and nodded to him. Lord Levenhorne was Heronvale's brother-in-law and the heir presumptive to Wexin's title and property, waiting only for the widow Lady Wexin to give birth to the child she carried. Tanner did not know if Levenhorne cared much whether he inherited or not.

It was said Levenhorne was deeply affected by the scandal around Wexin's death, but the person for whom Tanner felt the most sympathy was Lady Wexin. She had withdrawn from society, from the prying eyes and loose tongues so quick to condemn her by association. Tanner had heard she was in debt, but she had turned down his offer to assist her.

Bathurst was in danger of rehashing the entire day's debate

if Tanner did not stop him. He turned to Heronvale. "I have heard horses from your brother's stables are fetching top dollar."

Heronvale beamed. "Indeed. If you've a fancy for a race-horse, you should pay him a visit."

Tanner held up a hand. "Not at the moment, but I would not be averse to placing a wager now and then."

"A wise bet," Heronvale said. "Devlin's breeding pro-gramme promises to produce winners."

Bathurst recalled seeing one of the horses race and he launched in to a stride-by-stride description. Tanner spied his carriage finally appear at the end of the queue of carriages waiting to transport the lords from Westminster to their homes in Mayfair. He begged leave of his companions and walked to the vehicle rather than wait for it to reach him.

He greeted the driver and the footman who jumped down to hold the door open for him. Tanner climbed inside.

"Hello, my darling."

To his surprise, Marlena sat inside, looking beautiful in the light that filtered into the carriage. She wore a splendid carriage dress in deep blue with a pelisse to match. Her lovely face was framed by a matching hat with a tumble of white feathers on its crown.

"Ah, you are a feast to my eyes," he said, leaning over to give her a long, hungry kiss. When he broke contact, he murmured, "What the devil are you doing here? You must have been waiting an age."

She touched his face and lightly kissed him again. "Not that long, I assure you. I was pining to see you and took it in my head to ride in the carriage."

He wrapped his arm around her and held her close. "Very nice for me."

"How was the session today?" she asked.

He groaned. "The whole day was spent on the consolidated funds. Tedious in the extreme."

She looked at him with sympathy. "I am certain there was some good reason for such a discussion."

Tanner well knew that Marlena considered his activity in the House of Lords to be of very great value. He'd never thought much about it. It was an obligation, like signing papers, attending balls, answering a summons from the Duke of Clarence. If he was lucky, he had the chance to speak up about something worthwhile. Occasionally the debates became so loud and rancorous that bets were taken whether fisticuffs would break out. Those were the fun days. Mostly it was a boring obligation.

"The cursed bill was good enough," he told her. "To increase funds available for public service, but why they had to prose on about it all day was beyond me." He shook his head.

She laughed softly. "My poor husband."

He grinned at her then and tasted her lips one more time. "How has my wife been today?" He pressed a hand on her belly.

She covered his hand with her own. "I've felt splendid today. No queasiness at all. I even received callers."

To Tanner's great delight and Marlena's astonishment, she was with child. That physician who long ago pronounced her unable to conceive had been proven utterly wrong. There was a baby growing inside her. Tanner's baby. A son, a daughter, he cared not which. To have a child with Marlena seemed nothing less than a miracle.

Tanner asked her who had called upon her, and listened with half an ear as she told him about the ladies, most new to her acquaintance, those she liked, those she suspected of wanting merely to befriend London's newest marchioness, those who came to see the notorious Vanishing Viscountess.

Tanner enjoyed the sound of her voice. He had no right to feel so happy, to have so much to live for. His wife. His child.

After Wexin's death, they had travelled back to London, to clear Marlena's name once and for all and to do what needed to be done for her to assume her title as Baroness Parronley. One of Tanner's first tasks had been to dispatch his secretary to procure a special licence. Within a week of their return to London, he and Marlena were married by clergy at St George's Church in Mayfair. Many members of the *ton* witnessed the nuptials, as well as the Duke of Clarence and Tanner's much-relieved cousin, Algernon. Tanner wanted it very clear that he was really and truly married to Marlena, in the sight of God and everybody else.

Even before the wedding Tanner had taken Marlena shopping. Not at open clothes markets like in Liverpool, but at the finest shops Mayfair had to offer. He bought her jewellery at Rundell and Bridge, perfume at Floris, confectionery at Gunter's. He took her to all the best modistes—Madame Devy, Mrs Walters and others—and the best milliner, Mrs Bell. Marlena ordered a wardrobe of fine gowns and Tanner paid extra for them to be made for her as quickly as possible. Gloves, stockings, there was no item he did not wish to share in the purchasing, to make certain she knew she could have anything she desired.

To think he used to leave the purchasing of gifts to his secretary. He'd never enjoyed more what his money could buy than when using it to indulge Marlena in shop after shop after shop.

A lesser woman might have been overwhelmed by his attention and the attention of all of society upon their return. It had been somewhat like being plunged into the icy sea water, totally engulfing, hard to breathe. The newspapers carried the story and everyone from Mayfair to Cheapside was talking about the return of the Vanishing Viscountess. Marlena withstood the furore with the same fortitude she'd shown on their journey to Scotland, and Tanner was fiercely proud of her.

The consolation of all the tumult had been spending their nights together, full of lovemaking, full of joy, a haven in the midst of a storm.

"You are not listening!" she accused him.

He gave her a chagrined smile. "I was woolgathering, I admit." But what precious wool. "What did you say?"

"I had a letter from Laird Hay, with a message from Fia and Bram. Fia is increasing, too. Is that not splendid?" She squeezed his hand.

"Very splendid."

Tanner had had his secretary send money to all the people who had helped them during their flight to Scotland. When he took Marlena back to Parronley this coming summer, to await the birth of their child, he would find out what else he might do for Bram and Fia. Their own house, perhaps. Their own land.

He closed his eyes as Marlena sighed and relaxed against him. The carriage swayed as it rolled along, reminding him of the rocking of a ship.

Tanner thought back to standing in the cuddy of the packet boat from Dublin. He thought of his despair, his lamenting of his useless life. He had no doubt he would have let the sea take him if he'd not needed to save Marlena. He held her tighter.

She had saved him.

He lifted her face and his lips touched hers once more. He poured all the love in his heart into the kiss. Afterward he pulled her on to his lap and clung to her.

"What is it, Tanner?" she murmured, caressing his cheek, undoubtedly sensing his emotion.

"Nothing," he said. "Everything." He fixed his gaze upon her. "Thank you, is all. Thank you, Marlena."

They rode the rest of the trip to their Mayfair townhouse in contented silence.

LOVE INSPIRED HISTORICAL

*Powerful, engaging stories of romance,
adventure and faith set in the past—
when life was simpler and faith played
a major role in everyday lives.*

Turn the page for a sneak preview of
THE BRITON
by
Catherine Palmer

Love Inspired Historical—
love and faith throughout the ages
A brand-new line from Steeple Hill Books
Launching this February!

"Welcome to the family, Briton," said one of Olaf's men in a mocking voice. "We look forward to the presence of a woman at our hall."

Bronwen grasped her tunic and yanked it from the Viking's thick fingers. As she stepped away from the table, she heard the drunken laughter of the barbarians behind her. How could her father have betrothed her to the old Viking?

Running down the stone steps toward the heavy oak door that led outside from the keep, Bronwen gathered her mantle about her. She ordered the doorman to open the door, and he did so reluctantly, pressing her to carry a torch. But Bronwen pushed past him and fled into the darkness.

Dashing down the steep, pebbled hill toward the beach, she felt the frozen ground give way to sand. She threw off her veil and circlet and kicked away her shoes.

Racing alongside the pounding surf, she felt hot tears of anger and shame well up and stream down her cheeks. With no concern for her safety, Bronwen ran and ran—her long braids streaming behind her, falling loose, drifting like a tattered black flag.

Blinded with weeping, she did not see the dark form that sprang up in her path and stopped dead her headlong sprint. Bronwen shrieked in surprise and fear as iron arms pinned her, and a heavy cloak threatened to suffocate her.

"Release me!" she cried. "Guard! Guard, help me."

"Hush, my lady." A deep voice emanated from the darkness. "I mean you no harm. What demon drives you to run through the night without fear for your safety?"

"Release me, villain! I am the daughter—"

"I shall hold you until you calm yourself. We had heard there were witches in Amounderness, but I had not thought to meet one so openly."

Still held tight in the man's arms, Bronwen drew back and peered up at the hooded figure. "You! You are the man who spied on our feast. Release me at once, or I shall call the guard upon you."

The man chuckled at this and turned toward his companions, who stood in a group nearby. Bronwen caught hold of the back of his hood and jerked it down to reveal a head of glossy raven curls. But the man's face was shrouded in darkness yet, and as he looked at her, she could not read his expression.

"So you are the blessed bride-to-be." He returned the hood to his head. "Your father has paired you with an interesting choice."

Relieved that her captor did not appear to be a highwayman, she pushed away from him and sagged onto the wet sand. "Please leave me here alone. I need peace to think. Go on your way."

The tall stranger shrugged off his outer mantle and wrapped it around her shoulders. "Why did your father betroth you thus to the aged Viking?" he asked.

"For one purported to be a spy, you know precious little about Amounderness. But I shall tell you, as it is all common knowledge."

She pulled the cloak tightly about her, reveling in its warmth. "This land, known as Amounderness, once was Briton territory. Olaf Lothbrok, my betrothed, came here as a youth when the Viking invasions had nearly subsided. He took the lands directly to the south of Rossall Hall from their Briton lord. Then, of course, the Normans came, and Amounderness was pillaged by William the Conqueror's army."

The man squatted on the sand beside Bronwen. He listened with obvious interest as she continued. "When William took an account of Amounderness in his Domesday Book, he recorded no remaining lords and few people at all. But he did not know the Britons. Slowly we crept out of hiding and returned to our halls. My father's family reoccupied Rossall Hall. And there we live, as we should, watching over our serfs as they fish and grow their meager crops. Indeed, there is not much here for the greedy Normans to want, if they are the ones for whom you spy."

Unwilling to continue speaking when her heart was so heavy, Bronwen stood and turned toward the sea. The traveler rose beside her and touched her arm. "Olaf Lothbrok's lands—together with your father's—will reunite most of Amounderness under the rule of the son you are beholden to bear. A clever plan. Your sister's future husband holds the rest of the adjoining lands, I understand."

"You've done your work, sir. Your lord will be pleased. Who is he—some land-hungry Scottish baron? Or have you forgotten that King Stephen gave Amounderness to the Scots, as a trade for their support in his war with Matilda? I certainly hope your lord is not a Norman. He would be so disappointed to learn he has no legal rights here. Now, if you will excuse me?"

Bronwen turned and began walking back along the beach toward Rossall Hall. She felt better for her run, and somehow her father's plan did not seem so far-fetched anymore. Distant lights twinkled through the fog that was rolling in from the west, and she suddenly realized what a long way she had come.

"My lady," the man's voice called out behind her.

Bronwen kept walking, unwilling to face again the one who had seen her in her humiliation. She didn't care what he reported to his master.

"My lady, you have quite a walk ahead of you." The traveler strode forward to join her. "I shall accompany you to your destination."

"You leave me no choice, I see."

"I am not one to compromise myself, dear lady. I follow the path God has set before me and none other."

"And just who are you?"

"I am called Jacques."

"French. A Norman, as I had suspected."

The man chuckled. "Not nearly as Norman as you are Briton."

As they approached the fortress, Bronwen could see that the guests had not yet begun to disperse. Perhaps no one had missed her, and she could slip quietly into bed beside Gildan.

She turned to go, but he took her arm and studied her face in the moonlight. Then, gently, he drew her into the folds of his hooded cloak. "Perhaps the bride would like the memory of a younger man's embrace to warm her," he whispered.

Astonished, Bronwen attempted to remove his arms from around her waist. But she could not escape his lips as they found her own. The kiss was soft and warm, melting away her resistance like the sun upon the snow. Before she had time to react, he was striding back down the beach.

Bronwen stood stunned for a moment, clutching his woolen mantle about her. Suddenly she cried out, "Wait, Jacques! Your mantle!"

The dark one turned to her. "Keep it for now," he shouted into the wind. "I shall ask for it when we meet again."

* * * * *

Don't miss this deeply moving story,
THE BRITON,
available February 2008
from the new Love Inspired Historical line.

And also look for
HOMESPUN BRIDE
by Jillian Hart,
where a Montana woman discovers that love
is the greatest blessing of all.

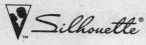

Romantic
SUSPENSE

Sparked by Danger, Fueled by Passion.

When Tech Sergeant Jacob "Mako" Stone opens
his door to a mysterious woman without a past,
he knows his time off is over. As threats to Dee's
life bring her and Jacob together, she must set
aside her pride and accept the help of the military
hero with too many secrets of his own.

Out of Uniform
by Catherine Mann

Available February wherever you buy books.

REQUEST YOUR FREE BOOKS!

Harlequin® Historical
Historical Romantic Adventure!

2 FREE NOVELS PLUS 2 FREE GIFTS!

YES! Please send me 2 FREE Harlequin® Historical novels and my 2 FREE gifts. After receiving them, if I don't wish to receive any more books, I can return the shipping statement marked "cancel." If I don't cancel, I will receive 6 brand-new novels every month and be billed just $4.69 per book in the U.S., or $5.24 per book in Canada, plus 25¢ shipping and handling per book and applicable taxes, if any*. That's a savings of close to 15% off the cover price! I understand that accepting the 2 free books and gifts places me under no obligation to buy anything. I can always return a shipment and cancel at any time. Even if I never buy another book from Harlequin, the two free books and gifts are mine to keep forever.

246 HDN EEWW   349 HDN EEW9

Name _____ (PLEASE PRINT) _____

Address _____ Apt. # _____

City _____ State/Prov. _____ Zip/Postal Code _____

Signature (if under 18, a parent or guardian must sign)

Mail to the **Harlequin Reader Service®**:
IN U.S.A.: P.O. Box 1867, Buffalo, NY 14240-1867
IN CANADA: P.O. Box 609, Fort Erie, Ontario L2A 5X3

Not valid to current Harlequin Historical subscribers.

Want to try two free books from another line?
Call 1-800-873-8635 or visit www.morefreebooks.com.

* Terms and prices subject to change without notice. NY residents add applicable sales tax. Canadian residents will be charged applicable provincial taxes and GST. This offer is limited to one order per household. All orders subject to approval. Credit or debit balances in a customer's account(s) may be offset by any other outstanding balance owed by or to the customer. Please allow 4 to 6 weeks for delivery.

Your Privacy: Harlequin is committed to protecting your privacy. Our Privacy Policy is available online at www.eHarlequin.com or upon request from the Reader Service. From time to time we make our lists of customers available to reputable firms who may have a product or service of interest to you. If you would prefer we not share your name and address, please check here. ☐

Silhouette® Desire

NEW YORK TIMES BESTSELLING AUTHOR

DIANA PALMER

A brand-new Long, Tall Texans novel

IRON COWBOY

*Available March 2008
wherever you buy books.*

COMING NEXT MONTH FROM

HARLEQUIN®
HISTORICAL

- **OUTLAW BRIDE**
  by **Jenna Kernan**
  (Western)
  Bridget Callaghan is desperate to save her family, stranded in the
  Cascade Mountains, but the only man who can help her is condemned
  to hang. With a posse at their heels and the mountain looming, Bridget
  wonders if the biggest danger might be in trusting this dark and
  dangerous man.
  *Jenna Kernan brings us not only a sensual romance, but also a thrilling
  Western adventure!*

- **THE WAYWARD DEBUTANTE**
  by **Sarah Elliott**
  (Regency)
  Eleanor Sinclair is thoroughly bored by high society. Sneaking out one
  night, dressed as a servant, to avoid yet another stuffy party, she meets
  the most handsome man—but her innocent deception will lead her to a
  most improper marriage....
  Sarah Elliott's defiant heroine will enchant you!

- **SCANDALOUS LORD, REBELLIOUS MISS**
  by **Deb Marlowe**
  (Regency)
  Charles Alden, Viscount Dayle, is desperately trying to reform—and
  the outrageously unconventional Miss Westby is a most inappropriate
  choice to help him. But Charles just can't seem to stay away from her!
  *Witty and sparkling—enjoy the Regency Season in Golden Heart Award
  winner Deb Marlowe's sexy debut.*

- **SURRENDER TO THE HIGHLANDER**
  by **Terri Brisbin**
  (Medieval)
  Growing up in a convent, Margriet was entirely innocent in the ways
  of the world. Now, sent to escort her home, Rurik is shocked to be
  tempted by the woman beneath the nun's habit!
  Surrender to Terri Brisbin's gorgeous Highland hero!

She neither wailed nor cowered from the storm.

She stood next to the Bow Street Runner, obviously his prisoner. Only a few hours ago, at the beginning of this voyage from Dublin to Holyhead, Tanner's gaze had been drawn to her, so dignified in her plight.

What crime had she committed to warrant her escort from Ireland? He'd been too blue-deviled to bother inquiring about her, however. Now he wished he'd spoken to her, or at least smiled at her. She seemed every bit as alone as he.

* * *

The Vanishing Viscountess
Harlequin® Historical #879—January 2008